POWER PLAY

MICHAELA GREY

For everyone who wants love but thinks they're not enough. I promise you are.

1

Gunner Ryan wasn't expecting the knock on his door at seven a.m. It was a day off and he'd been fully intending to sleep in, so he wasn't very happy as he clattered shirtless down the stairs and the dogs set up loud, excited barking. He locked them in the den, which they weren't thrilled about, and turned to see who was disturbing him at this hour.

He was even less happy when he opened the door to see a small child staring up at him, clutching some sort of stuffed animal to her chest. There was someone standing behind her, but Gunner didn't have time to acknowledge them, because the little girl said, "Mama says you're my daddy," and burst into tears.

It took a while to sort things out. He brought them both inside, into the living room. The little girl—Olivia, apparently—trailed off into snuffles that she tried to hide in the stuffed animal Gunner still hadn't managed to identify. The person with her was wearing a suit and introduced himself as Dexter Cane, a lawyer. He looked not very thrilled to be dealing with the whole situation. Gunner could sympathize.

"How—" He waved a hand at Olivia, who appeared to be talking to her stuffed companion—what *was* that thing?

"First things first," Cane said. "Are you indeed Gunner Ryan, formerly of the professional hockey team, the Indianapolis Racers?" His mouth was tight with distaste, and Gunner immediately bristled.

"Yes, and the stories are all true," he snapped. "I drank too much, partied too much, and fu—" He cut himself off just in time as Olivia stared up at him curiously. "What do you want?" he finally said, more moderately.

"I'm sorry, but I need to see some identification," Cane said. He didn't look sorry.

Gunner stared at him. "You came to *my* house before sunrise and now you want to see *my* ID? What's *your* ID? Why are you here and for that matter, how did you find me?"

Cane pulled his wallet from his back pocket and handed over a business card and his driver's license. ATTORNEY AT LAW, the card said, and the license confirmed this was indeed Dexter Cane, the photograph staring as sourly at him as the man himself.

"Fine," Gunner snapped. He'd left his wallet in the bowl by the door, so he stalked past them to get it and returned to hold it out between two fingers. Cane inspected it without touching and then nodded.

"Do you remember Stephanie Ratliff, in Indianapolis, seven years ago?" he asked.

Gunner couldn't remember seven *weeks* ago. He scrubbed a hand through his hair.

Cane coughed delicately. "Could you put a shirt on, please?" He gave Olivia a look, as if Gunner being shirtless would somehow offend her sensibilities.

Gunner could have pointed out again that they came to *his* house, at an ungodly hour of the morning, with no warning. He did not, because whatever the media said, he could be mature and reasonable. Instead he stalked upstairs and dug out a shirt, and if it was one of his oldest and rattiest, well… at least it covered most of his tattoos.

He stared at himself in the mirror briefly before going back downstairs. His reflection looked shell-shocked, curly white-blond hair going every which way and green eyes stunned. *You're not a father. You can't* be *a father. This isn't happening.*

Back downstairs, Cane looked only slightly appeased by the shirt but handed over an envelope. "This is for you."

Gunner, it said on the outside, and Gunner held it for a moment, knowing his world was about to drop out from under his feet and wanting, just briefly, to cling to normalcy.

Finally, though, he opened the envelope, turning his back on the unwanted guests to read it.

Gunner, it began in a smooth, looping script.

I'm so sorry. I never wanted this for you. I never wanted to ask *this of you. But there's no one else.*

Gunner didn't recognize the handwriting. *Maybe it's a mistake*, he thought, wild hope buoying him up suddenly. *Maybe it's a different Gunner.*

But the next sentence crushed that hope.

You probably don't remember much about our night together. You'd just won the Stanley Cup and were out with your team. God, you were so happy. I wanted to bottle that feeling and keep it with me, the way your eyes sparkled and how you stuck your tongue out and kind of curled it when you laughed at your own jokes. You were… intoxicating.

Gunner looked up, out over his backyard. The Cup. His rookie season. He barely remembered anything of the aftermath of winning—it was a blur of joyful screams and alcohol and laughter. They'd gone out, he knew that much. Of course they had. But had he picked up? He genuinely couldn't remember. He glanced back down at the letter.

I was a grad student, out for my birthday. Barely knew anything about hockey—my friends dragged me out to celebrate instead of studying. I wish I could say our eyes met across the crowded room or something, but you actually ran into me on your way back from the bathroom and knocked me flat on my ass.

Gunner had to admit that sounded like something he would do.

You took me to your place, after you made sure my friends knew where we were going, and you asked me to sign an NDA. Said the lawyers insisted on it even though you thought it was stupid. And I've kept to it, I have. People have asked me who Olivia's father is—Gunner's hands tightened convulsively on the paper—*and I haven't told them.*

Gunner glanced over his shoulder. Olivia had emerged from her deep conversation with *whatever* that thing was on her lap and was looking around the room. Her skin was light brown, hair wispy and wild with curls, and her eyes were darker brown. She asked Cane a question Gunner didn't quite hear. When Cane replied in a low whisper and Olivia jutted her chin out in a stubborn manner, Gunner felt like he'd been punched in the gut.

"Wanna see the *dogs*," she said.

"Oh, um," Gunner said. "Sure, I mean. They love kids. But they're big and they get excited, they might bump into you or knock you down."

Olivia tilted her chin and gave him a scornful look.

"Okay," Gunner said, almost amused. Nothing about this was funny, but he liked her grit. "Cane, the den is right through there. If you want to take her in while I finish reading this, that'd be great."

Cane's mouth tightened like he was tasting something bad but he got up and ushered Olivia out of the room.

Alone, Gunner turned back to the letter.

We were doing fine on our own. I fell in love with Livvy when they put her in my arms in the hospital. It was her and me against the world. We were going to do so many things. Climb the Eiffel Tower. See Machu Picchu. Visit the Easter Islands. (She loves geography, it's her best subject.)

And then I got sick. I told myself it was the flu,

that it would go away and I'd be fine again, but it didn't. And I wasn't. Olivia wanted to go out, to the park and the zoo and the aviary, and I… I just didn't have the strength or the energy.

Acute myeloid leukemia, the doctor said. 70-80% of patients under 60 go into remission after their first round of chemo. I wasn't one of them. It was aggressive. Is aggressive, I guess, I'm not dead yet. But it's going to happen soon, and Gunner… I'm so sorry. My family's not an option. They're hateful. They'd brainwash my baby and I can't—

There was a smudge on the paper. Gunner ran his thumb over it. He felt like he was floating just above his body. In the den, he could hear the click of the dogs' nails on the floor and happy panting, and Olivia giggling.

I've followed your career, of course. I'm sorry the Racers traded you but it seems like the Direwolves have been so good for you. You've grown up. Maybe you're still a little wild, but you're kind. *And that's what Olivia needs.*

You can do your own DNA test, of course, but I had one done as well, just to be sure. The results are included. I didn't do anything but study and go to grad school when I met you. And after—well, I still didn't exactly have time to go out and party. You were my first—not ever, don't freak out—in about four years, and then, well… you ended up being my last.

Gunner's eyes were stinging. He dropped the paper to rub them fiercely. This couldn't be happening. He couldn't even *remember* this fierce, funny, independent woman he'd spent a night with, and somehow that felt worse than anything else he'd been presented with today.

Finally, he bent to retrieve the letter, taking a deep breath.

I tried to call, Gunner, I really did. It wasn't easy getting your number and because of the NDA, I couldn't tell your agent why I needed it. My best friend is a lawyer—she convinced him when he stonewalled me, but I couldn't get through to you.

Half the time, Gunner didn't answer numbers he *did* recognize—the chances of Stephanie actually connecting with him were almost nil.

I left messages. I thought maybe if you listened to them, you'd call me back. But maybe you didn't get them. I don't know. I'm sorry—so sorry—it happened this way. I wish I could have met you once more, seen the man you've become. But the doctor said it's fast acting, aggressive. I have a week, maybe two.

Gunner doubled over and braced his hands on his knees, struggling to breathe. He'd forgotten his voicemail password over a month ago and just hadn't gotten around to changing it.

"Fuck, *fuck*," he choked. He'd fucked up *again*, without even realizing it. It took him a few minutes before he could straighten and focus on the letter again.

Now, on to my favorite subject. Our daughter. Gunner had to close his eyes briefly at that. *Olivia Anne Ratliff. You won't care about how much she weighed or how long she was at birth, but she's tall for her age—she basically had no chance there. I'm 5'10 and you're… well, yeah. And she's got all the moxie of a fucking mule. Don't try to fight her when she's got her mind made up—you won't win.*

She's… Gunner, she's so good. She fights a lot, you're going to get a lot of calls from whatever school you enroll her in. But I guarantee every single fight will be because she witnessed an injustice and was trying to right the wrong. She champions littler kids, protects them. Hell, she picked a fight with a fourth-grader *once because he was bullying a gay kid. She's like you—she knows no fear. She throws herself into anything wholeheartedly and never does anything by half-measures. Again—like you.*

Gunner half-laughed, digging the heels of his hands into his eyes. He didn't know how Stephanie knew him so well after just one night together, but she hadn't been wrong yet. Olivia shrieked with laughter from the next room.

"Slobber!" she complained, but she sounded delighted.

Well, at least they were getting along.

Right now she wears 8-10 year old clothes, in size. Look for the tags in the stores. Or order them online if you want to save the time and hassle, but be warned—if she doesn't like it, she won't wear it. I guess you could describe her style as punk lumberjack ballerina, but that'll probably change as she gets older.

Because she's half-Black, you're going to struggle with her hair. Find someone who has experience with curls like she has, or look up YouTube tutorials. She'll fight you on it—she hates her hair being brushed—but she knows it's not a battle she can win. Good luck though—you'll need it.

She loves geography, like I said. Not so great with math. And… she loves hockey. She didn't know who you even were until about a month ago, when the doctors told me how long I had and I knew I had to tell her something. *But she's been obsessed with the sport since she could hold a stick. Please, Gunner, if there's one thing you do for her—get her into a hockey program.*

There were several more smudges on the paper, wiped away like maybe Stephanie was crying as she wrote.

Take care of my baby girl, she said at the end. The letter wasn't signed.

Gunner looked at the letter in his hand for a very long time. And then he did the only thing he could think to do. He called Will.

"You look fine, what's the emergency?" Will said as he walked through the door. "I thought maybe one of your conquests didn't want to leave and you needed my help."

Gunner didn't dignify that with a response. Instead he wordlessly shoved the letter at him and sat down hard on the couch, head in his hands.

After a few minutes, Will sat beside him.

"Jesus," he whispered.

Gunner said nothing. What was there *to* say?

"Are you okay?" Will asked when he'd finished reading.

Gunner gave him an incredulous look.

"Stupid question, sorry. Um. God, Clancy's going to shit himself."

"Your brother is kind of the least of my concerns right now," Gunner snapped.

Will winced. "Sorry," he repeated. "What do you need from me?"

"I don't know," Gunner said, shoving his

hands through his hair again. "I don't *know*, I just —it just *happened* and she's *in the den*, and I'm *a father*? What am I going to *do*?"

"Well, can I meet her?" Will said, practical as ever.

So Gunner took him through to the den, where they discovered Cane sitting in a chair with his feet close together and hands tucked under his thighs while Olivia sprawled on the floor with both dogs mobbing her as she giggled.

They looked up when Gunner opened the door, and Ty broke away from the pack to come greet him. Gunner went to his knees and wrapped his arms around Ty's heavy shoulders, letting his oldest, dearest friend give him some silent comfort. Ty twisted enough to lick his face, which made Olivia laugh again.

"They give lots of kisses," she declared, sitting up. "What are their names?"

"This is Ty," Gunner told her, rubbing Ty's ears when he heard his name. "He's a pit bull, named after Ty Cobb, who was a famous baseball player, and I've had him since he was a tiny puppy. He's an old man now." He pointed at Babe, currently on his back in Olivia's lap, his mouth wide in doggy joy. "That's Babe. He's only two and he has lots of energy."

Olivia giggled. "That's a funny name for a *boy* dog. I like it."

"He's named after a baseball player too,"

Gunner said, but he could tell she didn't really care.

Instead she pinned Will with a curious look that morphed into recognition almost immediately. "You're Will Calder!"

Will smiled at her and stepped forward, holding out a hand like the earnest dork he was. "Yep. I'm—" He hesitated briefly and recovered. "I'm your—uh. I'm Gunner's captain."

Olivia nodded. "You tell him what to do, right?"

"Well, I try to," Will said, voice dry. "He doesn't listen very well."

"Hey," Gunner protested. Ty, the traitor, left him to go back to Olivia, and Gunner got back to his feet. "I listen."

"Sure," Will drawled. He winked at Olivia. "You listen, and then you do what you want."

Olivia laughed, clearly delighted, and grabbed her stuffed animal from the couch. She presented it to Will with an air that clearly said he should be properly impressed.

"This is Ferguson," she said gravely.

Will took one of Ferguson's legs—paws?—and shook it equally gravely. "Very nice to meet you, Ferguson." He leaned in. "What are you, exactly?"

Thank you, Will.

Olivia giggled, face scrunching up. "He's a anteater!"

Gunner didn't know much about stuffed animals, but he didn't think whatever that creature was had any relation to anteaters. A bear, maybe? Or a dog? He wasn't exactly qualified to decide.

"Not a snake, for the Racers?" Will's voice was teasing, gentle.

Olivia shrugged. "I like the Direwolves better anyway."

Something in Gunner's chest seized and he coughed to clear it. "Would, um—sorry I didn't offer before, but would anyone like something to drink?"

Olivia perked up. "Apple juice?"

"Uh—" Gunner had wine, vodka, rum, soda, and— "Is orange juice okay?"

Olivia made a face. "I guess."

They trooped through into the kitchen and Gunner poured orange juice into one of the only plastic cups he had. He gave Will Coke without asking and raised eyebrows at Cane.

Cane decided on Sprite and Gunner waited until things were quiet, the dogs making themselves comfortable in their favorite spots before he spoke.

"What happens now?"

Cane swallowed his sip of Sprite. "You sign papers taking custody. There are a few things you'll need to sign, but that's the main one."

Olivia reached across the counter and clutched Gunner's wrist. "Are you gonna be my daddy for real?" she asked, voice suddenly urgent.

Gunner hesitated, looking at Will. Will looked back at him, eyebrows raised.

"Um," Gunner said carefully. "Do you want me to be?"

Olivia released his wrist and nodded. "You're a good hockey player."

Will stifled a laugh in his drink.

"There are, um, other criteria you should consider," Gunner pointed out.

Olivia's face scrunched again. "Cri—what?"

"Things you should think about," Will said, helpful as ever.

"Mama—" Olivia hesitated and then visibly steeled herself as Gunner's breath shortened. "She says—" She caught herself and Gunner's eyes burned. "She *said* you were… good. Good at hockey but also… just good."

Gunner couldn't look at her. He turned away, staring unseeingly out the glass door at the dogs playing in the yard. He wasn't good. He'd never *been* good. *Wild. Chaotic. Party animal. Hotheaded. Undisciplined.*

There was a hand on his waist and Gunner turned without thinking to bury his face in Will's shoulder. Will held him, rubbing his back gently, and Gunner drew strength from him, clutching at his shirt.

Stephanie had thought he could do this. Will hadn't said, but Gunner knew he thought he could too.

When he pulled away, Olivia was watching them with wide eyes.

"Are you gonna be my daddy too?" she asked Will, sounding thrilled at the prospect.

Will stepped away like he'd been burned and Gunner buried the hurt, pushed it deep like he always did when Will reacted that way to the suggestion that he and Gunner were together.

"Ha, um, no," Will said, rubbing the nape of his neck. "We're just friends."

Olivia looked disappointed but didn't argue the point.

"Does this mean you're accepting custody?" Cane asked. He sounded like he couldn't wait to get away. Gunner could definitely sympathize.

He looked at Will, who looked back, calm and steady. His best friend, the man he'd been in love with for the better part of four years. Gunner took a deep breath. He thought he might puke.

"Yeah," he said. "I'm—uh… accepting custody."

The approval in Will's eyes almost made it worth it.

2

THEY SPENT the next hour signing paperwork as Will helped Olivia get her bags out of Cane's car. She didn't have much—just a couple of banged up suitcases and a backpack she dropped carelessly on the pile, and a cardboard box with Gunner's name printed on it that Gunner didn't open.

"Mama said I hafta go to school here," Olivia told Gunner. "Do I *really* have to?"

Gunner hid his smile. "Afraid so. But maybe not today." Was school even in? He had no idea. He went by 'hockey season' and 'not-hockey season' and all he knew was that hockey season was about to start.

Still, this perked Olivia up no end. "Can I play with the dogs some more?"

"Sure," Gunner said. "Why don't you take them outside? You guys can run around in the grass and get all dirty."

Olivia looked delighted at the prospect and bolted for the door, both dogs on her heels.

Cane finished signing the last paper and stood. "That's all I need, so I'll be going. All the documents you'll need to get her enrolled in school are here, as well as her shot records and medical history so you can find her a doctor."

Gunner had to resist the urge to clutch at Cane's perfect suit. "A doctor? Is she sick?"

Cane almost—*almost*—sneered. It was in the twitch of his threaded eyebrows and the downward quirk of his mouth. "No, of course not," he said, straightening his cuffs. "But she'll still need a doctor on file for her annual shots and anything else she might need."

"What else would she need?" Gunner knew he was starting to sound slightly hysterical, but given the circumstances, he thought he was justified.

"I'm sure I don't know," Cane said, taking a step back. "Thank you for your time."

"*Wait*," Gunner said. "You never said how you found me."

Cane's lips twitched. "Instagram. You really should be more careful about posting identifying information there. When we couldn't reach your number, we got a little more creative. It didn't take long at all. I really must be going now." He glanced out the sliding glass door to the backyard. "And… good luck."

He was gone before Gunner could ask what *that* meant, and Gunner and Will were alone in his dining room. Gunner looked at Will, who looked steadily back.

"What's in the box?" Will asked.

Gunner blinked and turned to open it. Inside, he found two carefully wrapped presents, one in red and green and the other in pastels, and another envelope with his name on it. Gunner eyed it like it was a snake poised to strike.

"Don't be a baby," Will said, and snatched the envelope out of the box before Gunner could protest. "Oh," he said after reading it, and Gunner grabbed it out of his hands.

Gunner, it said in Stephanie's now-familiar script. *Olivia's birthday is February 8. I'm sending you a present for her first Christmas and her first birthday without me. It's going to be hard for her. Please just be patient with her.*

Gunner looked up at Will. "Don't leave," he said. He felt like a drowning man clutching at a leaf, but Will didn't laugh at him.

"I'll stay until you ask me to go," he said instead. "But I have no idea what to do with a little girl, just so you know."

"Don't you have a sister?"

"An *older* sister," Will said. "Don't *you* have a younger sister?"

"Yeah but it's not like I raised her!" Gunner realized his voice was getting higher and he took a deep breath. "I was busy with, like, hockey shit!" He turned in a circle. "I have to—where's my phone?"

"Probably in your bedroom," Will said, and Gunner hated him a little for being so calm. "I'm going to make breakfast."

"I'm calling my mom," Gunner announced, and ran for his room.

In retrospect, he probably should have predicted his mother's reaction.

"You *what*?"

Gunner winced and held the phone away from his ear. "Mom—*Mom*. Stop yelling and *listen*. No, I didn't know. Mom, you think I would have kept this a secret? You think I *could* keep this a secret? I had no idea until she showed up on my fucking—sorry—doorstep! *No*, Mom, I'm not pranking you, I swear to God, I'm dead serious. Look, do you want me to take a picture of her? Will you believe me if I do that?"

He was already heading back downstairs, not listening to whatever Fay was saying. Olivia was flat on her back, wrestling with Babe as Ty watched. Gunner turned on the camera and trained it on her.

"Olivia!" he called.

Olivia jerked her head up. There were grass stains all over her dress and her hair had come out of its careful braids, curling in wild tendrils around her small face.

Over the speaker, Fay gasped. "Oh my god. Oh my *god*. Gunner, she looks *just like you*."

Gunner looked at Olivia doubtfully as she looked back at him, just as dubious.

Fay laughed, almost a sob. "You have made that exact face at me *so many times*. Gunner, *what* is going on?"

Gunner took the phone back in the kitchen and sat down at the counter to tell her everything

—or at least as much as he could. Will was cooking omelets, his broad back turned. Gunner had clearly woken him up too—he hadn't even stopped to style his hair, so it fell forward into his face in dark, shining waves as he flipped eggs. Gunner wanted to run his fingers through it.

"—is she?" Fay asked.

Gunner jerked. "What?"

"How old is she?" Fay repeated.

"Um. Six… and a half, or so, I guess?" He straightened on the stool. "Mom, is school in? Is she old enough for school? Where do I even take her? *How* do I enroll her? What do I do with her when I'm not here, or on the road? What do I do with her when I *am* here?"

He was starting to sound hysterical again, he realized as Will dropped the spatula and rounded the counter to grab Gunner's shoulders.

"Breathe," he ordered.

"Oh, is Will there?" Fay said. "Let me talk to him, honey."

Gunner handed over the phone on autopilot, dimly grateful that Will kept one hand on his shoulder as he straightened to speak to Fay.

"Yes ma'am," he said, ever the polite Canadian boy. "No ma'am, I had no idea. Guns called me this morning." He listened and then stooped to look in Gunner's eyes. "I think he's in shock," he reported.

"Am not," Gunner said vaguely. He tilted forward just enough that he could rest his cheek against Will's solid stomach. He could hear Olivia telling one of the dogs something in a very serious voice. Gunner closed his eyes. Maybe this was just… the worst dream ever.

Will pinched him and Gunner flailed upright. "Fucking—*ow*, Calder!"

"Language," Will chided, but there was laughter in his eyes. "You can't hide your way out of this one, Gunny." He held the phone out again.

"So the first thing you need to do is find her a school," Fay said. "And clothes—what's her wardrobe like?"

"How the hell should I know?" Gunner grumped. "She has a couple suitcases. They're pretty beat up."

"Single mother, didn't have much of a budget, did she?" Fay mused. "That baby probably needs an entire new wardrobe. And of course she'll need furniture for her room. And school supplies."

"*Mom*," Gunner protested. "How am I supposed to know how to do *any* of this?"

"I'll be there tomorrow morning," Fay said firmly. "Can you keep her alive for one day, Gunner?"

Gunner really wasn't entirely sure, but Will nodded at him, hand still on his shoulder.

"Okay," Gunner said. "Text me the flight details."

When he hung up, Will squeezed his shoulder and returned to the stove. "Go ask Olivia if she'll eat omelets with vegetables in them."

Gunner dragged himself to his feet and to the back door. Olivia was standing square on the grass, with the dogs sitting attentively in front of her, listening to every word. Gunner hesitated, unwilling to break the tableau. Olivia swung her arm, miming something—a slapshot, Gunner realized, his heart squeezing again—and then did a little miniature celly right there in front of the dogs, who immediately crowded around to get in on the fun.

Gunner cleared his throat and Olivia looked up, startled.

"Um, Will wants to know if you like omelets. With vegetables in them."

Olivia wrinkled her nose as Ty ambled over to flop at Gunner's feet. Gunner bent to rub his ears.

"She wearing you out, old man?"

"He liked my celly," Olivia announced, suddenly right in front of him.

"It was a very good celly," Gunner told her. "Omelets?"

Olivia sighed, put upon and world weary. "I don't want vegetables in mine though."

She and the dogs followed Gunner back inside as he tried to figure out a rebuttal.

"They're good for you?" he attempted.

This was met with the disdain it deserved as Olivia clambered onto the stool and swung her feet.

"They'll make you big and healthy" was Gunner's second sally.

Olivia snorted and Will nearly dropped his plate, eyes going wide.

"She sounds *just* like you," he said, setting the plate in Gunner's spot.

"No vegetables?" Gunner said, despairing.

Olivia shook her head firmly.

Gunner gave Will a helpless look and Will's lips twitched.

"She won't die if she goes one day without healthy food, Guns." He leaned in, hand curving around the jut of Gunner's hipbone, and put his lips to Gunner's ear. "Besides, maybe we can sneak some in without her noticing," he whispered.

Gunner was too busy trying not to have a very inappropriate reaction in front of the small child to do more than nod manically and pretend to taste the food Will had so thoughtfully made for him.

Olivia devoured her omelet and was done before either of them.

"I'm bored," she announced. There were twigs in her hair. Will reached out and gently pulled one free, clearly fighting a smile. "Can I explore the house?"

"Uh." Gunner tried desperately to remember if he left anything lying around. With a rush of horror, he remembered he'd left out the lube from two days before.

Will saved the situation.

"Why don't I show you the downstairs while —" He stumbled briefly. "Your, um. Gunner… goes and tidies up a bit upstairs? And then you can pick out what room you want to be yours!"

Gunner could *kiss* Will. Well. He could always kiss Will. But at that moment, he'd throw himself in front of a bus for the man. Will winked at him and he and Olivia left to explore the downstairs as Gunner hurled himself up the stairs like a madman.

He stuffed the lube under the mattress and tripped over his favorite dildo, big and purple with a flared head. He liked to imagine it was Will's dick when he fucked himself on it, which always felt great in the moment but usually left him defeated and miserable after. But now was *not* the time to be angsting about Will's dick.

Gunner grabbed the dildo, did a quick sweep to make sure everything else was put away, and shoved it under the mattress as Will and Olivia came up the stairs.

"This is your da—" Will stumbled again, grimacing.

"This is my room," Gunner said. He could do some rescuing too. "The guest rooms are down the hall. There are three of them and you can pick whichever one you want."

Olivia's face lit up. "*Any* of them?"

"Absolutely," Gunner told her.

Olivia squealed and dashed from the room as Will stepped in close. Gunner was not complaining about this sudden lack of personal space they seemed to be sharing, which made him miss what Will said.

"Sorry, what?"

Will gave him a weird look and leaned even closer, because God hated Gunner and wanted him to suffer. "I *said*, what if she picks the room beside yours?"

It was Gunner's turn to give him a weird look right back. "Why would that be a problem?"

Will rolled his eyes. "You're gonna have to learn to be quiet, aren't you?"

"Learn to be—*oh*." Gunner gave him a disgusted look. "You really think I'd bring anyone back here with a *kid* in the house?"

"Well I don't know, do I?" Will said, stepping

away. "I don't know what you get up to all on your own over here!"

"I'm *not* on my own now," Gunner snapped. He folded his arms across his chest because something was lodged under his breastbone at the thought of Will just *assuming* that Gunner would be that thoughtless, that careless.

Will's expression melted into concern and he took a quick step forward. "Guns, I didn't mean—"

"Yeah, you did," Gunner said, and brushed past him into the hall.

HE FOUND Olivia quickly and sure enough, she'd picked the bedroom beside his. She was sitting on the bed, legs crossed, staring around the room.

"What color would you like it to be?" Gunner asked, coming to sit next to her.

Olivia's eyes went wide. "I can paint it?" she breathed.

"Well," Gunner hedged, already envisioning the disaster of a small child set loose with a can of paint, "we can *hire* someone to paint it. Any color you want. What do you like most in the world?"

"Hockey," Olivia said instantly. She took his hand, not even looking at him, still gazing around the room as if trying to imagine it as hers, but Gunner held his breath and didn't move as she nestled her small fingers in his palm.

She looked up at him after a moment, though, frowning. "But I like jography too."

"Yeah," Gunner said, smiling. "Your mom told

me about that in her letter. All the places you were going to visit." He snapped his mouth shut, realizing what he'd said, and cursed himself as Olivia's lip wobbled. "I have an idea," Gunner said, not really sure what he was going to say but desperate to get the sheen out of Olivia's big eyes. "What if… what if we went to restaurants around Denver from the places you want to visit? We could get a big map," he continued, warming to the idea, "and you could put push pins in it for everywhere we eat. You can choose the places, and we can try them all if you want. And during the summer, we can visit some of them for real."

It had worked, he realized with a rush of delight and relief. Olivia bounced to her knees, clasping her hands together.

"Yes!" she said. "Yes, *yes*, can we start tonight? Please?"

Will appeared in the doorway. His hands were in his pockets, shoulders around his ears, and Gunner didn't meet his eyes. Instead he smiled at Olivia.

"Yeah," he said softly. "We can start tonight."

"Can Uncle Will come too?" Olivia asked.

Will visibly startled. "Oh, that's okay—"

"If you want Uncle Will there, then of course he can come," Gunner said firmly. Will wasn't weaseling his way out of this one.

"I need to talk to you," Will said.

Gunner patted Olivia's knee. "I'll be back in a minute. You think about what else you want in your room, eh?"

He followed Will into the hall and shut the door. Will was looking at the floor, the wall—

anywhere but at Gunner, who'd never seen such a big man look so much like a kicked puppy.

"I shouldn't have said that," Will blurted finally.

Gunner raised an eyebrow. "What, the part about me being a slut, or the part about me not being able to control myself to the point that I'd bring *strangers* into a house with a six year old?"

Will turned away, one shoulder going up as if to ward off the blow. "I don't—I didn't—"

He looked *miserable*, and Gunner couldn't stop himself from taking Will's arm and pulling him back around to face him.

"I haven't slept with anyone in four years," he said quietly. *Because of you*, he wanted to say. *Because of your big eyes and your stupid face and the way you fight for me, for the team, for the way you believed in me when no one else did.* He didn't say it.

Will looked poleaxed, mouth working. "But you—when we go out, you—and you always talk about—"

Gunner lifted a shoulder. "Imagine the chirping if the boys knew I *wasn't* sleeping around. So I find a willing girl, or guy, to leave with me. Give 'em a little money and make them sign an NDA, then come back here. Alone."

"But *why*?" Will demanded.

And there it was. His opportunity. He could tell Will, his captain, his best friend, his *linemate*, how he felt about him. Will had *asked*. He wanted to know *why* Gunner was celibate.

Gunner opened his mouth—and nothing

came out. He couldn't do it. Will didn't feel the same way. Gunner had known that for a long time, watching Will go through a string of girlfriends, each one sweet and pretty and smart, and he'd long since accepted that he'd never have more than he had right now, standing in his hall with a hand on Will's bicep and Will's eyes fixed on his face.

And so he shrugged, dredging up a smile. Because he couldn't lose this. He couldn't lose *Will.* He couldn't risk what they *did* have for some stupid, pointless declaration of love.

"It stopped feeling like fun and started feeling like an obligation," he said. He poked Will in the chest suddenly. "And don't you *dare* slutshame me, asshole. I've done shit I'm not proud of, but sleeping with people isn't one of them, so if you're going to—"

Will covered Gunner's mouth with one big hand. He was almost smiling, his eyes soft. "I'm not," he said quietly. "I *wasn't.* I never meant it that way, Guns, I swear. I just… I'm so sorry. I should have thought better of you."

"Story of my life," Gunner said, moving Will's hand. He tried for a smile but Will's face fell. He moved fast, pulling Gunner into his arms before Gunner could react.

"I'm an asshole," Will said in his ear. "Did I fuck it up? Did I fuck *us* up?"

Gunner couldn't stop himself from pressing his face into the crook of Will's neck for just a minute. He smelled so good, warm and spicy and like *home.* But then he eased back.

"We're good," he said quietly, holding Will's

eyes, and he saw the moment Will believed him, relaxing as a tiny smile quirked his mouth.

"'Uncle Will', huh?"

"It suits you," Gunner said, patting his cheek. "You look like an uncle." He went back into Olivia's room, grinning at Will's outraged sputters behind him.

3

Olivia was head and shoulders deep in the closet, inspecting the built-in drawers.

"Do you want to unpack?" Gunner asked her.

Olivia enthusiastically agreed and they spent a while figuring out where to put her belongings. She really didn't have much, and Gunner had to admit his mother was right—not that *that* was a surprise—and she needed a lot. Even Gunner, with his minimal knowledge of little girls and what they needed, could see she needed more than she had.

He managed to somehow persuade Olivia into a cleaner outfit before they went out to eat, but he admitted defeat when it came to her hair, looking at Will, who shrugged just as helplessly.

"What did your mama do with your hair?" Gunner asked.

Olivia, talking to Ferguson again, squirmed. "She liked to braid it. Or sometimes cornrows or pigtails."

What the fuck is a pigtail, Gunner mouthed to Will, who looked as baffled as Gunner felt.

Finally, Gunner located a hairband and sort of scraped the worst of the wild curls back into something resembling a ponytail while Olivia squirmed more and complained loudly.

"Sorry, sorry," Gunner chanted, trying to get one last strand under the elastic. "Okay, *done*."

He dropped his hands and Olivia inspected herself in the mirror. The twist of her mouth looked just like Gunner's when he was disappointed in something.

"I'll get better," Gunner said. "Sorry, I know it's shi—bad."

Olivia just grabbed Ferguson. "Let's go."

"Where *are* we going?" Gunner asked, following her from the house as Will trailed behind them. "Your first night, should be something special, right?"

"Efeopean!" Olivia announced.

"Fair enough, there's a good place not too far away." Gunner got Olivia in the backseat as Will climbed in the front. Gunner looked across the gearshift at him for just a minute, giving himself permission to look while Will fiddled with his phone.

When Will looked up, Gunner had put the car in gear and they were rolling out of the driveway.

"GUNS," Will said as they got on the highway. "We should talk about—"

Gunner threw a glance over his shoulder at

Olivia, who was deeply absorbed in talking to Ferguson. "About?" he prompted.

"Media," Will said. "What if we get recognized? What do we say if someone asks who she is?"

"The owners of this restaurant won't," Gunner said, changing lanes. "I've been there a lot, they know me and they keep their mouths shut. But —" He scowled at the road, turning options over in his head. "I don't want to lie and say she's a niece or family friend because when the truth *does* come out…."

"Yeah, doesn't look good for you," Will agreed.

"But I'm also not ready to drop that particular bomb," Gunner said. He shuddered at the thought. It was going to be a *circus*, and he'd be at the center of it, right in the mouth of the lion. Just because he'd been there before didn't mean he *liked* it.

"So we'll just rely on societal norms and expectations," Will said.

Gunner blinked at him. "We'll what now?"

Will pitched his voice higher, mimicking a stranger. "Oh, what a cute little girl, who are you?" He dropped his voice and added a growl, clearly pretending to be Gunner. "This is Olivia. We have to be going now."

"I don't sound like that," Gunner couldn't help pointing out.

Will just grinned at him. "We don't offer *any* information. We pose for a picture, sign whatever, and when they ask questions about her, we change the subject, and they're the assholes for badgering us."

Gunner turned that over in his head. It could work. It wouldn't work for *long*, but maybe it would hold off the worst of the invasive questions until he'd figured some stuff out. He nodded. "We'll go with that, then. But I still don't sound like that."

Will's grin just widened and he pitched his voice deep again. "What, you don't think it's sexy?"

"What's 'sexy'?" Olivia piped up and sheer panic flashed across Will's face.

"Um," Gunner said, fighting giggles as he took the exit. "It's when you think someone's cute or funny. But when you're older. Like if you want to date them."

"You mean like boyfriends?"

"Yeah, like that," Gunner said.

Olivia wrinkled her nose. "Boys are gross."

"They sure are," Gunner agreed. By some miracle, he found a parking space only a few blocks from the restaurant.

They walked down the sidewalk, Olivia between them, Ferguson under her arm. Suddenly she stopped and tugged urgently at Gunner's pant leg.

Gunner stopped too, and crouched to be at eye level. "What's up?"

Olivia looked everywhere but him. "Should I call you Daddy?" she finally asked, her voice small.

Gunner chewed on his cheek for a minute. "I feel like… maybe you're not ready for that." Olivia didn't look at him, pointed chin tucked down and away. "I feel like maybe *I'm* not ready for that," Gunner confessed, and that got Olivia to look up at him. Gunner smiled at her. "For now, why don't you just call me Gunner?" He leaned in, conspiratorial. "You can still call *him*—" pointing at Will, "Uncle Will, though. He loves it."

Will's eyes promised murder when Gunner stood up, and Gunner grinned at him. Olivia slipped her small hand into his and leaned against his leg briefly.

"C'n we go eat now?"

"Yeah, let's do this thing."

Dinner was delicious, and Olivia kept them entertained with running chatter, commentary on anything and everything that popped into her head, it seemed. She insisted on sharing her meal with Ferguson, who she reported was not a fan.

"Tragic lack of taste," Will said, shaking his head. "You'll have to teach him to appreciate good food, Olivia."

After the meal, Olivia dragged her feet. "I'm still hungry," she said.

Gunner looked at her, incredulous. "You ate your weight in lamb tibs, I was there."

"But there's a hole in my stomach," Olivia said. Her tongue peeked out between her teeth as she fought the smile. "An *ice cream* shaped hole."

Will burst out laughing as Gunner covered his face, trying to hide his own amusement. Olivia grinned, clearly pleased with herself, and made big, pleading eyes at Gunner.

"Okay," Gunner said finally. "Okay, *okay*. Look, there's a Marble Slab right there. Just this once though, okay? Ice cream's not good for you after every meal."

Olivia's expression begged to differ but she didn't argue.

IT WAS when they were standing in line in the ice cream shop that things began to break down. Olivia looked at the flavors of ice cream, and then examined the toppings, and then went back to the flavors. Her little face was anguished, even after accepting several tastings to settle on a flavor.

"There's so many," she said.

Gunner shifted his feet. A line was forming behind them, people starting to look bored and impatient.

"Just pick something," he suggested.

"But what if I don't like it?"

"Then you don't get it again next time," Gunner said, tone sharper than he intended. More people had just come in the store, which suddenly felt cramped and small. Any second now, they were going to be recognized and it was going to be a free-for-all.

Olivia looked at the ice cream, looked at Gunner, screwed up her face, and burst into tears.

Gunner was shocked into immobility for a minute. Will seemed equally frozen beside him.

Olivia sat down hard on the floor, crying harder, her face bright red, and Gunner moved on instinct, scooping her up and bolting. Olivia didn't fight him as he turned the corner and sat them both down on the steps of a rather majestic brownstone. She was still crying, fists wrapped in Gunner's shirt, and instead of calming, she seemed to be working herself up into a full on hysterical fit.

Gunner rubbed her back, praying none of the neighbors would come to investigate the noise. Will hadn't joined them, and Gunner wasn't sure if he was grateful or betrayed by that.

He realized after a minute that Olivia was talking, hiccupping gasped words through the tears, and he bent to listen.

"I—w-want… *Mama*," she sobbed, and suddenly *Gunner* was fighting tears.

"I know," he whispered, pressing their cheeks together. "I know, I know you do. I'm so sorry. I'm so sorry all you've got is me."

Olivia squirmed, but not to get away. She got her arms free and wrapped them around Gunner's neck, a damp, warm weight against his chest. She was still crying, but the worst of the sobs seemed to have abated.

"You must miss her so much," Gunner murmured, rocking her back and forth.

Olivia nodded against his throat, hiccupping.

"You poor kid," Gunner said. "Got ripped away from your home *and* your mother, dumped in a strange city where the people talk weird and with some tattooed dude who has no idea what to do, and on top of that, you had to spend all that time with *Cane*." He waited until Olivia looked up at him and then shivered theatrically.

Olivia almost smiled, ducking her face back down to press it into his shirt again.

"It's gonna get better," Gunner told her, hand

moving in rhythmic sweeps up and down her spine. "I promise. It won't hurt this bad forever."

"Gunner?"

"Yeah."

"Is Mama in heaven?"

Gunner leaned sideways to look into Olivia's face again. It was tear-streaked and miserable, and Gunner tugged the sleeve of his shirt up and gently wiped one cheek.

"Did your mama ever say what happened when someone died?" he asked, instead of answering.

"She…." Olivia hiccup-sniffled again. "She said. Th-that she'd always be with me. B-but I can't see her. Or h-hear her." Her lip trembled again. "I want to see her, Gunner."

"I know, sweetheart," Gunner said. He rubbed her back gently. "She loves you so much, you know?"

Olivia nodded, another fat tear sliding down her face.

"Gunner?"

"Yeah, kiddo."

"D-does she know I love her too?"

Gunner pulled her close again, blinking away tears of his own. "I promise she does, Liv. She always will."

And then Will turned the corner, face lighting at the sight of them. He had three ice cream cones carefully balanced in his hands, and he sat down beside them as Olivia swiped at her face and sat up, still on Gunner's lap.

"I had to guess what flavor you liked," Will said.

"But there's raspberry cheesecake swirl with white chocolate chips mixed in, and dark chocolate fudge with marshmallows and pecans, and sweet cream but that one's for me." His eyes twinkled as he licked the side of the ice cream and Gunner did his best to telegraph his gratitude with his facial expression alone. Will seemed to get it, from the way his lips curved.

Olivia opted for the raspberry cheesecake, but showed no interest in getting off Gunner's lap. They ate with her snuggled against him, wispy curls tickling his nose as Gunner tried to eat without dripping ice cream in her hair.

When they were done, Olivia sighed. "'M too tired to walk," she said.

"The car's like two blocks away," Gunner pointed out.

"So *far*," Olivia said, and somehow got heavier in Gunner's arms.

"I'll carry her," Will said, lips twitching. He gathered Olivia up and stood, Gunner following suit. He was man enough to admit that it did something to him to see Will holding a child—*Gunner's* child—but he said nothing, just dug out his keys and led the way to the car.

Olivia was asleep before they were on the freeway.

"Doing okay?" Will asked, his tone hushed.

Gunner focused on the road. "I'm… yeah. She misses her mom."

"Of course she does."

"I'm not enough," Gunner blurted, and immediately wished he could take it back.

Will was already shaking his head. "Not true. I

know you weren't *prepared*, but you're going to do fine."

"She misses her mom," Gunner repeated, and somehow Will got what he was saying.

"You're going to be a great father," he said, and his voice made the fact undeniable. This was happening. Gunner had a child, he'd become a parent, and he was going to be a good father. Will laughed suddenly. "I can't *wait* to introduce her to the team."

"Oh my god, they're going to spoil her *rotten*," Gunner said. His chest eased. Even if he fucked up —and he knew he would—at least he had Will.

"Is it okay if I tell Clancy?" Will asked. "He's already in Vancouver, but he'll want to know."

"Yeah, of course," Gunner said immediately. "Will you go with me to practice in the morning? *Shit*, how am I going to practice if I don't have a sitter?"

"Your mom's coming in early, remember?"

"Right." Gunner relaxed again. And then tensed. "But what about when she leaves?"

Will put a hand on his thigh. "Guns. Chill. She'll help you figure this all out."

Gunner nodded, focusing on the road and not on Will's hand where it was resting on his leg, and told himself he wasn't disappointed when Will took it back to type something on his phone.

HE TOOK Olivia when they got home, bundling her gently into his arms as she mumbled something, and followed Will up the walk to the front door. He blessed the fact that he'd given Will a spare key years ago as Will unlocked the door to let them in.

A quiet word hushed the dogs' happy greetings, and Gunner glanced at Will. "Can you let them out for me?"

He headed upstairs and gently shook a protesting Olivia awake in the bathroom so she could brush her teeth, which she did with her eyes drooping and shoulders hanging. Gunner could sympathize—he was feeling pretty wrung out too. He managed to get the hairband out of her hair without too much trouble and winced when his finger caught on a tangle. He'd known this child —*his* child—less than twenty-four hours and he already knew there'd be hell to pay if he tried to brush her hair right now.

One night without brushing it wouldn't kill her, he decided. Olivia insisted on help getting into her pajamas, which they'd put away in the closet armoire, so Gunner did his best to get her limbs in the appropriate holes and the pajamas zipped.

"What idiot thought a zipper was a good idea on children's clothes?" he muttered to himself as he tried not to catch the teeth on Olivia's skin.

Finally, he was done, and he helped Olivia up and into bed, pulling the blankets over her. She blinked up at him.

"G'night, Gunner," she murmured.

"Goodnight, Olivia," Gunner said.

Will was waiting in the hall, hands in his pockets and one foot up on the wall behind him.

He looked unfairly good and Gunner fought the urge to walk into his arms.

He rubbed his neck instead. "Dogs good?"

"Yeah, they did their business and they're downstairs." Will pushed off the wall and closed the distance between them. "*You* good?"

Gunner blinked, trying not to sway into Will's warmth. "Yeah. Yeah, I'm—it's a lot, you know?"

"You're doing really well," Will murmured.

Gunner wanted to kiss him. Wanted Will to hold him. *Wanted.* He pushed it away. "She lost her shit in an ice cream shop," he said.

"She's a kid. They're weirdly resilient right up until they're not. Maybe your mom would have been able to tell she was close to the edge, but we can't all be superhuman. You handled it right. You got her out, got her calmed down." Will smiled at him. "I'm really proud of you."

"I don't know if I can do this." Gunner closed his eyes.

"That twenty-one year old kid who showed up here angry and defiant and bruised?" Will said, making Gunner open his eyes. "*He* maybe couldn't have done it." He brushed Gunner's cheekbone with a knuckle. "You're not that kid anymore. *You* can do anything you put your mind to, and that includes raising a six year old girl."

Gunner wasn't strong. He was ashamed of his lack of self-control but he couldn't stop himself from leaning in and pressing his forehead to Will's shoulder.

Will just held him wordlessly, bracketing him in a tiny pocket of peace. "Do you want me to stay the night?" he finally asked.

God, did he ever. Gunner gathered the last of his willpower and stepped back, shaking his head. "We'll be fine. You should go home. Will…." Will's eyes were so warm, so kind. "Thank you," Gunner said. "I'd have lost my mind in a goddamn minute if it weren't for you today."

"I'll be over in the morning, say an hour before practice?"

Gunner nodded and watched as Will headed back downstairs. Then he brushed his teeth, changed, called the dogs, and climbed into bed. As always, Babe got in his own bed, while Ty curled up at Gunner's feet.

He fell asleep to the sound of them breathing.

He was awoken by the door opening in the middle of the night. Gunner sat upright as Babe growled but cut himself off as if recognizing the intruder.

"G-Gunner?" Olivia sounded miserable.

Gunner flicked on the lamp beside the bed. Olivia was standing in the doorway clutching Ferguson, her mouth drooping.

"What is it, what's wrong?" Gunner said.

Olivia's lip wobbled and she rubbed her eyes with a fist. "My room is… big."

"Well, it's a big house," Gunner said, and then felt like an idiot. "Do you want… um. Do you want to stay in here with me and the dogs, just for tonight?"

Olivia's face lit up and she scrambled onto the

bed in record time, giving Ty a kiss on the head in passing before squirming under the covers.

Gunner settled back down and turned off the light. He could just see the curve of Olivia's cheek in the moonlight. "I don't know any bedtime stories," he said apologetically. "And my singing voice is terrible."

"That's alright," Olivia said matter-of-factly. She snuggled down into the pillows. "G'night, Gunner."

"Goodnight, Olivia," Gunner said again, and this time he fell asleep watching his daughter as she dreamed beside him.

GUNNER HAD A CHILD. Gunner was a *father*. Will still couldn't quite wrap his head around this fact. The mental image of Gunner attending PTA meetings made him snort as he drove home from Gunner's house and pulled into his own driveway. He thought yet again about getting a dog or a cat —something to greet him when he got home. His house felt empty, cold, when he let himself in the front door, unlike Gunner's house, which was always so full of light and warmth and… dogs.

He headed for the kitchen and made himself some rooibos tea, leaning a hip against the counter as he thought and the water heated.

He'd never seen Gunner quite so panicked, not that he could blame him. He couldn't even imagine how he himself would react in the same situation. Still, Gunner had handled it like a pro, speaking to Olivia like a small adult instead of in the condescending way some grown-ups did. Olivia had clearly taken to him immediately, and Will couldn't blame her.

HE'D TAKEN to Gunner the minute he'd touched down in Denver and come through baggage claim, dark circles under his eyes and pale blond curly hair under a backward snapback, a forced smile on his unfairly handsome face.

Will had felt like he'd been punched in the stomach with Gunner's attractiveness, his chiseled cheekbones and the dimple in his chin. He didn't even know if Gunner was queer, certainly wasn't going to broach that subject with him when he was clearly still brittle and bruised from how Indianapolis had treated him.

Be careful with him, Horan had told him. *He's wild and undisciplined but something more than that is going on. I want you to find out if you can, but don't push him. Let him tell you when he's ready.*

Will had heard the stories, of course, seen the press conferences, read the articles. They all said the same thing. *Gunner Ryan is a ticking time-bomb. His talent on the ice doesn't make up for his behavior off it. Pity the team that takes him on.*

Will wasn't sure what to think, but he trusted his general manager. Horan had a keen eye for character that hadn't failed him yet. If he thought there was more to Gunner Ryan than the bad press that swirled around him like a cloud of stinging gnats, then Will was willing to give Gunner a chance.

So Will had taken him to his hotel, helped him drag his luggage upstairs, and then out for a mini-tour of Denver and some food.

"You're in Colorado now, you have to have a bison burger," he told him, and Gunner shrugged like he didn't care.

Will settled across from him on the wooden bench in the restaurant and watched as Gunner took his first bite. His green eyes went wide and he bit back a moan.

"That's more like it," Will said smugly, and dug into his own burger.

They ate in companionable silence for a while, neither feeling the need to speak. A country song was playing on the jukebox, the soft twangs soothing to Will's ears by now, but probably sounding foreign to Gunner. He wondered briefly if they had a lot of country music in Indiana.

He wasn't really expecting Gunner to put his fork down and say, "You might as well ask."

Will blinked. "Ask what?"

Gunner's chin went up. "You want to know what happened. Fine. Ask me."

Will fumbled for words. He wasn't good with words, dammit, but he could see the nerves in Gunner's tight shoulders, his white knuckles on the edge of the table. He needed to be careful.

"I want to know… whatever you want to tell me," he finally said.

Gunner's mouth twisted. "You want to know why they traded me? What I did to make them hate me? What a bad deal you got?"

"*No*," Will said, horrified, and Gunner must have heard the sincerity in his voice, because he took a slow breath. "Gunner, I don't—we *wanted* you here. I've watched... so much tape of you since I heard about the trade. We gave up two guys and next year's pick for you. You really think we didn't want you here?"

Some of the tension bled from Gunner's frame but he didn't say anything, eyes intent on Will's face, so Will continued, still fumbling for the right words.

"I don't know what they said to you. Or did to you." He didn't miss the flinch that got him, but he didn't follow it. "I think the press blew everything way out of proportion."

Gunner made an ugly noise. "Or maybe they got it exactly right."

Will just lifted a shoulder. "Even if they did, what would that have told me? That you like to drink, like to party, you have a lot of company, in and out of bed. You're also an incredible skater, your slapshot is a fucking wet dream, and you've got eyes in the back of your head on the ice. I don't care—" Gunner's eyes were sheened with something suspiciously like tears, and Will stumbled briefly. Was he saying the wrong things? What else could he say but the truth? "I don't think you're half the monster they painted you to be. I think you're young and made some bad choices and didn't have guidance from the guys who should have given it to you."

Gunner stood up so fast he nearly fell. "I have to—where's the bathroom?"

Will pointed silently and Gunner bolted.

Alone, Will put his head in his hands. He'd basically called Gunner stupid, hadn't he? He pulled out his phone and texted his brother. *Think I might have fucked up.*

Clancy's reply was swift. *Already?*

Will didn't rise to the bait. *We were talking about Indy and he got upset.*

What'd you say?

Will glanced toward the bathroom but there was no sign of Gunner yet. *Told him I wanted him here. That I didn't care about the press.*

Those sound like good things, Clancy replied. *Why do you think you fucked up?*

Because he just ran for the bathroom and he's not coming out, Will sent, frustration making his hands shake as he typed.

Clancy didn't answer for a few minutes, but Will didn't push him.

Finally, his phone buzzed. *Think you did better than you might think. Maybe he needed to hear it.*

Then why'd he run?

Will's phone rang and he answered immediately.

"You really are a dumb son of a bitch sometimes," Clancy said.

"Thanks, bro," Will said. "Love you too."

"How would you react when someone said something you needed to hear, something positive that you weren't expecting? How would you feel if you'd been kicked and beaten—metaphorically, I hope to God—and someone gave you a kind word?"

Will blinked, opened his mouth, closed it again. "Oh."

"Dumb son of a bitch," Clancy said, and hung up.

Gunner stepped out of the bathroom and made his way across the room to Will. His shoulders were loose, his stance easy again. He gave Will a bright smile as he sat down.

"Sorry, must have eaten something janky yesterday."

Will allowed him the out. "Feeling better now?"

"Yeah." Gunner met his eyes. "Yeah, I am."

They dropped the subject after that, talking about easier things, like Gunner's dog, his family up in Alberta. He had a younger sister in high school and his mother had raised them alone for most of Gunner's life.

"Walked out," Gunner said about his father with a shrug. "We got by fine without him."

Gunner asked about Will's family too, and Will told him about his mother in Ontario, his father who'd died in Will's teens, his sister studying for the bar and his brother Clancy.

"He's a D-man, and a damn good one, but if you tell him I said so, I'll deny every word to my grave."

Gunner's smile flashed again and something pulled low in Will's gut.

He was attracted to Gunner. It was probably inevitable, with that dazzling smile of his, the curls and the tattoos that peeked from under the collar of his shirt and covered both arms. Will was drawn to him, fascinated by him, wanted to make him smile more. He still had no idea if Gunner was straight or not—he'd given no sign in any direction. As much as Will wanted to find out, he didn't ask.

AND THEN GUNNER had gotten up on his locker after his first practice with the team and said loudly, "By the way, I like girls *and* guys, so if anyone has a problem with that, speak up."

There'd been a shocked silence and then Harnell had made an ugly noise.

"You checking us out, Ryan? Sneaking peeks at our dicks?"

Will had tensed to go to Gunner's rescue, but Gunner had it under control.

He laughed derisively. "Please, Harny, the day I need to look at that shriveled carrot you call a dick to get anywhere is the day I hang up my queer card for good."

That had dissolved the locker room into laughter, and Gunner had bounced to the ground, grinning. There were a few holdouts, of course, a couple of homophobes who thought they could take their aggression out on Gunner either verbally or physically.

Will had taken care of them when Gunner wasn't around—usually a firm talking-to from the captain was all that was needed anyway.

NOWADAYS, Gunner's sexuality was an open secret. No one talked about it outside the locker room, no one said anything to the media—not even the homophobes. Maybe Will had been a touch aggressive with his warning to be quiet, but he regretted nothing.

Still, Will had never made a move, much as he'd wanted to. *Teammates*, he'd told himself, and it had helped that Gunner had never made a move either, never showed any sign of interest, not in him or anyone else on the team. He'd slept around plenty—or Will had thought he had. Always with one girl or another for public events, often leaving the bar with a guy and showing up at practice with a cat-eating-the-canary smile the next day. After a while, Will's crush had faded, morphed into the steady affection that flowed between them like water, sweet and life-sustaining. It was better that way. He told himself that a lot.

The kettle beeped at him and he poured the water over the tea with one hand as he dialed his brother with the other.

"Willy-boy, it's late, you not keeping to your schedule?"

Will rolled his eyes, carrying his tea through to the bedroom. "Can we be serious for a second?"

"I don't know, can we?" Clancy shot back, but he sobered at the sound of Will's sigh. "Sorry, little brother, what's up?"

"Um." Will kicked off his shoes and settled on the bed, careful not to spill his tea. "So something kind of… happened today. With Gunner."

"You finally tell him you love him?" Will could *hear* Clancy's infuriating grin. "Wait, no, you don't sound happy enough for that to have happened. Unless he said he didn't love you back, which I guess would make you sound like a sad puppy, but I can't imagine he'd—"

"*Oh my god shut up*!" Will shouted. "I have told you and *told* you, asshole, it's not *like* that, and that's *not* why I'm calling so could you please just shut the fuck up because *Gunner has a daughter*."

There was a stunned silence. Will blew out a breath, scrubbed a hand through his hair.

"Uh."

"Pretty much," Will said, leaning back against the pillows.

"*How*? Is he seeing someone? I thought he was single. Is he—"

Will gave him the rundown as he understood it, Clancy listening intently.

As he was talking, he heard typing.

"Keep going, bud," Clancy ordered. "I'm just buying a plane ticket."

"What, *now*?"

"Season isn't starting for another week, I can take two to three days to come meet this kid who's turned my buddy's world upside down, not to mention made *you* sound like a doting grandpa."

"I do not," Will protested.

"Your voice goes all soft and gooey when you say her name," Clancy said. "It's disgusting. Oh hey, I can catch a flight tonight if I hurry. Don't worry about picking me up, I'll get a car from the airport, gotta go, bye!"

The phone cut off before Will could argue, and he was left holding a cooling cup of tea, staring at the far wall in bemusement.

4

GUNNER WOKE up with a heavy weight across his chest and hair in his mouth. He dragged his eyes open to find Olivia face down on top of him, her face buried in his shoulder. She was a tiny furnace, pumping out so much heat Gunner was sweating, so he gently eased her off to the side and slipped out of bed to use the bathroom.

Olivia was still asleep when he came out, so he took the dogs downstairs and let them out, thinking despairingly about food he might be able to make that a six year old would eat.

The doorbell rang and Gunner froze, glancing at the clock. It was barely six o'clock in the morning—Fay's plane wasn't due for another two hours, and Will wasn't coming over until nine.

But sure enough, Fay was standing outside his door, beaming at him. She looked the same as ever—petite and put together, maybe a few more smile lines around her eyes and a little more silver in her blonde hair. Gunner's heart lurched and he stumbled into her arms.

"Mom," he said, holding her tight. "*Mom.*"

"I know, baby, I know." Fay stroked his hair and then released him. "I got an earlier flight."

"You could have called," Gunner said, diving to pick up her bags and usher her inside. "I would have come and got you."

"And wake Olivia up, make you drag her out this early?" Fay snorted. She looked around the living room and nodded. "At least you're keeping the place nice."

"The housekeeper is," Gunner mumbled. "I mostly just stay out of her way, she scares me."

"So where's Olivia?" Fay asked.

"Gunner?" Olivia sounded uncertain, standing at the top of the stairs, her hair a wild aureole around her face.

Gunner darted up the stairs and knelt beside her. "Hey," he said softly. "My mom wanted to come meet you. Is that okay?"

Olivia's eyes widened. "Your mom?"

"Yeah, your grandma. Do you want to come downstairs and meet her?"

Olivia nodded and then caught herself. "Is she —" She chewed on her lip as Gunner waited, confused. "Is she nice?" she finally said in a rush.

Gunner flashed back to the letter, the way Stephanie had talked about her own parents. "She's *so* nice," he told Olivia. "She takes care of everyone and she'll love you exactly as you are, she'll never try to change you."

Olivia digested that and started down the stairs. She marched up to Fay and held out one small hand. "I'm Olivia," she said clearly. "You're my... Gunner's mom."

Fay sank to her knees and took Olivia's hand. "I am, which makes me your grandmother." Her eyes crinkled when she smiled. "You're a very beautiful young lady and it is absolutely lovely to meet you."

Olivia considered, and then threw herself forward, into Fay's arms. Fay caught her, tears welling in her eyes, and Gunner had to look away and clear his throat.

"Is—um, Olivia's got the room you usually sleep in, but you can have either of the other two," he said. "Do you care which?"

Fay shook her head, careful like she didn't want to dislodge Olivia. Gunner already knew it was nearly impossible to budge Olivia if she didn't want to be, but he'd let his mother figure that out for herself. He took her bags upstairs and put them in the guest room opposite his room.

When he got back downstairs, Olivia was sitting at the counter, talking at high speed while Fay looked through the fridge.

"And then I played with the dogs and showed them my slapshot, and then Gunner and Uncle Will let me pick out my room and we unpacked my stuff and then we went out for Efeopean and *ice cream*." Olivia's face dropped. "I cried in the ice cream store and upset Gunner."

"What? No!" Gunner said. He rushed to her, tilting her pointed chin up. "You didn't upset me. I was *worried* about you. But I wasn't upset. You didn't do anything wrong, okay?"

Olivia's mouth worked but she nodded. "And

then we came home and I got scared in the night and Gunner let me sleep with him and Ty."

Gunner caught Fay's amused eye. "Just for the night," he said defensively. "She'd had a really rough day."

"Olivia, how do you feel about pancakes?" Fay asked, and Olivia lit up.

It was easier, after that. Gunner could sit back, watch the way his mother treated Olivia—gently, with care for the obvious trauma she'd been through, but also briskly, with purpose, the way she approached everything in life. It was good, clearly effective, he thought, taking mental notes as Fay and Olivia argued about the inclusion of vegetables in the scrambled eggs Fay was making.

"I don't *want* them," Olivia said, storms brewing in her eyes.

Fay, slicing mushrooms, raised an eyebrow. "Gunner told me you want to be a hockey player."

There was a mutinous silence, as if Olivia knew where she was going with this.

"Gunner, what do hockey players eat?" Fay asked sweetly.

"Protein," Gunner said, hiding his smile. Why hadn't he thought of that yesterday? "Lots and lots of protein, and… vegetables."

Olivia sighed, tiny shoulders slumping.

The scrambled eggs had cheese, onion, mushrooms, and spinach in them, and they were delicious. Olivia ate every bite and accepted a second helping when it was offered.

THE DOORBELL RANG as they were cleaning up the breakfast mess and Gunner ran to answer it. Will was standing there grinning at him. He opened his mouth to speak and was sharply hip-checked by Clancy, who barged into the house before Gunner could react.

"Where is she?" he demanded. His beard had somehow gotten even thicker since the last time Gunner saw him. "I gotta meet this mini-Gunner. Is she as ugly as you?" He dismissed that. "Not possible. Is she in the kitchen?" He dashed that way without giving Gunner time to answer.

"How…," Gunner said, staring after him.

"Sorry," Will said, rubbing his hip. "He's been unbearable since I told him. Got a flight down last night. We should probably—"

"Go make sure he's not corrupting my daughter?" Gunner said. "Good thinking."

They found Clancy in the kitchen, staring at Olivia, who looked thunderstruck.

"Oh my God, she *does* look just like you," Clancy breathed. "Olivia, I'm Clancy, the handsome Calder brother. Is Gunner treating you okay? Blink twice if you need me to rescue—"

"Why is there so much *hair* on your face?" Olivia interrupted.

Gunner couldn't stop the laughter and didn't try. He clung to Will and *howled* as Clancy straightened, attempting to regain his dignity.

"Definitely your daughter," he said. "Hi Mrs. Ryan, it's nice to see you again."

"Shouldn't you be in Vancouver?" Fay asked,

her lips twitching. "Not that it's not lovely to see you too. We were all very sad to hear you got traded."

Clancy shrugged. "Gunny's my friend too, and the season hasn't started. I wanted to be here to offer moral support." He made a face. "Ugh. Emotions. Gross."

"How long can you stay?" Gunner asked, his throat tight. Will rubbed his back silently.

"Flying back out tomorrow. Figured I'd go to the rink with you guys today, say hi to everyone."

Olivia perked up. "Rink? Are you gonna skate?"

"May even play a little hockey," Clancy told her with a wink. "You wanna come watch, sprout?"

Olivia was about to vibrate right off her stool as she looked at Gunner and then Fay as if unsure who to ask permission from.

Fay coughed. "I can come with her, if you want. Let her watch some practice and then maybe take her shopping after?"

Gunner looked at Olivia and knew there was no way he could say no to that face. "But the guys can be a little… rough," he warned her as she squealed with delight. "They might scare you."

Olivia tilted her chin. "But you'll be there too." That seemed to be all there was to say on the matter, and Gunner had to turn away, clearing his throat.

"I'm gonna… go get ready," he said vaguely, in the direction of the kitchen, and escaped upstairs. It took him a minute to realize Will had followed him up.

"You look a little less like you've been hit by a train this morning," he said, sitting down on Gunner's bed.

Gunner averted his eyes from *that* sight and shrugged, pulling clothes out of the dresser. "I'm… dealing. Shit." He stiffened. "I gotta tell Frank first. Should I call him or go by his office when we get there?"

"Call him," Will advised, so Gunner sat down beside him, still determinedly not thinking about Will in his bed, and dialed Frank Horan's number.

"Gunner!"

His GM always seemed delighted to hear from him, like he genuinely liked Gunner and looked forward to their conversations. It made it easier for Gunner to take a deep breath and blurt out, "So apparently I have a daughter."

Dead silence on the line, and Gunner shifted his weight, glancing at Will.

"Congratulations?" Frank finally offered, his voice careful. "I thought you were single. When… how…."

"I am. Single, I mean. She, um. Indianapolis, after we won the Cup?"

"Ah. And you're just now telling me?"

"I just now found *out*," Gunner said. "I would have said—I would have told you, I swear."

"I see." Frank was silent for a minute, considering in the way he had. "So what's the deal?"

Gunner told him everything, the letter and Stephanie's illness and her reluctance to leave Olivia with her own parents. "She said—" He swallowed. "She said I was good. And that Olivia would be safe with me."

"You are, and she will, if that's what you want," Frank said.

"What I—what does that mean?"

"I just mean there are options," Frank said soothingly. "You being thrown in the deep end of the single parent pool isn't the only course of action here."

"Do the other *options* include taking her away? Giving her up for adoption or to Stephanie's parents?" Gunner's throat was tight and he suddenly wanted to punch something.

"Maybe your mother would take her," Frank said carefully.

"*No,*" Gunner exploded. He was on his feet, not sure how he got there, fury blinding him. "I'm not—not giving her away or passing her off like she's something to get rid of. She *needs* me. And I know I'm not responsible and *mature* and whatever, maybe she *would* be better off with someone else, but Stephanie asked *me.* I'm not giving up on her, okay? She's *my* responsibility." He stopped, swallowing hard, as Will rose to his feet, eyes sympathetic.

"That's all I needed to know," Frank said, and he sounded warm. Approving. "I'll let the appropriate departments know. I take it you're not going to hide her existence or pretend she's a niece or cousin?"

"No," Gunner said simply. Will was standing in front of him, just watching, and Gunner steeled himself against the urge to step into his arms again.

"I can't wait to meet her," Frank said, and when he hung up, Gunner let out a huge breath.

Will was still standing there but he looked unhappy.

"It's okay," Gunner told him. "Frank's cool with it."

Will shook his head. "I wish you wouldn't do that."

"Do what?"

"Get so down on yourself," Will said. "The only one saying you're not responsible and mature is you."

"And every media outlet from here to Indy," Gunner flung at him.

Will didn't flinch. "They don't matter. Your friends, your *family,* we know the truth. *Stephanie* knew it, Guns, after being with you for one night. So don't you think you should start listening to us, and stop believing the media?"

Gunner couldn't breathe. He dug the heels of his hands into his eyes, gulping for air. "I've fucked up so much," he managed. He could *hear* Mateo's voice, thick with tears and betrayal. *How could you?*

Will's hand was warm on his arm as he pulled Gunner against him. "You won't fuck this up," he said, and the calm certainty in his voice made the tears in Gunner's eyes sting harder.

There were footsteps outside, and then Clancy's voice.

"Are we going or what?" He stopped dead in the doorway as Gunner hastily stepped back, out of Will's arms. Delight dawned on Clancy's face and Will pointed at him.

"No."

"Oh *yes,*" Clancy said, grinning. "Is this finally

happening? Can I *finally* collect on my bet with Belsy?"

"*Nothing* is happening," Will said, sharp and vicious. "Except you fucking off downstairs to wait for us."

He shut the door in Clancy's face and turned back to Gunner. "Sorry, every time I think he's dropped that stupid idea of his—"

"So stupid," Gunner agreed. He was distantly proud of keeping his voice steady, but he couldn't look at Will's face. Instead he held up his change of clothes. "Gonna, um—" He escaped to the bathroom.

Inside, the door closed, he braced his hands on the counter and stared at his reflection. "So stupid," he whispered.

5

Six years ago

He liked the team. More than he'd thought he would, honestly. He hadn't known what to expect —what the Racers management or Jefferson had told them before he came to them, and he'd been braced for the worst, for derision and exasperation bleeding into anger when Gunner just couldn't— wouldn't, if Jefferson was asked—do what was expected of him.

Instead he found a coach who seemed actively interested in what Gunner thought of the plays he drew up. He found a captain in Will who watched what Gunner did, who complimented him on especially nice moves, who seemed almost able to read his mind.

And he found a team of guys who welcomed him in as if they had no idea they were inviting a viper into their den, a disaster just waiting to strike.

The wives and girlfriends were friendly too, and Gunner found himself flirted gently with by multiple women who clearly appreciated his looks but had no intentions of actually pursuing him. It was a new experience, and one he found he enjoyed. It felt… safe, somehow, like he could be himself, be *liked*, without feeling the need to close the deal.

His favorite was Cady, he decided early on. She was short, verging on plump, with a heart-shaped face and dark hair in a pixie cut.

She was Belmont's girlfriend, and she was sharp and funny and had fascinating observations on everything. She was in culinary school, and everyone on the team was her guinea pig when it came to testing her latest creations.

Most importantly, she didn't seem starstruck by him at all. His first week in Denver, she got his number from Will and called him.

"Sorry," she said, sounding not at all repentant. "Jason's got an interview and I need to have my car looked at. Do you think you could come with me?"

"Wait, who's Jason?" Gunner asked.

"Belmont, you doofus!"

"Oh, right. Why do you need me?"

"Because I'm a girl, and because of that I clearly know jackshit about cars. So I need you to come with me, preferably in a sleeveless shirt so they can see your tattoos, and stand silently beside me while I bully them."

So Gunner had gone with her and done as she asked. He'd folded his arms and looked forbidding as Cady did exactly what she'd said she would do —bullied the technician into giving her exactly what she needed.

"It's not the carburetor!" she exclaimed. "Do you even hear yourself? It's the timing belt! It's so simple, I just need it replaced. Look, if you can't do it, I'll take it somewhere else."

The technician opened his mouth, a patronizing smile on his face, and Gunner cleared his throat. That was all it took.

"Sure," the technician said, deflating. "It'll be done in an hour."

"Perfect," Cady declared, and turned to Gunner. "Tacos?"

"Absolutely," Gunner agreed.

THE RESTAURANT WAS bright and cheerful and Cady smiled at him over her soda.

"How are you liking Denver?"

"It's beautiful," Gunner said honestly. "Hard to breathe, kinda, but they say I'll acclimate."

"Yeah, the altitude will bitchslap you at first," Cady agreed. "Finding your place on the team?"

"So far." Gunner dunked a chip in salsa. "They're good guys."

"How do you like Will?"

Gunner glanced up. "Why?"

Cady shrugged. "Because he's your captain, and he's not always comfortable leading, from what Jason's told me. 'Course, Jase hasn't been here much longer than you at this point, but still. Seems like Will's still trying to find his way too."

"Well, he just got named captain what, a month ago?" Gunner asked. "He's probably still figuring a lot of shit out. He's—I really like him. He's kinda dorky, you know? Awkward, I guess. I know he hates the media, not that I blame him. But he met me at the airport, and he took me around Denver and out to eat, and he—" He said they want me here, he thought but didn't say. "He made me feel welcome."

"You should have heard them freaking out when they got you," Cady said, smiling fondly at the memory.

Gunner stared at her. "What?"

"Oh, it went around the group chat like wildfire. Jason showed me some of it. They were super excited. Apparently something something puck sense something footwork something—to be honest, I know more about cars than I do hockey at this point, although I'm sure I'll learn. Suffice it to say, it was all very complimentary."

Gunner's ears were burning. He ducked his head and took a drink of his water, struggling to find words.

"So, are you single?" Cady inquired. She flashed a smile when Gunner glanced back up at her. "If you're wondering whether or not I manufactured this outing in order to mine you for gossip, you'd be partially correct. My car really does need a new timing belt, but you were a nice… bonus."

"Well, at least you're honest," Gunner said, amused in spite of himself. "Yes, I'm single. And I guess the news has gone around?"

"What, about you playing for more than one

team?" Cady took a gulp of soda. "Yup. That took some balls, I gotta say."

"Better to get it out of the way," Gunner said. "That way I know early on who's gonna have a problem with it. What about, um… Will? Do you think he's okay with it?"

"I know he is," Cady said firmly. "Just ask him if you're worried. So you're not seeing anyone?"

"Pretty sure that's what single means," Gunner agreed. "And I'm really not interested in being set up with someone, just for the record."

Cady deflated, pouting briefly. "You sure? Because I think he'd be perfect for you."

Gunner managed to summon a smile. He was too raw from what had happened with Mateo to even think about dating without flinching. "I'm sure. But thank you. Is Will dating anyone?"

"Why, you wanna take a shot at him?"

Gunner did flinch that time, and Cady sobered.

"Fuck, I didn't mean—I'm sorry. I was just teasing, okay?"

Gunner stirred his drink, not meeting her eyes. "It's okay. But no teammates. Ever. I was just curious."

"Okay. As far as I know, he's single right now. He dates occasionally but he's so shy I think it's hard for him to pick up."

"Are we talking about the same guy?" Gunner asked. "Will, shy?"

Cady looked startled. "You think he's not?"

"Well, he's weird, sure. And awkward, like I said. But he's not *shy*. He just doesn't like talking to people he doesn't know."

"Isn't that the definition of shyness?" Cady asked, lips quirking.

"Pretty sure it's not," Gunner said, smiling back at her. "Tell me more about yourself. Belsy said something about cooking school?"

6

Olivia chattered the whole way to the rink, telling Clancy all about her skating lessons and how she was going to play pro hockey.

"Who are your favorite players?" Clancy prompted.

"Gunner, duh," Olivia said, rolling her eyes as if that was a given. "And Saint, and Uncle Will. And Scout Jackson, I love her!"

"Scout Jackson is talented *and* hot," Clancy agreed. "And I'm gonna ask her out now that we live in the same city, you watch. But I digress. Uncle Will." Clancy turned to look at Will, who was staring determinedly out the window. "*Uncle* Will. It fits you, William." He leaned into Olivia's space. "But what about me?"

Olivia shrugged. "You're okay, I guess."

Gunner couldn't stifle the snort as Clancy clutched his chest, mortally wounded.

"I'll just have to change your mind on that," he said. "Because I'm the best, and these two chumps got nothing on me. I'll give you Saint though."

"Mama took me to a Seabirds game once!" Olivia told him. "We were really far away but I could see Saint on the great big screen, and Carmine got in a *fight*!"

"Ever seen the Direwolves play?" Clancy asked.

Olivia shook her head regretfully. "I wanted to, but Mama said she couldn't afford it. She looked so sad, so I stopped asking." She brightened. "We watched all your games on the TV, though! At least last season. Before that I was little and didn't understand much."

Clancy appeared fascinated. "You're not little now?"

Olivia gave him a scornful look. "I'm *six,*" she said in withering tones.

Will grinned at Gunner, soft and private between them. "This kid is great," he said, voice pitched low under Olivia and Clancy's conversation.

"Yeah," Gunner said, smiling. "She kind of is."

FAY HAD FOLLOWED behind them in Will's truck. After practice, they'd decided, she was going to take Olivia shopping in Gunner's car while Gunner rode home with Will. Olivia was bouncing on her toes the second she was out of the car, tugging on Gunner's hand to make him walk faster.

Fay laughed, beside him. "You were just like

that at her age," she said fondly. "Bursting with energy and unable to contain it."

"C'moooon," Olivia said, pulling harder. "You're walking so *slow*."

Inside the building, though, she got quiet, and crowded close to Gunner's leg. He bent to see her face, which she'd tucked against his thigh.

"Hey," he said softly. "You okay?"

Olivia nodded wordlessly but she didn't let go. Gunner couldn't really walk with her clinging to his leg, so he swung her up into his arms.

"Better?" he asked.

Olivia looped her arms around his neck and beamed at him. "Better," she agreed.

The first person they saw was Belmont, walking out of the dressing room with a towel draped around his neck, brown hair damp and disheveled. He saw Gunner, opened his mouth to greet him, then did a comic double-take at Olivia on his hip.

"You—uh."

"Olivia, this is Jason Belmont. Don't believe a word he says about me."

Olivia waved.

Belmont looked thunderstruck. He waved back, mouth working but nothing coming out. Will stepped up beside him and whispered something in his ear. Belmont's eyes shot wide.

"Holy *shit*!"

Gunner immediately covered Olivia's ears, glaring at him, as Belmont went bright red and stumbled over an apology.

"That's a bad word!" Olivia chirped.

"It sure is," Gunner agreed, still glaring. "The rest of the guys in there?"

Belmont nodded, still staring at Olivia.

"I'll go in first," Will said. "Make sure they're decent."

He slipped through the doors as Clancy joined them and Belmont's eyes somehow got even bigger.

"You're here too?"

"Like I'd miss this," Clancy scoffed.

"Jason plays defense," Gunner told her. He wasn't sure how solid her hockey knowledge was, at six years old. "He plays with Uncle Will's line a lot."

Belmont's eyes were bulging at this point. *Uncle Will*, he mouthed to Clancy, who looked positively devilish with glee.

Will put his head through the door. "All clear, come on in."

Gunner walked into a bubble of silence. Most of his team was there, in various states of undress, but thankfully no one was naked. And they were all staring at him. Or rather, they were all staring at Olivia, who'd put her head down on Gunner's shoulder at the full force of the attention trained on her.

"Guys, this is Olivia. Olivia, these are my friends." He cleared his throat. "Olivia's, um. My daughter. She came to live with me yesterday. So, like… you'll probably be seeing a lot of her. Also she loves hockey and she came to watch us practice, so don't let me down out there."

No one said a word. Gunner shifted his weight, unsure what to say. Belmont, Clancy, and

Will were behind him, Belmont whispering urgently in Will's ear.

Arseni broke the silence first, rising to offer a big hand to Olivia. "Arseni Kutepov," he told her when she hesitantly accepted it, and gave her a gallant little bow. Gunner could have kissed him. "Can call me Sonny." He smiled. "You look like your papa."

With that, the dam burst and the others crowded around to introduce themselves. Olivia was clearly bowled over by the amount of attention, and she clung even tighter to Gunner's neck, but she didn't seem afraid, so Gunner stood still and answered questions from the team for her.

"Six. She's from Indianapolis. No, she's not a Racers fan. I'll explain later. *Later*."

Lukas came over toward the end, and Olivia gasped.

"You're *so tall*," she marveled.

"Luke's a goalie," Gunner told her. "Helps him stop a lot of pucks, being so tall. Means he can reach a long way."

"Plus you ride on shoulders, you can touch ceiling," Lukas said, smiling at her.

Parson showed up then, pushing through the doors. He'd clearly been warned, as there was no surprise on his face as he strode up to Gunner and Olivia.

"This is our coach," Gunner said. "He's very nice, I promise, but he sometimes yells at us."

"Only when you don't listen, which is always," Parson retorted, but he smiled at Olivia. "Nice to meet you, kiddo. It's time for the boys to get out on the ice."

Gunner took the not very subtle hint and turned to find Fay, who'd waited in the hall. She collected Olivia and they waved goodbye to him as he dove back into the dressing room to change.

And was immediately pounced on by several very large men, all wanting to know what the *fuck* was going on.

"I didn't know until yesterday," Gunner said over and over. Belmont was looking a little manic, Arseni mostly confused, and Lukas was grinning openly, flashing his missing tooth. "It was a one night stand thing, okay? Happened in Indianapolis. The mother never told me, never told anyone until she got sick."

That shut them up briefly.

"Wait, hang on." Schulz was clearly doing math in his head. "You said she's six. Born when?"

"Uh, February."

Schulz's mouth dropped open. "*Guns.* You had a Stanley Cup baby!"

"Not intentionally!" Gunner protested, but no one seemed to hear him, everyone talking over each other.

It took Parson using the whistle to shut them up. "Not that this isn't fun," he said dryly, "but we really do have practice. So get your asses in gear, maybe?"

THEY HIT the ice and Gunner spotted Olivia and Fay immediately, sitting up against the glass. Gunner pulled a face at Olivia as he skated by, getting a giggle from her, and then Coach's whistle blew and it was time to get to work.

Gunner's awareness shrank to the ice under his blades, the puck on his stick and the burn of his muscles as he powered through the drills. He was sweating and exhausted when Coach called them in to complain about the holes in their defense for a while before sending them off to cool down.

Fay and Olivia were waiting in the hall.

"She didn't get bored once," Fay told him.

Olivia grinned up at him. "You were *great*," she said.

Gunner grinned back, running a hand through his sweaty hair. "I've gotta cool down and shower and then we have strategy stuff. Mom?"

"I've got her for the rest of the day," Fay said. "We'll see you at home."

Clancy grabbed Will and pulled him into the showers, pushing him toward the far showerheads as Will protested.

"How many times do I have to tell you, I don't like you like that!" he said, and Clancy snapped him with the towel.

"You're disgusting," he informed him as Will rubbed the stinging spot, unable to stop the grin. "We're talking about Gunner."

The grin slid off Will's face. "Nothing to talk about." He turned the water on and waited for it to heat, avoiding Clancy's eyes.

"He's in love with you," Clancy said, and Will choked on air.

"He *what*?"

"You heard me. How you don't see it is beyond me." Clancy scowled. "Kid or not, he's head over heels in love with you. He watches everything you do. When you're not looking, his eyes—" He shook his head. "Dumbass has shit taste, but that's neither here nor there. Question is, what are *you* going to do about it?"

Will stepped under the spray, tilting his face into the water. "I'm not going to do anything," he said after a minute. "Because you're wrong." Around them, the other players were coming in, turning on their own showers and talking back and forth, but Gunner hadn't appeared yet. Still, Will kept his voice low. "It's not like that, and you know it. Besides, even if it *were* true, I'm the captain. It would be inappropriate."

Clancy threw his hands in the air. "You are *infuriating*," he snarled. "Stubborn fucking jackass, when are you going to see what's right in front of you? Are you only going to figure it out once it's too late?" He stopped sharply and Will looked up to see Gunner, carrying a towel and looking bemused.

"Everything okay?"

"Fine," Will said shortly, and turned back to the water as Clancy growled something under his breath and stomped to a different showerhead.

"You guys fighting?" Gunner asked, joining him, and Will would never check out a guy in the shower or locker room, it was incredibly bad manners, so he resolutely didn't look at the long line of Gunner's throat as the water streamed through his hair.

It took him a minute to remember Gunner asked a question. "Just a difference of opinion," he said, and reached for the shampoo. "He thought

Val Kilmer was the best Batman. Can you believe that?"

Clancy dragged Gunner aside after the strategy session. "We're going out," he announced.

This brought protests from several people, all of whom wanted to dig as many details of Gunner's new situation out of him as possible. Clancy growled at them.

"I'm leaving tomorrow, and I want to spend time with my friend," he said. "You buzzards can have him later." And he stalked away, pulling Gunner along behind him.

Gunner put up a protest most of the way, but truth be told, he was relieved to be away from the team's questions. Clancy held up Will's keys.

"We're going for nachos, and we're going to talk," he said, and the glint in his eye boded no good for man nor beast.

The ride to Clancy's favorite nacho joint was silent. Gunner spent it on his phone. Fay was sending him pictures of Olivia trying on clothes, others of them in the food court of the mall, and Gunner couldn't help but smile as he flicked through them.

A text from Will popped up. *Sorry.*

For what? Gunner sent back.

My brother, mostly.

Gunner didn't answer. He wasn't sure what he'd say, in any case, but they'd arrived and Clancy was waiting for him to get out.

Inside, they placed their orders and sat down.

"First things first," Clancy said. "That kid is adorable and you're gonna be a great father."

Gunner gaped at him. That wasn't even in the *realm* of things he was expecting to hear, and he had no idea how to respond.

Clancy waved a hand, looking disgusted. "I'm not going to repeat myself but I said what I said. Now." He flattened his hands on the table and leaned forward, holding Gunner's gaze. "We're talking about Will."

"Nope," Gunner said immediately. "No, we are not. That's a thing we're very much not talking about."

"Yes," Clancy said. "We are. How long have you been in love with him, Guns?"

Gunner slumped forward, folding his arms on the table and hiding his face in them. "Fuck my life," he moaned.

"Don't change the subject," Clancy said.

Their food arrived and Gunner struggled to marshal his thoughts.

"It's just, like… hero worship," he said weakly after a few minutes.

"Bullshit," Clancy said around the chip he'd shoved in his mouth. "Hero worship tends to fade with proximity. This—whatever it is, it's not fading. If anything, it's getting stronger."

"Shut the fuck *up*," Gunner pleaded, but Clancy was unmoved.

"You have to tell him, man."

"*No*." Gunner clenched his fists, suddenly panicked. "No, I can't, I *won't*."

"Why not?"

Gunner fought the flight reflex. "Don't ask me. Don't—please don't."

Now Clancy looked sympathetic. "This is your alternative? Pining for him? Wishing for what you can't have?"

"It's better than not having him at all," Gunner spat, and scrubbed at his face. When he dropped his hands, Clancy was regarding him seriously.

"You really do love him." It wasn't a question.

"Have for a while, yeah." It was a relief, somehow, to finally say it aloud, to admit to the open air and someone who wouldn't reject him that he was in love with someone who didn't love him back.

Clancy shook his head and picked up another chip. "My brother is a fucking dumbass."

"He's *not*," Gunner said instantly. "It's not his fault."

Clancy rolled his eyes. "For not seeing what's under his nose? He's supposed to be the fucking *captain*, and he's so oblivious it's embarrassing!"

"Will doesn't…." Gunner stopped and took a breath. "Will loves me. I know he does. Maybe not the way I want him to, but that's okay, because it's still something. I'd be a fool to ask for more, not when I know he can't give it."

"*How* do you know he can't give it?" Clancy demanded.

Gunner met his eyes, steadier now. "Because if he could, he would have by now."

Clancy sighed. "You're giving him way more credit than he deserves, Guns." His eyes sharpened. "Or maybe you're giving yourself *less* credit."

"Do not," Gunner warned.

"Is this a self-sacrificing thing?" Clancy asked. "Oh my god it is, isn't it? You think you're like, not good enough for the golden boy, so you're never going to tell him how you really feel." He sat back in his chair, looking stunned. "I can't believe I cracked the code."

"Stop it," Gunner hissed. "Just fucking *stop it.*"

But Clancy shook his head. "I'm your friend too. I'm one of your best friends and you know it. And that means sometimes I have to say stuff you don't want to hear." He leaned forward again. "Whatever shit you did in your past, it's in your past. It's not you anymore. It hasn't been you in a long time. You deserve love, goddammit, and I won't sit by and watch you sacrifice yourself like this." He made another face. "I can't *believe* you're making me talk out emotions. You're so buying lunch."

Gunner stuffed a chip in his face and didn't respond. That didn't seem to deter Clancy at all.

"When are you going to forgive yourself?" he asked quietly. "When is enough enough?"

Gunner's traitorous eyes stung and he blinked hard. "When I stop thinking about the people I've hurt," he whispered. *Mateo, eyes sheened with tears he won't allow to fall, voice wobbly, arms wrapped around his waist and shoulders hunched against the pain.*

"Who'd you hurt, Gunner?" Clancy's eyes were intense suddenly. "Hm? Because from where I sit, I saw a kid who helped his team win a Stanley fucking Cup *despite* liking to party too much. Did you ever hit anyone, off-ice? Hurt someone physically?"

Sometimes Gunner thought he *had* hurt Mateo physically, the way he'd curled around himself as he'd stared at Gunner across the crowded bar. But he couldn't say that to Clancy.

"No," Gunner said, shaking his head. "No, I —" He swallowed hard. "I let them down. The Racers. My mom. My fans. I let the fame go to my head and I forgot what I was there for, and I—" It was hard to breathe. "I fucked it all up. They couldn't trust me, Clancy. I deserved to—" He swallowed it back but it was too late. Clancy's eyes were already sharpening.

"Deserved what, Gunner?"

Gunner clammed up, shook his head again.

"It's been six years," Clancy said, still watching him with laser focus. "Don't you think it's time to let go of some of that load you're carrying?"

"What's the point?" Gunner managed, hating the way his voice wobbled. "It's done. I'm a big boy and I'm over it."

"Because if they hurt you," Clancy started, and then stopped, clutching the table. "More than just emotionally, I mean—that's bad enough but—if they hurt you physically too—I'd—*we'd*—"

"You'd what?" Gunner asked. "Fly to Indy and beat up everyone on the team?" He'd rather have his toenails pulled out than be having this conversation, but still his heart ached with a fierce love for the man currently sitting across from him, clearly trying not to lose his composure.

"Does Will know?" Clancy asked.

Gunner lifted a shoulder. "Some of it. More

than most. He wants to beat them all up too, but you and Will can't fix my past, as much as I appreciate you wanting to try. Can we just… let it go?"

Clancy searched his face for a long moment, and finally nodded. "Let's talk about your kid," he said. "How soon can you get her into a hockey program?"

"She'll be enrolled in one before I find her a school, probably," Gunner said, managing a smile.

Clancy shook his head. "Can't believe you have a kid. This is gonna either be awesome or terrifying. Possibly both."

7

Six years ago

IT WASN'T AS if no one had asked him about Indy. Will had tried a few times, before getting the hint. Clancy did too, with all the subtlety of a sledgehammer, until Gunner shut him down. A few of the other guys brought it up occasionally, but Gunner kept his answers short until they got the point. *No talking about Indy.*

He was regretting that when they hosted Indy in Denver the first time. If he'd told someone—if anyone else knew what had happened in Indy, maybe Gunner wouldn't have felt like this, like he was grasping at dead leaves in a whirlpool intent on sucking him down. He didn't sleep during the pregame nap, lying on his back and staring at the ceiling, resolutely not thinking about the upcoming game.

The players were in the locker room when he arrived, talking and laughing and throwing things at each other. Gunner ducked a flying roll of sock tape and headed for his locker.

He was focused on getting his pads in place and didn't notice Will crossing the room toward him at first, not until he sat down beside him. Gunner jumped, and tried to cover it with a cough.

"Um. Hey."

"Hey." Will's eyes were sharp, missing no detail of Gunner's appearance. "Feeling okay?"

"Sure, yeah." Gunner's left elbow pad wouldn't settle into position. He tugged on it, swearing under his breath, and finally yanked it down and off. Will said nothing, watching him. Gunner clenched the elbow pad in his fist and gritted his teeth. "I'm fine, really."

"Okay," Will said simply, and left.

Gunner watched him walk back to his locker and his stomach slowly settled. Will understood. Maybe he didn't know exactly what had happened, but he still got it somehow, and Gunner took a deep breath for the first time all day.

You're not in Indy anymore, he reminded himself. *They* want *you here.*

"Alright," he said aloud. "Alright, let's do this."

"Fuck yeah!" Belmont said from beside him, and held out his fist for Gunner to bump.

IT GOT HARDER when he stepped onto the ice though. The black and green on white of the Racers' away jerseys blurred in front of Gunner as he went through his warmups. He could hear

Mike shouting something—he sounded cheerful, at least—to Tim as they worked on a passing drill down the ice. Mike had never been the problem in Indy, although he'd never stepped in and stopped anything, either, and Tim had been traded to the team just before Gunner was shipped out, so he barely knew him.

Still, hearing their voices made something clench deep in Gunner's gut. He went to his knee and practiced his breathing, trying to pretend he was stretching his quads.

Someone in a Denver gray, red, and black jersey settled to his left, and Gunner glanced over to see Will stretching beside him, looking straight ahead. He said nothing, and Gunner followed his lead. They ran through the stretches in silent unison, and it didn't escape Gunner's attention that Will had put himself between Gunner and the end of the arena the Racers were currently on.

Gratitude swelled in his chest but he kept his mouth shut. He was able to join the team to take shots on goal against Lukas, but still he couldn't help feeling tuned to the other side of the arena, listening for one voice in particular.

He heard it in the face off circle, in position behind Will. Dean Jefferson smirked at Gunner over Will's head, his pale blue eyes as cold and sharp as ever.

"Settling in?" he asked. He glanced at Will before Gunner could respond. "Has he offered to suck your dick yet?"

Acid churned in the pit of Gunner's stomach.

Will lost the face off. Jefferson grabbed the puck and eeled past him, quick as a flash.

It went downhill from there.

The play the first period was sharp and chippy. Both teams were on edge, and Gunner hadn't missed the way Will was clutching his stick, muscle jumping in his jaw.

Belmont got a breakaway and raced down the ice with it, but he was flatly denied by the Racers goalie, who caught the puck midair and slapped it down.

The Racers were taking their lead from Jefferson, which meant every opportunity was seized to subtly trip Gunner, hook or slash him without the refs noticing, or crosscheck him brutally into the boards.

Gunner picked himself up each time, teeth clenched just a little tighter, but he said nothing.

"Are the refs fucking blind?" Belmont snarled as Gunner wiped his face where a stray stick had caught him and inspected his fingers for blood. "I'm going to kick some ass, these motherfuckers—"

"No," Gunner interrupted. "That's what they want. You start a fight, you're the one in the box. Just leave it. I'm a big boy, Belsy, I can handle a little rough play."

Belmont growled as Parson gestured for him to take the ice.

"If you need help figuring out how to handle him, I can give you my number," Jefferson said in the next face off.

Gunner bit back all the things he wanted to say. Will lost the face off again.

This time, Jefferson sent it to Mike, and they played tic-tac-toe with it right into Lukas's crease, where Jefferson tucked it home short side.

It was his fault, Gunner knew. The team was off balance, scrambling to find their rhythm, their feet, and every time Jefferson faced off with Will, he had another comment ready.

"He's deadweight, you know," he said, tone conversational, as the ref readied himself to drop the puck. "He'll pull your whole team down."

Gunner shot the ref an imploring look, but the ref just shrugged fractionally. Chirping was a time-honored tradition, after all, and Jefferson hadn't actually done anything over the line.

The puck fell and Jefferson snatched it out from under Will's nose again.

By the end of the second period, they were down by two and had yet to even get on the board. Gunner trailed after the team into the locker room, his stomach in knots.

He barely heard Parson's speech, too caught up in his own misery. When Will sat down beside him, Gunner flinched. He opened his mouth to apologize—for what, he wasn't entirely sure—but Will beat him there.

"You and I are going to talk, after the game." That was his captain voice; absolutely no room for argument.

Gunner slumped and nodded. As the players

stood and began to file back onto the ice, Gunner found Parson.

"Coach?"

Parson turned to him. "What is it, son?"

"Maybe it would be better if—" Gunner swallowed. "If I'm not out there."

"And why is that?"

"You saw the way they're playing," Gunner said. Everyone was out of the room except for Will, who lingered by the door out of earshot. "You know it's—because of me."

Parson's brows drew down, his lips tightening. "So you think we should give 'em what they want?"

Gunner hunched his shoulders, half turning away. "Forget it," he said over his shoulder. "I—I'm sorry. It's nothing."

Parson caught his arm, pulling him to a stop. "Gunner," he said. "You are part of this team now. This family. When we go out on that ice, we play and fight and bleed for each other, do you understand? I will not hide you away in the locker room as if I'm ashamed of you. So you'll go out there with your head up, and you'll look that weaselly asshole in the eyes and you'll tell him to go fuck himself, in the nicest way possible, while we all stand behind you. Are we clear?"

Gunner's throat was too tight for him to speak, but he managed a nod. Parson squeezed his forearm and let him go.

"Go on then," he said.

Gunner headed for the door Will held open for him, and they walked up the tunnel shoulder to shoulder. At the top, Will slapped him on the back.

"Come on, liney. Let's show them how it's done."

They didn't win. Jefferson's line sank another goal on Lukas in the first few minutes, then another at the halfway mark. It was impossible to come back from that, but they tried. Schulz scored the only goal for the Direwolves, two minutes before the period ended, but it was no use. The Racers had them scrambling, no way to close the gap in scoring.

Gunner kept his mouth shut, misery choking him, as they straggled down the hall. He was halfway out of his sweaty gear when Parson stepped into the middle of the room.

"A minute of your time, gentlemen."

Everyone stopped to listen.

Parson continued, turning in a slow circle. "Does anyone here blame Gunner?"

Gunner froze.

Lukas blinked, like maybe he hadn't understood the question. Belmont scowled thunderously. Schulz looked angry, but not at Gunner. Will's face was blank, neutral, but Gunner could read tension in his shoulders, in the muscle that jumped in his jaw.

"So it's not his fault we all played like shit?" Parson said when no one answered. His eyes were sharp and searching as he scanned each face in turn.

"Course not, Coach," Clancy said, dragging his shirt off over his head.

Gunner stared at his lap. No matter what they said, he knew it was his fault. He just had to find a way to fix it.

"Right," Parson said. "Because we're a team. That shit performance out there? That absolute train wreck of a goddamn hockey game? That's on all of you. That was terrible and I hope you're well and truly ashamed of yourselves for letting those pricks get in your head like that." He glared at Gunner. "Next time we'll do better." It wasn't a question.

Gunner nodded silently.

"Shower and go the fuck home," Parson said. "I don't want to see you for a while."

GUNNER DIDN'T SEE Will when he left the arena. For the best, he told himself, and drove home. Every part of him hurt from being knocked into the boards so many times, and all he wanted was a hot bath and maybe some whiskey to numb the worst of the pain.

But when he pulled into his driveway, Will's truck was parked in front. Gunner's heart sank. Will stepped out when Gunner did, his dark eyes serious.

Gunner led him up the path and opened the door silently. Will brushed against Gunner's shoulder as he went inside, and Gunner closed his eyes. *Stop wanting what you can't have.* The dogs were thrilled to see them, but Gunner gave them only a brief greeting before letting them into the backyard.

He and Will headed for the den without a word, and Gunner curled up in one of the armchairs, drawing his feet under him. Will settled on the arm of the sofa beside him, almost close enough to touch.

"Get it over with," Gunner said after a minute, when Will didn't speak. "Just—"

"Tell me what happened," Will said quietly.

Gunner pressed his cheek to one knee. "It wasn't sexual," he said.

"Okay," Will said.

"He was just—he was fucking with your head." Gunner closed his eyes. "He never—I didn't—" He couldn't find the words, so he shut his mouth.

"Then what did happen, Gunner?"

Will never used his first name, not like that.

"I was wild," Gunner said. He looked up, into Will's eyes. "I needed—discipline."

Something flickered across Will's face but he said nothing.

"That's all it was," Gunner whispered. "He was trying to help me."

"What did he do to you," Will said flatly. Thunder was brewing in his eyes, in the way his big hands clenched and unclenched in his lap.

"He… they… helped me get better," Gunner said. "Will, I'm not a child. I knew I needed to improve. I couldn't control myself, so they—"

Will pushed himself to his feet in one quick movement. He took several long strides away, then back, hands in his hair. Gunner watched him pace, unsure what he'd said wrong.

"You're *not* a child," Will finally said. "But they treated you like one."

Gunner shook his head, but Will wasn't finished.

"They told you it was your fault," he snarled. "But did anyone actually show you how to channel your energy, help you figure out how to work it off without making stupid decisions? No, they just punished you when you did fuck up." He kicked the sofa with an inarticulate roar, but this time Gunner didn't flinch.

Will wasn't angry at him. Will would never hurt him. *Never*. Gunner stood up too and closed the distance between them. Will stopped in his tracks and Gunner put a hand on his forearm.

He was safe. He didn't know how it had happened, how he'd found this, but he knew, deep in his bones, that Will would die before letting anything or anyone hurt Gunner again. Tears stung his eyes but he didn't let them fall. Instead he took a shaky breath and stepped forward, right up into Will's space.

He slipped his arms around Will's waist and pressed his face to his shoulder. Will didn't move for a long, breathless moment, and then his arms were circling Gunner's shoulders, pulling him even closer. He smelled like sweet, spicy cologne and hair gel, and Gunner relaxed into his warmth, closing his eyes.

He was falling for Will Calder, and there was nothing he could do about it except pray Will had the sense to not feel the same way.

8

Present day

WILL WAS WAITING when they got back to the rink. He climbed in the back, glanced at Gunner, then stiffened and leaned over the seat to look at him.

"What?" Gunner said. "Something on my face?"

"Are you okay?" Will said quietly.

Gunner froze. Clancy was sitting *right there*, and Will was up in Gunner's space, clearly aware he was upset.

"Can we—not now," he begged, and he was really getting tired of pleading with the Calder brothers, but Will seemed to accept it and sat back.

Clancy said nothing, but he started the truck with a distinctly self-satisfied air that made Gunner want to punch him just a little bit.

That feeling intensified when they got back to

Gunner's house to realize that Fay and Olivia were still out.

"Oh," Clancy said casually. "I left something at your place, Will. I'm gonna run over and get it, I'll be back in time for dinner." And then he was gone and Gunner and Will were staring at each other.

"Sorry," Gunner said nonsensically, and headed up the path.

"Why are you apologizing for *my* brother?" Will said, right behind him. "And while we're on the subject, what did he say to you that upset you so bad?"

Gunner's shoulders climbed up around his ears and he bent to greet the dogs, doing his best to ignore Will, who was still standing there waiting for a response.

"You guys wanna go out?" he asked them. "Go outside, run and play? Maybe we should go swimming?"

"*Gunner.*"

Gunner straightened.

Will looked miserable, fidgeting with the hem of his T-shirt. "Talk to me?" he said, and all Gunner wanted was to kiss him into smiles again, make his eyes crease up at the corners the way they did when he was really happy.

Instead he backed away, heading down the hall to let the dogs into the backyard. They charged outside and Gunner stood for a second and watched them. When he turned, Will was right behind him and Gunner nearly ran face-first into him.

Will caught him with a hand on his elbow and the other on his waist but he didn't move back.

Gunner was pinned between the glass door and Will's solid bulk, and Will… wasn't backing away.

"Something's going on with you," he said, his voice low.

Gunner rolled his eyes, opting for humor. "I just acquired a daughter, did you notice?"

Will's expression, so intent and serious, didn't change. "You tell me everything, Gunny. Don't shut me out now."

"I don't tell you *everything*," Gunner protested. *I haven't told you I'm in love with you, for instance.*

He licked his lips and Will's eyes followed the motion, darkening. His hand was big and warm on Gunner's ribs, thumb stroking slowly, almost absently, across the fabric. He looked into Gunner's eyes, then back to his mouth, and Gunner could almost see the decision crystallize in his head. He was going to do it, and Gunner didn't know if he was strong enough to stop him. His knees had turned to water and he couldn't move.

The front door opened and Olivia shouted something happily from the yard.

Will let go like he'd been burned, putting three feet of space between them. He was on the other side of the kitchen when Fay walked in and Gunner was still sagging against the door.

She looked back and forth between them. "Everything okay?"

Will nodded, wiping his palms on his jeans. "Yes ma'am. Everything is, uh. Great."

"Good. Then you can help me get stuff out of the car." She raised an eyebrow at Gunner. "Both of you."

Gunner managed to drag his brain back online and straightened. Outside, he stopped at the sight of his car, stuffed to the brim with packages, bags, and boxes.

"Holy sh—did you buy several stores?" he asked Fay, who'd come out for another armful.

Olivia tugged on Gunner's leg. "Gunner, *look*." She spun in a circle, making the frilly skirt of her dress fly out and showing off the heavy black boots she had on underneath.

Gunner applauded. "*Very* nice," he said when she stumbled to a stop, out of breath. "Absolutely gorgeous. I especially dig the boots with the dress, perfect combination."

Olivia dimpled. "Gramma Fay and I bought me clothes. And stuff for my room. You wanna see it?"

"Gramma Fay, huh?" Gunner smiled at his mom and then flinched as Will bumped into him on his way up the path. It wasn't much contact but it was enough to remind him—he cleared his throat and scooped up as much as he could carry, staggering and groaning under the weight for Olivia's amusement.

It took a while to get everything in, sorted, and put away. Fay told Gunner to be expecting furniture deliveries in the next few days.

"We picked out what she wanted together. I think you'll like it." She clapped her hands. "Who's hungry?"

Gunner sent Clancy a quick text—*my mom's back, asshole, get over here I'm mad at you*—and followed her into the kitchen.

"Please don't cook," he said as she opened the refrigerator.

Fay gave him a look. "You've never complained about my cooking before. Wait, that's not true."

Gunner couldn't help his snicker at that. "No, seriously. You've been on your feet all day. Will and I are beat too. Why don't we just order in? We can get anything you want, and no one has to cook except the people we're paying."

Fay seemed faintly relieved at the idea. They discussed menus and placed an order. Gunner threw in an entree for Clancy he knew Clancy hated, just on general principle, and then he brought the dogs back inside and they all headed to the living room to wait for the food.

Olivia claimed the settee for herself, and Babe got up on it with her, his head on her ribs. She had Ferguson tucked into her elbow and she was dividing her conversation between the anteater and Babe equally. Babe seemed enthralled, darting his tongue out to lick her face whenever she paused.

Fay settled in a recliner, so Gunner kicked off his shoes and collapsed on the sofa, leaving the other recliner for Will. He was entirely unprepared for Will to sit down on the end of the sofa and pull Gunner's feet into his lap.

Gunner jerked his head up but Will wasn't even looking at him, one forearm resting on Gunner's ankle as he thumbed through his phone with his free hand.

"So, Gunner," Fay said.

Gunner twisted sideways to look at her. She smiled at him.

"I'm going to help you find a nanny for Olivia over the next week or so. I'll want you there for the interviews, because it's important for you to mesh with whoever we pick as much as Olivia. Do you want a live-in or part-time?"

Gunner thought about it, or tried to, as Will began absently stroking his ankle with one thumb. He shifted, willing himself not to react.

"Um. With my schedule… probably better to have a live-in, don't you think? Especially since some weeks I'll be gone completely."

"So they'll need to be able to drive, and have a clean driving history." Fay was writing on a notepad in her lap. "Preference for male or female?"

"Whoever fits best," Gunner told Fay honestly. "It's about what works. I don't care who they are or what they look like, as long as they pass a background check, have good references, and sign an NDA."

Will stroked his ankle bone with a thumb. He hadn't looked at Gunner at all, seeming absorbed in whatever he was reading on his phone, but he had one hand wrapped almost entirely around Gunner's ankle, and Gunner couldn't *think*.

He heard Will's truck in the driveway, and Will's hand left his ankle just as Clancy appeared in the doorway.

"Hey sprout!" he said to Olivia. "Didja get a lot of good stuff?"

"So much!" Olivia told him, bouncing upright. "Wanna see?"

Clancy followed her upstairs and Will's hand

returned to Gunner's leg, this time a little farther up, as Fay got up too.

"I'm going to set out plates for dinner," she announced.

When she was gone, the room was quiet. Gunner had his phone out, ostensibly looking at it, but all he could process was the feel of Will's palm on his shin, the slow trace of a finger along his calf muscle.

Will *still* hadn't looked at him. His brow was furrowed as he read something. Gunner wanted to jerk away, snap at him to stop. He wanted to melt into his hands and beg him to keep going forever. He was frozen, and he realized with horror that Will's hand was inching higher, and Gunner was getting hard.

He rolled off the couch so fast he nearly landed on Ty, napping on the floor at Will's feet, and scrambled upright.

Will blinked up at him, looking confused. "Something wrong?"

Gunner straightened his shirt. "Gonna… go help Mom." He escaped, knowing he'd left his dignity back in the living room but unable to care.

But it didn't stop there. All evening long, Will found reasons to get close to Gunner, to let a hand graze over his lower back, or touch his knee, or bump into his shoulder as he was passing behind him. He sat next to him while they ate and pressed their legs together, but when Gunner looked over, Will was focused on his food or bantering with Clancy.

It was driving Gunner up the fucking *wall.* He was strung tight with nerves and anticipation, wondering where Will was going to touch him next, what excuse he'd come up with. If Gunner called him on it, he'd be acknowledging that something was going on between them, and he was—he was terrified. He didn't know what Will was doing, or *why* he was doing it. All he knew was he didn't hear a word of the dinner conversation, eating mindlessly and trying not to jump out of his skin every time Will touched him.

Olivia began rubbing her eyes and yawning halfway through dinner, but managed to stay awake until she'd cleaned her plate.

"I can take her, Mom," Gunner said when Fay got up, but she smiled at him.

"Let me? I'm not going to have many chances."

Gunner settled back into his chair as Fay shepherded Olivia upstairs. Clancy was looking at him over his glass of wine, eyes amused, and Gunner glared at him, which just made Clancy's smile widen.

"So when are you leaving?" Gunner asked, just to be a dick.

"In the morning," Clancy sighed. "Gotta get back to whipping those boys into shape."

"Good luck with that," Will commented, leaning across Gunner to steal something off Clancy's plate and balancing himself with a hand on Gunner's thigh.

Gunner closed his eyes and prayed for patience. When he opened them, Will was innocently eating whatever he'd stolen and Clancy was openly laughing at him. *Fuck you*, Gunner mouthed. Clancy blew him a kiss.

"You have to try this," Will said, and held out the fork to Gunner, who'd had enough.

He stood abruptly and started picking up plates. When he headed for the kitchen, Will, of course, followed him.

Arousal was slipping into anger, a frustrated hum in Gunner's veins. Did Will think this was a game to him? He dropped the plates in the sink a little too roughly and turned to find Will right behind him again.

"Move," Gunner said.

Will's eyebrows went up and his eyes narrowed. He leaned past Gunner and set his plate in the sink and then brought his other hand up and rested it on the counter, effectively trapping Gunner in his arms.

"You gonna make me?" he purred.

The anger boiled over into white-hot fury all of a sudden and Gunner *shoved* Will's chest, hard.

Will stumbled backward, shock rounding his eyes.

"I am *not playing this game*," Gunner hissed, and stalked out of the kitchen.

He headed straight upstairs to say goodnight to Olivia, who was dressed in her pajamas and curled up in her bed. She looked a little uncertain about sleeping alone, so small in the too-big bed, and Gunner had a sudden idea.

"Hey," he said, sitting down on the bed beside her as Fay puttered around the room, picking up and straightening. "How would you like it if one of the dogs slept with you?"

"Oh yes," Olivia said, clasping her hands. "Please can it be Babe?"

"I had a feeling you'd want him," Gunner told her with a wink. He whistled and both dogs came thundering up the stairs. Fending off Ty, Gunner motioned Babe up onto the bed, where he bathed Olivia's face with rapturous kisses as she giggled but didn't do much to fend him off. "Down, Babe," Gunner told him.

Babe collapsed obediently to the bed and wagged his tail, thumping it against the mattress. Olivia already looked more settled, clutching Ferguson in one arm. Gunner sat down beside her again.

"Better?"

Olivia nodded. "I like Gramma Fay," she said through a yawn.

"She likes you too," Gunner said. He gave into impulse and stroked her soft hair off her forehead.

Olivia snuggled into her pillows. "I like *you*," she announced, her eyes half-closed.

Gunner's breath caught. "I like you too," he whispered, and Olivia smiled and fell asleep.

Gunner motioned to Babe to stay and tiptoed from the room, pulling the door closed behind him.

Clancy, Will, and Fay were all talking downstairs in the living room when he joined them. Gunner, still on edge and frustrated with Will, deliberately chose the farthest seat from him to start a conversation with Clancy about the sad state of his new team's defense.

"That fancy goalie of yours can only do so much," Gunner said.

Clancy halfheartedly kicked at him. "You wait

and see. I'm taking them to the playoffs all by myself if I have to."

Will was talking to Fay, but he kept shooting looks at Gunner, who ignored them.

Finally, Fay made her excuses and went to bed, giving both Calder brothers hugs before she left.

With her gone, Gunner suddenly didn't know what to do.

"I should sleep too," he said, too abruptly. "Clancy, you're an asshole. Thanks for coming down to be backup." He pulled him into a hug because no matter how irritated he was with his meddling, they didn't get much better than Clancy Calder.

Clancy hugged him back. "Go get 'em, tiger," he whispered, and Gunner groaned and pushed him away.

"Get the fuck out of my house," he said, but he was smiling as he followed them to the door.

Clancy stepped through and Will moved like lightning, shutting him out and spinning in one smooth motion to catch Gunner's shirt and shove him against the wall.

Gunner's breath sputtered and died as Will leaned close, his eyes dark and unwavering on Gunner's face.

"This is *not a game*," he growled. He let go just as fast and walked out the door, leaving Gunner trying to stay upright with watery knees.

He slept like shit, of course, jolting awake at every sound until he wanted to scream his frustration. He finally rolled over and shoved a hand down his pants. It was embarrassing how quickly it happened to the thought of Will's big body covering him, his mouth on Gunner's—he spilled silently into his palm, eyes squeezed shut as he shook through the aftershocks.

When he was cleaned up, he found himself closer to sleep, yawning as he curled up under the covers. *This is not a game*, Will had said. He wasn't fucking with Gunner's head for the hell of it, not that Gunner had ever really believed he would.

He didn't know what had changed, or how, but Gunner trusted his captain and best friend. He fell asleep looking forward to the morning.

"Hi, I'm Mateo." The man in front of him had dark, sparkling eyes and a wide smile that flashed dimples in his olive cheeks. "Glad to have you on the Racers."

Gunner took his hand. He was young and stupid and flushed with pride at having gone second in the draft, at being wanted, *so he wasn't subtle about the once-over, and Mateo flushed, but by the way his smile widened, he didn't actually mind.*

"Good to be here," Gunner said. "What position are you?"

"Right wing. Coach is making noises about putting us together, seeing what we can do."

Gunner raised an eyebrow. "I think I'd like to see what we can do too."

He woke from a tumbled dream of kissing Mateo, who somehow became Will halfway through. Mateo-Will cupped his face, eyes sad. *I always wanted it to be you,* he said, and turned into a purple unicorn.

Gunner opened his eyes and stared at the ceiling. "What the fuck," he said out loud.

All the turmoil of the last week had dredged up memories, stirred up all the emotions he'd been able to mostly repress for the past six years.

Who was he kidding? Whatever Will's reasons for torturing him like that, the fact remained that he was team, and Gunner wasn't about to go down that road again. He couldn't risk it, not when he knew how it would turn out. How it *had* to turn out.

He had to pretend everything was fine and pray Will would let it go.

Gunner pressed the heels of his hands to his eyes and sucked in air, his throat suddenly tight. *Why* couldn't he have this?

Because you don't deserve it. It was Mateo's voice, soft but uncompromising. *Not after what you did to me.*

Gunner swallowed hard and sat up.

9

He barely saw Will that day, so swept up in getting Olivia sorted, taking furniture deliveries, helping his mother look at schools and figure out schedules. Will smiled at him in the dressing room, brushed against him on the way to the shower, but they didn't have time to talk.

That was fine by Gunner. The longer they went, the better his chances that Will would just let go of whatever had possessed him that night and let their relationship go back to the way it had been.

By afternoon, Olivia was crabby and fretful. The house had had a near constant stream of people through it, working on her room and coming for interviews, and Gunner was starting to tell, now, that she was nearing the end of her rope.

So he made an executive decision, grabbed his iPad and scooped her up, whistling for the dogs.

They headed out into the backyard, Olivia blinking in the bright sun but not protesting.

"Where are we going?"

"I thought you might want a break," Gunner told her. Olivia's hair was soft against his cheek, and she smelled like strawberries from the shampoo Fay bought her.

They walked through the yard to the gate on the far side, where the dogs were already waiting. They knew this routine, and Gunner felt guilty for neglecting it with them lately.

Outside the yard, he let Olivia down but she reached up for his hand. The woods were peaceful around them, birds chirping and a squirrel chattering somewhere up ahead at the dogs. Gunner had bought his house partly because of the location—acres and acres of state park backed up to his yard, miles of trails he liked to run with the dogs early in the morning, before the sun burned off the mist.

It was cool under the trees. Olivia had perked up as well, looking around with interest as they walked the trail. Gunner took a right turn down a smaller path.

"This is my favorite hidey-hole," he said, holding a branch aside so she could duck under it. The trees' branches meshed together above them, forming a lacy green canopy over the small clearing where Ty was already rolling blissfully in the grass while Babe chased down an interesting smell on the perimeter.

"Oh," Olivia breathed.

"Even extroverts need time alone sometimes," Gunner said. "This is where I go."

"What's an ex—extro—"

"Extrovert," Gunner said, sitting down in a

patch of shade. "It's someone who likes a lot of people around them."

"I like people," Olivia said, flopping down cross-legged beside him. "But they get so *loud* sometimes."

"They sure do," Gunner said. Without thinking, he wrapped an arm around Olivia's waist and pulled her close. "Better?"

Olivia nestled against him trustingly. "Better."

"Do you wanna watch game tape with me?"

"Oh, *yes*!"

"I had a feeling," Gunner said, grinning down at her. "So this is a pre-season game, I'm not in it, but since I've got an A, I'm expected to watch the tape and see how the rookies and call-ups are doing."

Olivia nodded very seriously, small face screwed up in concentration.

Gunner settled her against him and hit play on the iPad. He expected her to get bored within the first ten minutes, but she stuck with it much longer than that, asking questions about why a player made a certain move or hit the puck like that, and Gunner found himself pausing to answer as in-depth as he could without getting too technical and confusing her more.

Finally, she yawned and slumped into his side, and the questions petered off. After a few minutes, Gunner realized she was sound asleep, her face pressed against his ribs. Gunner felt the now-familiar squeeze of his heart and he brushed a kiss to the top of her head. Then he hit play on the iPad again and went back to watching the tape.

IT WAS ALMOST dark when they got back to the house. Olivia had begged to be carried and Gunner couldn't say to her big brown eyes, so they went home with Olivia's arms around Gunner's neck, a sleepy, heavy bundle in his arms.

Fay fussed when she saw them—he'd texted her they were leaving, but he still got an earful about nap times and messing up her sleep schedule and paying better attention to these things. Gunner pulled a face at Olivia behind her back, making her giggle, and then solemnly promised Fay he'd do better.

DINNER WAS JUST the three of them, and Gunner and Olivia washed dishes while Fay rested. Olivia got more soap suds on her than the dishes, but they had a great time. Gunner took a picture of her, covered in bubbles and grinning at the camera, and sent it to Will.

He got a reply immediately. *Having fun without me?*

You could come over, Gunner said. And then realized his mistake. *Wait, fuck, you can't.*

Uh… k?

Sorry, Gunner sent. *We've got one more person scheduled for an interview and then it's Olivia's bedtime and Mom wants to talk about school shit once she's asleep.*

Will's answer didn't take long. *I'll see you tomorrow :)*

Missed you today, Gunner sent, and regretted it immediately. He shouldn't have said that. Why had he said that? He was so *stupid*.

He died several thousand deaths before he got Will's response.

I always miss you when we're not together.

Gunner clutched his phone as his traitorous heart leapt. He didn't know what to say.

See you at practice, Will sent, and Gunner put his phone away as the doorbell rang.

He liked this one, he realized on the spot when she stepped over the threshold. She was short, in her forties, and—round was the best way to describe her, he thought. Round cheeks, round face, round, blue eyes and a smile that reached from ear to ear when she spotted Olivia peeking out from behind Gunner's legs.

"Lane Gibson," she introduced herself. Her handshake was firm and she crouched to meet Olivia's eyes on her level. "You must be Olivia. My name is Lane." Her tone was gentle but not patronizing, and Olivia accepted her proffered hand without hesitation. Lane straightened. "I should warn you, Mr. Ryan, I know absolutely nothing about hockey."

"I can teach you!" Olivia piped up.

"She could," Gunner said, and gave her his full-wattage smile, leaving her blinking.

"I might have looked you up on Youtube," Lane confessed. "Not that I understood very much of what was happening."

"I'm gonna play hockey," Olivia told her. "Gunner's enrolling me in a mite league!"

"That sounds amazing!" Lane said as Fay came in from the living room and introduced herself.

They settled in the den to talk. Gunner watched Lane's reaction to the dogs—positive—and the way she spoke to Olivia—calm and friendly—and the way Olivia blossomed as she told Lane about her hockey dreams and how she got to see Saint Levesque play. He caught his mother's eye and gave her a subtle nod, about half an hour into the conversation, just as Olivia yawned.

Fay took over the conversation as Gunner ushered Olivia up to bed. He was starting to get the hang of the bedtime routine down, he thought, coaching her through brushing her teeth and then easing a brush through her wild curls—Olivia's least favorite part by far.

Olivia talked throughout, asking questions that Gunner answered as patiently as possible and chattering about stuff he couldn't follow and didn't really try.

"Did you like Lane?" Gunner asked as he tucked her into bed.

Olivia nodded.

"Would you like her to take care of you when I'm not here?"

Olivia's eyes widened. Then her lip wobbled and fat tears began to roll down her cheeks.

"Oh, fu—" Gunner had no idea what to do. He reached for her, hesitating—maybe she didn't want to be touched—but she hurled herself into his arms, clinging to his neck and she wasn't crying, she was *sobbing,* heaving breaths dragged out of her lungs as Gunner held her, helpless and bewildered.

"What did I do?" he begged her. "What did I say? Help me out, Livvy, I don't *understand.*"

"I d-don't w-want—" She sucked in air and wailed, "*I don't want a new mommy.*"

Gunner's heart cracked in half in his chest, tears springing to his own eyes. He pulled Olivia even closer, crooning in her ear.

"That's not what I meant, she's not replacing your mom, sweetheart, she's just helping us! She's going to watch you when I can't, but your mother will *always* be your mother, you hear me? I'm so sorry, Liv, I didn't think—"

Olivia just clung tighter, hiccupping helplessly against Gunner's throat, and he folded himself over her, rocking her gently back and forth until she'd cried herself out, limp and heavy in his lap. He was afraid to move, afraid to disturb whatever fragile peace had been drawn over her, when she stirred.

"Gunner?"

"Yeah," Gunner murmured into her hair.

"You'll still be my daddy, right?"

Gunner's arms tightened so sharply Olivia made a muffled squeak of protest. He relaxed with an effort, whispering an apology.

"Always," he managed, his throat thick.

"Okay," Olivia said, and fell asleep.

Six and a half years ago

"You love me as much as I love you, right?" Mateo's voice was drowsy, almost asleep. His arm was slung across Gunner's waist. It had been comforting a minute ago. Now it felt like an anchor, pulling him into the deep.

From somewhere, Gunner forced a laugh, grateful Mateo couldn't see his face. "Sure, bud," he said, and felt Mateo go still.

GUNNER WAITED until his back was protesting the position he was in, until he was positive she was asleep and not waking up anytime soon. Then he eased her into the bed, tucking her under the covers and smoothing her hair off her flushed face. She looked impossibly small, and Gunner felt panic, black and sticky, coating the back of his throat. He couldn't do this. He wasn't enough. Good enough, smart enough, *kind* enough—

Somehow, he made it to the door and down the stairs. He could hear Fay puttering in the kitchen, having sent Lane home.

Gunner couldn't face her. If he opened his mouth, whatever was forming in his lungs was going to—was going to—

He grabbed his keys off the rack and slipped out the door. Halfway down the drive, he sent his mother a text.

She's asleep. Goin to Will's 4 a bit.

It was dark, but Gunner was a good driver,

careful on the curves, muscle memory keeping him controlled and steady even though he wanted to shake out of his skin. He could *feel* it, clawing at his chest from the inside and he pressed his foot down a little harder on the accelerator.

Most of the lights were off in Will's house, but there was one on in his bedroom. Not asleep yet then. The rush of relief propelled him up the steps. He didn't wait for Will to answer, just used his spare key and let himself in.

Will must have heard his car, because he was halfway down the hall when Gunner stepped inside.

"Hey," he said, and he was smiling, soft and private, and for one horrible minute Gunner thought he'd made the wrong decision, that coming here was the worst thing he could have done, but then Will took in Gunner's no doubt disheveled appearance, the way he had one hand on the wall to keep himself upright. Will's eyes sharpened and it was Gunner's captain who spoke. "What happened?"

Gunner opened his mouth but nothing came out.

"Olivia?" Will demanded, and he was already reaching for his shoes, but Gunner managed to shake his head.

"She's okay," he got out.

Will subsided, but the worry was stark on his face. He reached out and Gunner took a quick forward step, into his arms. Will hissed a breath as he pulled him close.

"You're shaking," he whispered.

Gunner put his face down on Will's shoulder, just like Olivia had done to him. Will smelled so good, a hint of spicy cologne and hair gel and the cotton of his T-shirt mingling in Gunner's lungs, and he could feel the panic receding bit by bit.

"I just… need a minute," Gunner said vaguely, closing his eyes. Will seemed to get it, and they stood quietly in the hall until Gunner's breathing slowed and the trembling stopped.

Then Will took his hand and led him to the kitchen, where he put him in a chair.

"Coffee, tea, or something stronger?"

Gunner didn't let go when Will tried to straighten. "Just—"

"Okay," Will said, and pulled up a chair in front of Gunner's, bracketing Gunner's knees with his own. "Tell me when you're ready." He wasn't touching Gunner other than with his knees, but Gunner felt safer than he had all night.

"I—we had the interview for the nanny."

Will nodded, eyes intent.

"She's nice. I think she'll work for us. She's great with Olivia, the dogs don't scare her. Doesn't know hockey but she's supportive, you know?"

"No one's perfect," Will said, deadpan, and Gunner almost smiled.

"I was putting Olivia to bed and I asked her what she thought of Lane and if she'd be okay with Lane living with us and taking care of her." Gunner's throat tightened. "She—" He swallowed. "She… freaked out. Thought Lane was replacing her mother, that Lane was her *new* mother."

"Oh shit," Will breathed. "Is she okay?"

Gunner nodded, jerky and uncoordinated.

"She c-cried for a while. I think… it needed to come out, maybe."

"Cathartic," Will agreed. "Poor kid. Are *you* okay?"

Not remotely. Gunner shook his head mutely.

"Can you tell me why?" Will's voice was always so gentle, and right then it was like a feather stroking Gunner's skin, soft and barely there.

"I can't do this," he blurted, and held up a hand before Will could argue. "I know, we've had this conversation. But I can't, Will, I *can't*. I c-can't be a father, I'm barely a functioning human being, how am I supposed to raise a *child*? I don't know the answer to half the shit she asks me, when I get home after practice I'm exhausted and the season's almost here so it'll be so much worse, I can't *do* this. I didn't *want* this. She's—" He covered his face, fighting back the panic again. "She's counting on me, and I'm just going to let her down, because that's what I *do*."

Will's fingers circled his wrists and pulled them gently away from his eyes. Gunner let him, suddenly exhausted.

"Don't tell me I won't," he muttered, mostly to his lap.

"Okay," Will said, startling Gunner into looking up. Will shrugged, still holding Gunner's wrists. "You're gonna let her down, Gunny, is that what you want to hear? You're going to fuck up, and you're gonna do things wrong." Gunner tried to jerk his hands away but Will's were suddenly like iron. "Because *you're human*," he continued. "You think your parents did it all right? You think they didn't fuck up? I know mine did. My dad *forgot me* once. Left me behind in a grocery store. Got all the way home before he realized. Shit *happens*, Gunner. People fuck up. They try their best and sometimes it's not enough."

"But it has to be," Gunner said, almost pleading. "She needs it to be. She needs *me*."

"She *has* you," Will said. "And she has me. And Lane. And your parents. She has a family." His hands loosened until his thumbs were stroking slow and gentle over Gunner's pulse points. "And you have a safety net, Guns. You're not alone. Besides, you have money, and that makes a big difference, doesn't it?"

Gunner nodded unwillingly.

"If you can't figure out how to do it, you can hire someone to do it or teach you how," Will continued. He was *still* holding Gunner's wrists, eyes steady on his face. "Olivia adores you. You'll make it work."

Gunner squeezed his eyes shut against the stinging tears.

"What do you need from me?" Will asked, and *God*, Gunner loved him so much. It was the only reason he had the courage to say what needed to be said.

"I need my friend," he whispered. He looked up, into Will's beautiful, beloved face, and swallowed the shards of glass in his throat. "I need you to be Will and me to be Gunner. Like we were a week ago. Not whatever we were the other night. I don't—I don't know what that was, and I—I can't find out. I can't be all twisted up like that right now. I need to know you're there, Will. As my friend. And nothing more, so I can be Olivia's father." He thought vaguely like he should be bleeding from wrenching the words out, but he wasn't—his skin was smooth and unblemished. How could he say these things and they not leave a visible wound, he wondered briefly, but Will just nodded, his face blank.

"Alright, Guns." He was drawing away, letting go, putting the space Gunner had asked for between them, and Gunner—Gunner thought he'd die if Will stopped touching him. But he didn't. His traitorous heart continued beating, and Will was standing, Will was turning away as if he couldn't bear to look at Gunner anymore.

"Will," Gunner whispered.

Will said nothing.

Gunner stood up, wavering. He ached to touch Will's broad back, but he thought it would genuinely break him if Will flinched from his hand.

So he walked on careful legs that only wobbled a little out of the kitchen and down the hall.

He heard quick footsteps behind him before he reached the door, and turned just in time for Will to yank him into a hard hug.

Gunner choked on the sob of relief as Will held him tight, standing there in the dark hallway, everything Gunner so desperately wanted and couldn't have.

"You're still my best friend," Will said. "You always will be. *Always*, Guns. This is non-negotiable."

"Good," Gunner managed through the tears burning his throat. He gave himself one more long minute of his face pressed to Will's throat, scratchy with the stupid beard he seemed to love so much, feeling Will's pulse racing under his lips, and then he eased away. "I'll… see you at practice."

"Yeah," Will said, and watched Gunner leave with dark, unreadable eyes.

10

Six years ago

Will hated Mariah Carey. It was nothing personal, not really. But having to listen to her croon about all she wanted for Christmas for a solid month every time he turned on the radio made him want to punch something.

Somehow, listening to Gunner sing it, Santa hat sliding off his curls and alcohol making his cheeks flushed, it wasn't so bad. Even though Gunner really did have a terrible voice.

Gunner caught his eye and grinned, putting a sway in his hips as he hit the chorus again. Will smiled back and made his way across the crowded room, stepping over teammates and girlfriends and wives to find himself a drink and a comfortable spot to sit and listen to the rest of Gunner's performance.

Winning looked good on him, Will thought as he pushed a napping Belmont over so he could squeeze onto the couch. It gave him confidence, an extra bounce in his step that Will was delighted to see.

Gunner finished the song with a flourish and a deep bow that knocked his hat off. He straightened, that heart-stopping smile as wide as ever, and made a beeline for Will on the couch.

"Move, Belsy," he said.

Belmont muttered something and slouched against his girlfriend, so Gunner grabbed his legs and dragged him off the couch. Belmont yelped and flailed as Cady laughed at him, but Gunner had already stolen his spot, pressed up against Will and beaming at him from a few inches away.

Will took a drink of too-sweet punch. "You're a terrible singer," he said.

Gunner's smile somehow widened. "But I'm a hell of a performer."

"That you are." Will glanced around the room. "Half the women in here want to jump you right now, terrible singing be damned."

Gunner pushed his lower lip out. "Only half, and only women? I'm too young to be losing my touch already."

"Maybe more than half," Will allowed. "Although I couldn't give you a number on how many teammates want to jump you." *There's at least one, though.*

"Well, it's probably good anyway," Gunner said. He draped an arm casually around Will's shoulders. "I have a strict 'no teammates' policy."

Will's stomach dipped. "Is that so?"

Gunner hummed, rubbing his cheek against Will's shirt. "You smell good. What was I saying?"

"You were saying you don't date teammates," Will said through his teeth.

"Right," Gunner said. "There was this one guy —" He shook his head. "Not worth getting into. But I learned my lesson." His teeth flashed in a smile. "At least about that. Not about anything else."

Will somehow dredged up a smile in return and downed the rest of his punch in a single gulp.

Present day

Olivia had bounced back from her meltdown by the next morning, her eyes bright as she chatted to Fay and Gunner tried to drown himself in his coffee.

He hadn't slept at all, of course, staring at the ceiling and berating himself for his stupidity until his eyes burned with the tears he wouldn't allow to fall.

Fay tossed him some worried looks as Olivia instructed Ferguson on how to properly eat waffles, but Gunner pretended not to notice. He ate breakfast mechanically and took his plate to the sink, Will's bowed shoulders the night before all he could see.

"Bye Mom," he said, dropping a kiss to her temple, and then glanced down to see Olivia staring up at him with those melted chocolate eyes that Fay swore were shaped just like Gunner's.

Without stopping to think, he stooped and pressed a loud, smacking kiss to her syrup-sticky cheek. Olivia burst into giggles, swiping at her face, and Gunner winked at her.

"Now you know where the dogs get it."

But his smile faded as he got in his car. He had to look at Will today, pretend he hadn't told him they could never be together. *Fake it till you make it.* A coping mechanism that had gotten him through many of his younger years. Gunner took several deep breaths, pushing away the hurt on Will's face, the twin ache in his own heart, and thought about what mattered. Olivia. Hockey. The team.

When he was in control of his expression enough, he drove to the rink.

Most of the guys were in the locker room, loudly bantering as they stripped down to get in their gear.

Belmont found Gunner first, sitting down beside him. He looked unhappy, and Gunner stifled unease, plastering on a smile.

"'Sup, man?"

"What's going on with Will?" Belmont asked without preamble.

Gunner froze and then tried to shake it off with a cough. "I'm—how would I know? We're not in each other's pockets."

Belmont looked genuinely startled at that. "Yes you are? In fact, most of the time you guys get here at the same time, if you don't ride together. You always leave together, you're always at each other's houses—we've been saying for years that you guys should just move in together."

"Is there a point to this?" Gunner said loudly.

"My *point* is that if anyone knows what's going

on with him, it'll be you. So...." Belmont gazed expectantly at him.

Gunner sighed and shoved his feet into his skates to avoid having to meet Belmont's eyes. "I don't know, man. Sorry."

"Well, can you find out? Because he's grumpy as fuck and it's making the rookies nervous."

Gunner glanced toward Will's stall. He was settling his gear over his head, not looking at anyone, his jaw set. Gunner sighed again.

"I'll see what I can do." It was his fault, after all.

Schulz leaned over Belmont. "You know what, Belsy—all that stuff you said about them getting here and leaving together... they haven't done that much lately."

"The fuck did you come from?" Gunner demanded.

"You're right," Belmont said, considering Gunner.

"Stop looking at me like that." Gunner turned away to grab his pads.

"Has Gunner posted anything about Will on Instagram lately?" Belmont asked.

Schulz gasped theatrically. "Mom and Dad are fighting!"

"Oh, for fuck's sake." Gunner strapped the pads into place, ignoring the hushed discussion beside him.

"Wait," Volly said from across the room. "Which one's Mom and which one's Dad?"

"Will's Dad, obviously," Shore put in. "He's got that 'disappointed but not surprised' face down cold."

"And Gunner's Mom," Schulz added. "Because he's always got to look pretty and take his selfies and he *looooves* fashion."

"Way to fucking stereotype," Gunner snapped.

"Is not nice, put women in box," Arseni chimed in, making everyone turn and stare at him. He turned red but lifted his chin. "Is true."

Gunner slapped him on the shoulder and dragged his jersey over his head. Will still hadn't looked at him. Gunner told himself it was for the best and headed for the ice.

Parson had been trying different things with the lines, and he'd shuffled them around again so it was Gunner, Volly, and Arseni working through drills with Foster and Schulz. It felt good, they were mostly meshing, but Foster couldn't seem to get the trick of the pass they were working on. Over and over they tried it, and every time Gunner sent it through the forest of blades and sticks to where Foster was supposed to be waiting, he missed it.

Gunner pulled up sharply after the sixth time, stifling frustration.

"Sorry, Guns," Foster said, hanging his head.

Gunner took a deep breath. "It's okay, Foz. Let's try it again."

This was usually the point where he'd pull Will aside, ask him for help getting through to Foster, maybe demonstrate what he was going for. Will always knew what Gunner was going to do on the ice. He was there, ready, every time Gunner had the puck on his tape.

But Will was on the far end of the ice, leaning on his stick and talking to several rookies. He hadn't been on Gunner's unit all practice, nor had he spoken to him once.

This is what you wanted, Gunner told himself, but he couldn't help the feeling of betrayal that gnawed at his stomach. If the *team* suffered because of his stupidity, that was going to make it so much worse. Will knew better than to let his personal life get in the way of his hockey. And if he couldn't—it was going to be Gunner's fault.

"Again!" Gunner shouted, and grabbed the puck.

Foster got it that time, rifling it past Lukas's glove, and Gunner whooped and collided with him as Foster threw his arms in the air.

"I told you!" Gunner said, and Foster beamed at him. Gunner patted his helmet as Parson blew his whistle and they headed in.

Parson was switching up the lines again, and Gunner and Will were back on the same unit. Will looked focused, hands easy on the stick, and Gunner felt cautious hope. Maybe it would work.

Gunner stole the puck and dodged Shore, bolting through a hole to race down the ice toward Lukas. He was aware of Will off to his left, and Gunner knew he had no chance of scoring with Schulz and Volly breathing down his neck the way they were. He ducked Volly and sent the puck to Will, who reached for it too late and missed.

Gunner was so shocked he stopped skating and Schulz collided with him, sending him into the boards.

"Shit, sorry," Schulz said, helping him up. "You okay?"

Gunner shook it off. Will had gone after the

puck and was currently trying to get it away from Shore. He succeeded and spun, but he missed the chance at a wrister as Volly neatly scooped the puck off his stick.

"Jesus," Schulz said, staring as Will chased Volly up ice. "Are you guys *actually* fighting?"

"*No*," Gunner said. His stomach twisted. "We're not… it's not—everything's fine."

"Sure," Schulz said, gesturing to where Will still hadn't gained any ground against Volly.

Gunner sighed.

Will kept playing like that every time he and Gunner were put together. He fumbled several passes, missed Gunner's cues, and finally slammed his stick against the ice in frustration, cracking it. He hurled it at the boards and skated off the ice, everyone watching him go silently.

Gunner caught Schulz's eye and hunched his shoulders.

Will was already in the showers by the time the rest of them got in from their cool-off. The mood in the locker room was subdued and Gunner focused on getting stripped out of his sweaty clothes.

I'll talk to him when I'm out of the shower, Gunner told himself.

But Will was gone when he got out.

11

"I CAN'T DO THIS," Will said when Clancy picked up the phone. He was in his truck, pulled off in the parking lot of a small gas station where he hopefully wouldn't be recognized.

"What, be a responsible, functioning adult? Tell me something I don't know."

"I'm fucking serious, Clance."

Clancy sighed. "What happened?"

"I—you remember the night we had dinner with Gunner, before you went back to Vancouver."

"'Course. You drove the poor kid out of his mind. You haven't closed the deal yet?"

Will pinched the bridge of his nose. "I was trying—I wanted to know if you were right."

"Well of course I was. Am. So what is it you can't do? What happened?"

"I was going to—" Will gripped the wheel. "I thought there was a possibility you were right. I wanted to… try. To maybe… I don't know—date him or something. But he—he said he couldn't."

"Didn't want to?" Clancy's voice was sharp.

"No," Will whispered. "*Couldn't*. Olivia had a… she freaked out, I guess, thought the new nanny was going to be her new mother and she didn't want that, she panicked, and it scared Gunner so much. He needs to give her as much stability as he can right now. So he asked me to… not. For us to be just friends again. He said he can't risk… anything, not with her to think about."

Clancy was silent for a long time. "So he's as stupid as you," he finally said.

"He's *not*," Will protested, stung. "He's taking care of Olivia, putting her first. It's what he *should* be doing. I can't fault him for that."

"So what is it you can't do?"

"Be his friend," Will spat. "I can't—it's killing me, Clance, that he's so close, and he wants this —*me*—too, but he won't let us have it. I don't know how to be his friend again. Or *just* his friend."

Clancy groaned. "God, how is this my life. How did I end up your own personal Oprah?"

"Sorry for asking for your *help*," Will snapped. "Forget it, I'll figure it out on my own." He hung up, and when Clancy immediately called back, Will hit Ignore and put the phone on silent. He stared out the window for a minute.

He didn't know what to *do*, and the worst part was, he couldn't figure out what hurt most—not being able to touch Gunner, or the lost look on Gunner's face when Will pulled away.

He was only human. He couldn't be what Gunner needed, not if he wanted to stay whole himself. If that meant keeping some distance until he could figure out how to handle the situation, then that was just what he'd have to do. And if Gunner hated him for doing it, well, Will deserved it.

He was starting the truck when there was a rap on the window. Will jumped, turning to see a young Black man with crooked teeth and a charming smile. He was wearing a hoodie and seemed harmless, so Will cautiously lowered the window a few inches.

"Will Calder, right?" the young man said. "Spence Ogilvie. I run a pretty popular blog that covers the Denver Direwolves and I was wondering if I could get a quote from you."

"About what?" Will asked warily.

"About Gunner Ryan's daughter coming to live with him."

Will's brain fuzzed out briefly. Spence was still talking but he couldn't hear him.

"Sorry, no comment at this time," he said, and pulled out of the parking lot before Spence could protest.

His first instinct was to head straight for Gunner's house, make sure he was okay, but he stopped himself. Gunner had years of media training. He had more experience than Will when it came to media doublespeak and polite nothings. He could handle a few reporters, and he wouldn't want to see Will right now, not after that morning.

So he drove home, hating himself, and he didn't answer his phone when it rang.

GUNNER WAS HELPING Olivia out of the car in front of the Indian restaurant she'd picked for lunch. The world map was in the trunk, as were push pins that she'd agonized over for a long time. They had to be the right colors, she'd told Gunner, who'd been amused but stood back and let her decide.

Olivia was talking as Gunner closed the car door behind her, slipping her small hand into his immediately, and Gunner didn't immediately notice their surroundings.

"Gunner! Gunner Ryan, can I have just a minute?"

Gunner took a quick step back, tucking Olivia behind him. There were four people with their phones out, clearly recording as they headed his way, and before he could move, they'd formed a loose semicircle in front of him.

"Is this your daughter, Gunner?"

"What's her name?"

"How old is she?"

"How long have you known about her?"

"Gunner?" Olivia sounded terrified.

Gunner swung her up into his arms and she put her face against his shoulder, clinging for dear life. "Guys, back up," Gunner said, forcing himself to stay calm. "You're scaring her."

Thankfully, they cooperated, backing away a few feet to give them some breathing room. Gunner assessed his options. Clearly, someone had leaked the news before the team's PR agent had a chance to put out the official press release. Gunner was going to have to be very careful to stay on script.

"We're about to have lunch," he said, summoning a smile. "Can we make this quick? I'll take one question from each of you."

A heavyset older man raised his hand and Gunner nodded at him.

"Is this really your daughter, then?"

"Yes," Gunner said. Olivia tightened her grip and he rubbed her back. "Her name is Olivia. She just came to live with me."

"Did you know about her before?" someone else asked.

"No," Gunner said. "Complete surprise." He tilted his head sideways and caught Olivia's eyes. "A happy one, though." A smile flickered briefly over her face before she tucked it back down against his shoulder.

"Why is she here?"

Gunner silently swore at that. "Her mother got sick. Olivia had nowhere else to go. Last question, guys."

"How many more kids you got running around out there?" The asker grinned at his companions as if expecting them to share the joke.

Gunner stared at him flatly.

"What kind of a question is that, man?" one of the other reporters muttered. "Jesus."

"We have to go," Gunner said. "Thanks for respecting our privacy." He strode away, Olivia clinging like a burr, and ducked into a nearby store. He headed for the back and knelt between the aisles of clothes to put Olivia on her feet. "Can you look at me, Liv?"

Olivia rubbed her eyes with a small fist but obeyed. "They were loud," she said, sounding ashamed.

"Yeah, they get excited. And sometimes we'll get recognized. Kind of a lot, honestly. Denver's proud of their hockey team and they think of us as part of the family. Which means they also think they can stop us and talk whenever they want."

Olivia looked thoughtful, chewing her lip. "Will the kids at school know?"

Gunner winced. "Probably. It's not going to be easy to keep it a secret. But we'll find you the *right* school, okay? One where they don't bother you all the time. Gramma Fay is helping me look. And there will be other hockey kids there."

"Okay," Olivia said.

"I'm sorry," Gunner told her, and Olivia wrinkled her forehead.

"Why?"

"Because we can't just be… us. We have to stop and talk to people and I have to sign stuff and be friendly and it'll be that way for a long time."

"It's okay," Olivia said simply, and slipped her hand back into his. "I don't mind. They just scared me for a minute but I'm brave again now."

Impulsively, Gunner leaned forward and kissed her on the cheek, making her giggle. "Ready for Indian food?"

"Yes!"

"It's spicy," he warned her, standing. "Sure you can handle it?"

Olivia tilted her chin up. "I'm tough."

"You sure are," Gunner agreed, and they left the store.

12

Will stayed away from him for the next week, while Gunner was distracted with getting Lane up to speed on his household routines and Olivia into the school she joined late. They found a well-reviewed private school with children of many local celebrities, including a few teammates' kids, and Gunner was promised Olivia wouldn't be bothered.

But there were reporters everywhere, crawling all over Gunner for quotes, pestering his teammates, following Gunner's car when he went to the grocery store or out to pick up dog food, and Gunner couldn't *breathe* through the frustration that choked him. He swallowed it back, answered every question they threw at him with the same polite half-smile on his face.

"Total surprise," he said over and over. "I had no idea. Yes, I'm very excited to have her here with me. A lot of time to make up for."

He was asked about Will's reaction to Olivia's

appearance, and gave that about as much attention as it deserved. "Will's very supportive of me. He's one of my dearest friends. He and Olivia are already close." *He hasn't talked to me in a week,* he thought bitterly as he recited yet another sound-bite the PR team put together for him. *But sure, he's supportive.*

The team's playing was suffering, the vets frustrated and the rookies worried as Will studiously avoided being in the same room with Gunner until Gunner was grinding his teeth. Every time he tried to get Will alone, Will had a reason why he couldn't talk. Gunner couldn't decide if he was angrier at himself or Will. *What happened to best friends,* he wanted to scream, but he kept his mouth shut and his head down, focusing on getting his line clicking.

THEIR FIRST GAME WAS A DISASTER. The Riptide nearly got a shutout against them, until Volly put one top shelf on their goalie just before the end of the last period. They were distracted, out of sync, and unable to find each other for plays.

Will spent most of the game on seeming autopilot. Gunner was forced to call plays when Will didn't, rousing the stragglers and trying desperately to pull them into a cohesive unit, but it was useless.

They were dejected as they shuffled into the locker room. Gunner looked up as he left the ice —Olivia and Lane were sitting in the players' families' section, and Olivia was against the glass, hands flat against it. She was saying something, but Gunner couldn't hear her over the crowd. Still, she looked happy, so Gunner dredged up a smile for her and tapped the glass with his stick before heading down the tunnel.

He made it through the cooldowns and media scrums, acutely aware of Will handling his own mess of reporters a few feet away. Gunner answered questions, drank water, tried to keep the bland media face in place, and went through the now familiar digging about Olivia on autopilot. A lot of them asked about her mother, and Gunner repeated the spiel the PR team had given him. He could do it in his sleep now. "Grad student, this was her decision and I respect that. No, I don't resent her for not telling me sooner. Yes, Olivia loves hockey, she wants to go pro."

He was also unsurprised when Parson pulled him aside after he was out of the shower.

"A word," he said, and Gunner sighed and followed him.

In his office, Parson leaned against his desk and crossed his arms.

"What's going on with my captain?" he asked without preamble.

Gunner had played a long, grueling game and he was exhausted. He dropped into a chair and rubbed his face.

"He's not talking to the boys on the ice," Parson said. "They're getting more captaining from *you* than him. Which, glad to see you stepping up, son, but *what* is going on?"

Gunner wanted to sleep for a week. They had

a game the next day. If his shit tanked their chances of a Cup run, he'd never forgive himself.

"You'd have to ask him, Coach," he said woodenly.

Parson made an irritated noise. "I did. He said it was personal, nothing to worry about. Let me tell you, Gunner, I'm fucking worried."

"Sorry, Coach," Gunner mumbled.

"Talk to him," Parson said.

"What good would that do?" Gunner demanded. "He's avoiding me too!"

"Not a suggestion." Parson's voice softened. "Fix whatever's broken between you before it breaks the team, Gunner."

Gunner nodded, eyes on the floor.

HE WASN'T SURPRISED to find Will gone by the time he got outside. Olivia and Lane had already gone home, so Gunner headed for his car.

Halfway home, he took the turn to Will's house on impulse, lips tight as he punched in the gate code.

Will appeared about as thrilled to see him as Gunner was to be there.

"Do you want me to be traded?" Gunner flung at him before Will even had the door open all the way.

Will looked stunned. "You—what? Why would I want that?"

"You obviously don't want me here. As in Denver. And it was your town first, so if you want me to go—"

Will grabbed Gunner's elbow and hauled him bodily over the threshold into the house, slamming the door behind him. Gunner stumbled, catching himself on the wall, and turned. Will was looking at him, just looking, but his eyes were dark and Gunner couldn't help the way his breath shortened.

"You said," Gunner started, and couldn't finish. Will didn't move but Gunner was suddenly, acutely aware just how big he was, standing there just out of arm's reach.

He licked his lips and tried again. "You said I was still your best friend. That that was non-negotiable. But you've been treating me like shit ever since. So I guess you changed your mind, and if you want me to go, then—"

"You can't just go," Will said. "You signed a seven year contract. I was the first person you told. Remember?"

"I'll figure out a way out of it," Gunner said desperately. "I fucked us up, and I want us back, but I guess I can't have that so if you want me to go to another team—"

"Stop *saying* that," Will hissed. He took a step forward. "It's killing me, Gunner, okay? It's fucking *killing* me. And I'm sorry, I know what I said and I meant it, I still mean it, but you're—" He gestured as if helpless. "If I touch you, I'll never stop." He snapped his mouth shut as if he hadn't meant to say that last part.

"What *happened*?" Gunner demanded.

Will blinked, startled. "You—what?"

"We were nothing but friends two weeks ago," Gunner said, feeling his way. "And then Olivia came, and… my mom, and Clancy….” The light dawned. “Clancy said something to you, didn’t he?”

Will didn’t answer, which was answer enough.

“What did he say?” Gunner asked. “It was the day I introduced Olivia to the team, I’ll bet you anything. You were different, after.”

Will scrubbed a hand through his hair, making it stand on end. “It just—he made me realize I’ve been taking you for granted all this time.”

Gunner stared at him.

“How long have we been friends?” Will asked.

“I mean… since I stepped off the plane, pretty much.”

“Pretty much,” Will echoed. “Six years playing beside you, watching you play the field, but you never once made a pass at me even though you *literally* stood on your locker after our first practice to announce your sexuality to the team.”

Gunner couldn’t help the soft huff of laughter at the memory. “Figured it was best to get all the surprises out in the open at once.”

Will was smiling, his eyes warmer. “But you never hit on me. You remember the Christmas party, first year you were here?”

“Vaguely,” Gunner said. “I think I drank a lot.”

“You really did.” Will sounded amused, but then he sobered. “You also told me you didn’t date teammates. Ever.”

Gunner stared at him. “I did?”

“You did. And I got the message.” Will ran a hand through his hair again. “You slept around with people *not* on the team, played the field—or I thought you did. And then you told me you hadn't been with anyone in awhile, and right after that Clancy showed up and tore me a new one for stringing you along."

"Stringing me… what?"

"He said it was obvious you were in love with me, and if I didn't want you, then I needed to cut you loose. And I just—" Will took another step forward and Gunner tensed but Will was brushing past him, out of the hall into the kitchen. Gunner followed, unsure what was going on. He found Will rummaging in the liquor cabinet. "I need something if I'm going to finish this fucking conversation," he said, half to himself, half to Gunner. "Want anything?"

Gunner shook his head automatically. "Driving."

Will resurfaced with a bottle of whiskey and a shot glass. He poured himself one and downed it, Gunner helpless to stop the way he traced the line of his throat as he swallowed. Then he poured another.

"I couldn't stop thinking about it," Will said. "About you." He looked up. "I didn't know, Guns. How you felt. Because you said that at the party, and you never *once* indicated that you'd be down with…." He gestured with the hand holding the bottle. "Anything."

"I make it a habit not to shit where I eat," Gunner said, struggling to keep his voice even. "So I stayed away from teammates, and that included you, with a neon sign above your head that said DO NOT TOUCH, and I had fun that didn't involve you guys. *Any* of you. Because I couldn't risk it, Will—if it went sideways—*when* it went sideways, we'd still have to play together. Pretend it hadn't happened, whatever, and I—you were too important."

"I just… never knew," Will said, and it was almost like he was pleading for Gunner to understand what he was trying to tell him. "You were always… you never once let me think I might have a chance."

Gunner shrugged. "By the time I realized you weren't straight, and that—" He shut his mouth abruptly.

Will's eyes narrowed. "That what?"

Gunner shoved his hands in his pockets. "It doesn't matter. That's not what I'm here to talk about anyway."

"I think it is," Will said. "Because Clancy told me I've taken you for granted, all these years. You're always here when I need you, but you're… stuck. Because of me." He took the third shot and set it back on the counter before turning to Gunner. His eyes were determined, his mouth set the way it got after he argued a penalty with a ref and was shot down. "I needed to know if… if you *did* feel the way Clancy said. If I *did* have a chance. So I… touched you."

"Is that what we're calling it?" Gunner said. "You drove me out of my fucking *mind* that night, Will."

Will's grin was fierce and possessive and it lit a fire in Gunner's gut. But then the smile dimmed, and he looked at the ground. "Olivia's the most important thing in your life," he said quietly. "I get that. If she were mine, it would be the same way. But Gunner—" He glanced up. "Not touching you, especially after you admitting you wanted it as bad as I did—" He shook his head. "I couldn't do it. I couldn't pretend."

"You said I was your best friend," Gunner repeated, his throat thick. "And you've treated me like garbage for a *week.*"

Will crossed the kitchen in several quick steps and yanked Gunner into his arms. Gunner's eyes were burning, *again,* and he had to bury his face in Will's throat and breathe through his mouth in rapid gulps to keep from breaking down.

"I've been trying so hard," Will said into his hair. "I've been trying to stay out of your way so you can raise Olivia and instead all I've managed to do is make you feel *worse* but Gunner—" His voice was unsteady. "It's killing me not to touch you."

Gunner leaned back enough to see him. Will's eyes were so dark he couldn't see his pupils. "You can still touch me," Gunner said quietly.

Will's arms tightened but he shook his head. "Can't." His throat bobbed when he swallowed.

Gunner buried his face in Will's throat again. "Touching me now," he pointed out. His lips brushed Will's skin, and Will shivered.

"Shouldn't be," he managed.

He was right. Gunner knew that. He didn't trust himself so close. But he also couldn't make himself move back. So they stood quietly, until their breathing synced up and Gunner could feel the misery and uncertainty of the past week dropping off his shoulders.

"I'll go to another team if you want me to," he said after a few minutes.

Will tightened his grip and shook his head. "Never."

"Then will you stop avoiding me?"

Will took a deep breath. "Yeah." He pressed his cheek to the top of Gunner's hair. "I'm sorry. I'm an asshole."

"Sometimes," Gunner said.

He could feel the faint vibration of Will's laughter against his cheek and cautious hope unfurled beneath his breastbone. Maybe he could work with this.

13

The next day at practice, Gunner walked into the locker room to a remarkably different mood. The boys were talking to each other, their tones still serious but their expressions lighter. Gunner realized why when he made eye contact with Will on the other side of the room and Will *smiled* at him. Gunner smiled back, somewhat helplessly.

Belmont was the first to greet him.

"So you guys made up, huh?"

Gunner sighed. "Don't you have better things to do?"

"Not when Will calls me after the game to apologize for being an asshole and asking for my input on how to bring the team back together. Everyone's going out for paintball tomorrow, by the way."

Gunner looked at the ground, fighting another smile. "Good," he said. "That's… good."

Turned out Will called everyone on the team,

even just for a minute or two, checking in, reassuring, promising to do better. Gunner felt like the weight on his shoulders had eased and he could breathe for the first time in a week.

Practice went much better. Will was on Gunner's line again and this time caught everything Gunner sent him, slapping it right back or sinking it behind Lukas's knee, chirping the vets relentlessly and pushing the rookies for more.

Halfway through, Gunner realized he was smiling and couldn't stop.

Parson didn't demand too much of them, mindful of their game that evening. They had an intensive strategy and planning session after practice, and then everyone dispersed for their game day naps.

When they got to the arena, the mood in the room was sober but Gunner saw hope on a lot of faces. He made the rounds himself, talking to everyone in turn and lingering with a few of the rookies. Volly he wasn't too worried about, but Foster still hadn't settled into his bones yet. He had a tendency to bambi-leg it when he got too tired. Gunner offered to show him a few drills between games to help with that.

"You'll hate me, after," he warned. "But they'll help, I promise." He patted Foster's knee. "Coach and Will wouldn't have you here if they didn't think you were ready."

Foster nodded, looking determined, and gripped his stick tighter as Gunner went back to his stall. He was halfway through getting his skates on when Will sat down beside him.

"Hey," Gunner said cautiously.

Will's eyes looked tired, like he was still short on sleep despite his nap, but he smiled. "Hey." He didn't say anything else.

Gunner waited, but Will seemed content to sit beside him, looking at the team as they got into their gear and talked over and around each other.

"They're good guys," Will said.

"Yeah," Gunner agreed.

"Coach talked to me," Will said next. His shoulders slumped briefly. "I'm sorry I put that on you, Guns. Making you have to lead without me."

"Don't be stupid," Gunner said, keeping his hands in his lap. "I knew you'd get your head out of your ass eventually."

Will's laugh was startled and genuine, and Gunner ducked his head to finish putting his skates on, not bothering to hide his smile.

THEY WON 4-2, Will getting a goal off Gunner's assist and then Gunner scoring off a breakaway less than a minute later. He collided with Will after, breathless and triumphant, arms in the air as Will swung him around, roaring something in his ear.

It was going to work. He had Will back. Olivia was in the stands, beating her small hands against the glass, delight all over her expressive face, and Gunner pointed right at her, making her somehow light up even more. Gunner threw his head back and laughed as the rest of the line slammed into them.

Six years ago

Will called an emergency team meeting the day before their first game in Indy, with everyone but Gunner.

"Someone is with Gunner at all times once we touch down," he said. "I'll take point, but if I can't be there, I want one of you with him. This is non-negotiable, understood?"

The guys nodded, looking uncharacteristically somber.

Schulz raised a tentative hand and Will nodded at him.

"Can we ask what happened?"

"No," Will said flatly. "If he wants you to know, he'll tell you."

"What if he sends us away?" Volly asked.

"You come get me immediately." Will looked around the room at them, studying their faces. "Does anyone here still have a problem with Gunner?"

No one spoke.

"Harny," Will said.

Harnell jumped. "No, man, it's… I'm cool. It's fine. Guns isn't checking us out. And he plays damn fine hockey."

Will nodded. "If anyone else has a problem, find me in private. For now, let's keep him safe, alright?"

On the airplane, Will took the seat beside Gunner. He had his earbuds in, eyes closed as he listened to music, but his fingers were tapping restlessly on his thigh and his foot was jiggling. Will touched his knee and Gunner's eyes snapped open.

"Don't fidget," Will said. "It's annoying."

Gunner studied him for a minute with his clear green gaze, but finally his lips quirked and he nodded.

A thought occurred to Will and he nudged Gunner's knee again. "Hey."

Gunner pulled an earbud out.

Will fidgeted, searching for words. "That, um. Guy you mentioned."

Gunner's brow furrowed.

"The—" Why were words so *hard*? "At the Christmas party, you said something about an ex. That it didn't end well. Is he—"

Comprehension and surprise dawned on Gunner's face. "I mentioned him?"

"Not by name or in any detail, but in passing, yeah. Is he on the Racers still? Are we going to have a problem?"

Gunner shook his head. "He got traded a few months before I did, went to Scottsdale. He's not there anymore."

Will relaxed. "Okay. Good."

The rest of the plane ride was silent, but Will couldn't help noticing that Gunner stuck a little closer than usual on the tarmac and onto the waiting bus. They'd flown in late and were heading straight to the hotel, although a few of the younger guys were talking about going out to grab a drink. Gunner shook his head silently when Will suggested they go too, so they shouldered their bags and found their rooms, next door to each other.

Will hesitated at his door as Gunner fumbled with his key card. "Do you want to… I don't know, watch a movie or something?"

Gunner was nodding before he was done. He opened the door to his room, dropped his bag inside, and was by Will's side immediately. Will almost laughed, but there was nothing funny about the shadows like bruises under Gunner's eyes, or the way he was hugging his ribs.

Inside the room, they took off their shoes and got comfortable on the king-size bed. Gunner was still a ball of tension, but Will had the feeling that if he tried to touch him, it might snap the clearly brittle thread holding him together.

So instead he turned on the television and started flicking through channels.

He landed on one where Will Ferrell was standing outside a bakery. Gunner made a noise and Will glanced at him, then back to the channel.

"This good?"

Gunner nodded. "I love this movie."

He was asleep before it was over, head pillowed on his arm. Will turned the television off and slid down on his side to face him. Gunner's face was soft in sleep, the lines of worry and tension smoothed out. The lamplight painted his cheekbone gold, a curl falling forward over his brow, and Will fought the urge to smooth it back.

Instead he got up and found the extra blankets, shaking one out and tucking it around Gunner's shoulders. Then he turned off the light and slid under his own blanket.

They won't hurt you again, he told Gunner silently.

When he woke up the next morning, Gunner's blanket was folded at the end of the bed and Will was alone in the room. There was a text on his phone from Gunner.

Thanks. See you at breakfast.

Will hurried to shower and headed downstairs with his hair still damp. He found Gunner in the dining room, eating obscene amounts of breakfast meat. He looked tired but not as fragile as he had the night before, and a genuine smile crept across his face when he saw Will.

The only other one there from their team was Volly, who looked like he'd much rather still be asleep, his head propped on a fist and eyes closed.

"Hey," Will said, sliding into the chair opposite.

"Hey," Gunner said, smile widening a fraction. "Hungry?"

Volly blinked and yawned. "'M goin' back to bed," he announced, and left.

Alone, Gunner and Will looked at each other.

"I don't know how he knew I was down here," Gunner said, cutting a sausage into pieces. "He just showed up and fell asleep sitting there."

Will hid his smile. "How are you feeling?"

"Fine," Gunner said. Something in the word warned Will not to press, so he dropped it.

"Any friends you're gonna look up while we're here?"

Gunner shook his head. "Burned those bridges, I think." His smile was rueful, self-deprecating, and Will wanted to kiss him. Instead he stole a piece of bacon off Gunner's plate, grinning at the sputter of outrage that got him.

THEY SPENT the day sticking close to the hotel for the most part after morning practice, although Will did manage to wheedle Gunner into taking a walk with him close to lunchtime. Gunner kept his hands in his sweatshirt, the hood up and sunglasses on. Still, he talked easily enough, pointing out sights as they strolled, and his body language was loose and relaxed. Will bumped him with a shoulder.

"You look like you're hiding from paparazzi."

Gunner's smile flickered. "Maybe I am," he retorted. "I was a pretty hot commodity around here, you know."

Will feigned being starstruck. "Oh, Mr. Ryan sir, can I get your autograph, sir?" He fluttered his eyelashes and Gunner shoved him with a snorted laugh.

"You're an idiot."

14

THE ARENA WAS ALREADY FILLING up when they arrived that afternoon. Gunner rolled his shoulders as they walked down the back halls to the dressing room, and Will glanced at him.

Gunner's smile seemed forced. "Crowd probably won't be thrilled to see me."

"Fans have a pretty short memory," Will said. "You might be surprised."

Gunner looked skeptical and didn't answer.

He couldn't help but notice the way the others found reasons to talk to Gunner as they dressed and warmed up. Volly, looking much more awake, flopped down beside him and they discussed a TV show he apparently wanted Gunner to watch. When he moved on, Schulz was there, asking Gunner if there was a good place to eat near their hotel.

Will watched, getting his UnderArmour on and bouncing on the balls of his feet, swinging his arms back and forth as his muscles slowly warmed up. Gunner was looking slightly less tense by the time Will fetched up beside him and slapped him on the shoulder.

"Kickball time."

A group of them ended up in the hallway, bouncing the ball back and forth to each other. Will made sure he was next to Gunner, bumping him companionably as he lunged for the ball, laughing when Gunner tripped and went sprawling.

By the time they were ready to go back and get their gear on, Gunner's smile was much easier. Still, he began to tense again as they readied to take the ice.

Will caught the front of his jersey and pulled him in until their helmets bumped. Gunner's eyes were wide and startled, his breath warm on Will's face. Sound faded away around them until all Will could see was Gunner's eyes.

"Let's show them what they lost," he murmured, just for Gunner's ears.

Gunner blinked rapidly and pressed his mouth into a flat line. He nodded, sharp and jerky, and Will let him go.

The game was a blur. Will was still finding his place on the first line, but Gunner's presence on his wing was a steadying influence. The worst part was the face off. Dean Jefferson was in fine form, quick as ever with a vicious barb right before the puck dropped.

"Guess you figured out how to get him in

line," he said conversationally the first time, bent over with his stick balanced on his knees as they waited for the ref. "Did you bend him over for you or did you use the belt?"

Will was achingly aware of Gunner's silent presence behind him but he kept his mouth shut.

Jefferson won the face off. Will went after him immediately and somehow got in front of the puck when Jefferson tried to pass it. He sent it behind him without even looking, knowing Gunner was there and would intercept it.

He spun to see Gunner charging up ice, and Will bolted after him, keeping pace on the far side of the rink. They hadn't practiced this move, but somehow Will just knew, he *knew* if he could get to the sweet spot at the precise moment Gunner needed him—he put his head down and poured on speed, dodging a hapless Racer.

He was closing on the net fast, and he didn't even see Gunner make the pass, but somehow the puck was there, slicing through the traffic, and all Will had to do was turn his wrist and tip it in, up and over the goalie's knee before he had a chance to react.

Gunner collided with him behind the net, flinging himself into Will's arms. Will caught him, yelling something incoherent about how fucking incredible Gunner was, and Gunner clung to him and laughed, head thrown back in delight.

JEFFERSON DIDN'T HAVE anything to say during the next faceoff. Will grinned at him, still buzzing with glee.

"I think he's gotten himself in line just fine," he said, and snaked the puck out from under Jefferson's nose.

THEY WON in a resounding 5-1 victory. Gunner was named first star, and Will watched as he took to the ice to salute the crowd and then talk to the broadcaster.

"How's it feel, being back in Indy?" she asked.

Gunner took his helmet off and shook out his curls before answering. "Lotta memories," he said. He looked up and found Will, standing by the gate. He smiled. "It's good to be back."

THEY WERE GREETED in the locker room with cheers and shouting, everyone crowding around to hug Gunner as Will stood back, unable to stop his grin.

After the media scrums and cooldowns, Will found his way back to Gunner's side as he got dressed.

"How's it going?" Will asked, and Gunner shot him a sideways smile as he bent to tie his shoes.

"Better." He straightened. "That felt good."

"What, spanking the team that didn't appreciate you properly?" Will bumped him with his elbow and Gunner laughed.

It cut off abruptly though, and the smile slid off his face as he looked past Will toward the open door.

There was a man standing there—he was a Racer, Will knew that much, but he didn't know most of them by name. All he knew was this wasn't Dean Jefferson, which was probably good because Will didn't actually want to spend a night in jail for assault.

But Gunner didn't look happy, staring at the man with a pinched mouth and furrowed eyebrows as he shifted his feet in the doorway.

"Who is that?" Will asked quietly.

"Mike," Gunner said through tight lips.

"Did he—"

Gunner shook his head.

"Do you want to talk to him?"

Gunner shook his head again.

"Okay." Will headed for the open door. He caught Mike's arm and pulled him through and out into the hall with very little effort as Mike protested but didn't struggle much. Will hauled him down the corridor until he was sure they wouldn't be overheard and then let him go. "What do you want?"

Mike swallowed audibly. He wasn't very tall, slim-framed and built for agility and speed more than power. Will wasn't even remotely ashamed about looming over him as he waited for an answer.

"I—I just wanted to talk to Gunny."

"You don't get to call him that," Will said flatly.

Mike flinched. "I didn't—sorry. I just. Look, I wanted to tell him—"

Will waited but Mike couldn't seem to find the words.

"Tell me, and I'll consider passing it on," Will said. Part of him wondered if this was the right approach—protecting Gunner like he was a helpless child who couldn't take care of himself—but he also hadn't missed the stark relief on Gunner's face when Will had taken charge.

Mike's shoulders drooped. "I wanted—I know how they treated him, man. I know what they did."

"And you wanted, what? To dredge it all up again?"

"No," Mike protested. "No, I wanted to tell him I was sorry. I didn't—" There were tears in his eyes, Will realized with a jolt. "I didn't stop them. I was too scared, too new and too m-much of a coward. I didn't want to be sent down. So I told myself it wasn't happening, I l-looked the other way, I tried not to hear what they were doing, and —" He swallowed, sharp and convulsive. "I fucked up. I—he didn't deserve any of it, he n-needed someone and I didn't—" He dashed a hand over his eyes and turned away. "I shouldn't have come," he said over his shoulder. "Just forget it."

"Wait," Will said.

Mike froze in place.

Will heaved a sigh. "You're right, you fucked up. And I don't know if I can forgive you."

Mike tucked his chin to his chest and said nothing.

"But it's not up to me. It's Gunner's choice. I'll tell him what you said. If he wants to reach out—does he have your number?"

Mike nodded, something like hope in his eyes.

"Then if he wants to talk to you, he knows where to find you. Now get the fuck out of here before I punch you on general principles."

Mike nodded again and bolted.

Will waited until he was gone and then went back to the room. Belmont and Schulz were sitting on either side of Gunner, talking casually about a video game they were obsessed with, and Gunner met Will's eyes.

Will just nodded fractionally at him and Gunner's posture eased. Will pulled out his phone and sent him a quick text.

Tell you on the plane.

Gunner dug out his own phone, read the text, and put the phone back in his pocket. "Can we get this show on the road, gentlemen?" he asked. His voice sounded almost normal, Will thought with a strange sense of pride. "I don't know about you, but I want to sleep in my own bed tonight."

15

Present day

October gave way to November and Gunner went on his first set of away games. He was a nervous wreck the whole time, texting Lane constantly, until she called him in exasperation while he was supposed to be napping before the game.

"She's *fine*, Gunner," Lane told him firmly.

Gunner was in bed, flat on his back staring at the ceiling. "Is she—" *Does she miss me?* he wanted to ask, but he didn't.

"She asks about you all the time, and I've promised her we'll watch your games," Lane said. She laughed quietly. "She misses you, of course she does. But she's *so* excited. She told all her friends and teachers about you. And she's eating her vegetables. I promise."

"Okay," Gunner said, a lump in his throat but

his chest easing. "Um. I'll try to call after the game, if—if it's not too late."

"I'll let her stay up for this one," Lane said, sounding amused. "But when you're on the east coast, she'll just have to watch them the next day. Can't throw off her sleep schedule too much."

Gunner couldn't help smiling. "I'm glad you're with us, Lane."

Lane laughed again. "I didn't expect to enjoy this job as much as I have. Now go to sleep, Gunner. We'll be watching the game."

Gunner fell asleep almost immediately.

THEY WON three of their four away games, losing the fourth and returning exhausted but still hopeful.

Gunner spent as much time with Olivia as he could, but she was busy too, enrolled in a mite league that kept her out a lot. But she was glowing and happy and talked nonstop when they were together, and Gunner soaked up every minute, taking her swimming or to the park with the dogs every chance he got.

Will was almost back to his old self, as he'd promised. A little quieter, maybe, somewhat less inclined to touch Gunner, but he was *there,* he sat next to Gunner on the plane more often than not, discussed game plays and lines and joked with him. If he didn't get too close, didn't touch Gunner as often, well, Gunner tried not to mind.

The lines were gelling, their powerplay unit coming into its own. They were rising through the standings of the Western Conference, and people were beginning to whisper about playoffs as the months spun out.

"First Christmas party with the team!" Gunner said, picking Olivia up and swinging her around the room to make her shriek with laughter. "Are you excited?"

Olivia nodded, wispy curls falling into her eyes. "Lane's gonna do my hair all pretty."

Gunner tucked her under his arm so he could tousle her head. "Your hair's *always* pretty, silly."

Olivia squirmed and giggled until Gunner set her back on her feet. "I gotta go get ready." She dashed for the stairs as Gunner followed at a more sedate pace to get dressed himself.

Will was hosting the party, so it was a short commute to his house, Olivia talking nonstop in the backseat. Ferguson was with her, of course, with a bow made from the same fabric as her dress tied around his neck at a jaunty angle. Gunner had learned by now when Olivia expected a response and when she was just talking to hear her own voice, so he hummed acknowledgment in the pauses and made encouraging noises as she told a mostly incomprehensible story about a girl in her hockey league. Something to do with her skates, Gunner thought as he turned into the driveway and found a spot to park.

Will opened the door before they made it up the walk, and Olivia bolted straight for him. Will stooped and caught her, swinging her up into a hug. He was wearing a red and green Christmas sweater, his dark hair styled carefully off his brow, and he looked unfairly good. Gunner wanted to kiss him, or bite him.

"You look like a princess!" Will was saying to Olivia, who preened.

"D'you like my hair?" She patted the perfect braids. "Lane did them."

"They're beautiful," Will told her. "Did you cry when she brushed your hair?"

Olivia scowled and then her expression cleared as she realized he was teasing. "I'm not little anymore," she said loftily, nose in the air.

"You sure aren't," Gunner said, joining them in the doorway. "Why don't you go show Sonny your dress? I told him about it last week."

Olivia wriggled down and dashed inside as Gunner stepped up onto the doorsill.

"Hi," Will said quietly. "You look nice too."

Gunner smiled at him. They were just a few inches away and it would be so easy to lean in—

"Gotta keep up appearances," he said lightly. "Everyone here already?" He slipped past Will into the house and down the hall to the huge living room, where Olivia was already holding court, Sonny, Luke, and Belmont all talking to her at once.

Gunner was greeted with cries of delight and hugs from several wives and girlfriends, perfectly groomed and smelling like flowers. The house was decorated with silver garlands and softly twinkling lights, a huge Christmas tree in the corner of the living room.

"It's very festive," Gunner said as Will came up behind him. "Did you decorate the tree yourself?"

Will snorted and handed him a cup of eggnog. "You kidding me? I paid someone. Same person who did the Christmas decorations. You want her number? Your place could use a tune-up."

"Hey, my place is just fine, asshole."

"Language!" Sonny said, glaring at him.

Olivia was deep in the middle of what sounded like the story she'd been telling Gunner in the car and clearly hadn't heard, so Gunner just stuck out his tongue and turned to investigate the kitchen.

He found Cady inspecting what smelled like a pie in the oven. "Hey!" he said, already grinning.

Cady spun. "Gunny!" She threw herself at him, a solid bundle in his arms. Gunner hugged her back.

"Where've you been?" he asked when they finally separated. "Thought maybe you'd gotten sick of Belsy's shit and moved on to better things."

Cady tucked a strand of dark hair behind one ear and rolled her eyes. "Something keeps dragging me back. I think it's all the smelly gear—you know it's like catnip to me."

Gunner laughed and hugged her again. "It's good to see you. You need to come visit more often. What've you been up to?"

They chatted as Cady checked a pot on the stove and Belmont wandered in. He wrapped his arms around Cady's waist and she absently tilted her head so he could kiss her neck while she stirred the potatoes.

Gunner looked away just as Will walked in, Olivia perched on his shoulder.

"Look how tall I am, Gunner!" Olivia said. Her arm was around Will's head, messing up his hair, but Will didn't seem to mind. He carried her in a circuit around the room and Olivia clutched his head harder as the mistletoe on the ceiling caught her eye. "What's that, Uncle Will?"

Will looked up, careful not to dislodge her. "Oh, that's mistletoe."

"That's a funny word," Olivia said, sounding delighted. "It doesn't have *toes*!"

Will shot a grin at Gunner.

"Why's it up there?" Olivia wanted to know next.

"Well, it's a Christmas tradition," Will said. "When two people are standing under it, they have to kiss. Grownups will usually kiss on the mouth, but if it's a kid, it's like this." He swept Olivia down off his shoulder and planted a noisy kiss on her cheek as she shrieked happily and clung to his neck.

Gunner applauded and Will straightened, tossing Olivia back up onto her perch like she weighed nothing at all. Olivia waved as she was paraded out of the room in style, and Gunner laughed quietly and took a sip of his eggnog.

"She's adorable," Cady said. Belmont had disappeared and it was just the two of them again. "How are you handling everything?"

Gunner shrugged. "I'm surviving. The learning curve has been brutal, but she's really great."

"Let me know if you ever need a babysitter," Cady said, and turned back to the potatoes.

GUNNER WANDERED BACK out to the living room and settled on the couch to watch the rookies, who'd dug out a board game from somewhere and were currently arguing about the rules. Olivia was watching raptly, Ferguson tucked in the crook of her elbow.

"No, if your counter thingy lands at the bottom of a ladder you can go up it!" Volly said, and Foster groaned.

"That's Snakes and Ladders, dumbass!"

"Language!" three people said simultaneously before Gunner could even open his mouth.

Gunner didn't bother trying to stifle the laugh. The eggnog had been spiked and he was feeling very comfortable and relaxed, bones warm and a little melty.

Will sat down beside him and Gunner squinted at him.

"How much rum was even in that?"

"Why, is it working?" Will's grin was devilish.

"I'm gonna have to get Lane to drive us home," Gunner muttered, and Will handed him a refill.

"Hey look!" Olivia said, pointing above their heads. "Mistletoes, Gunner! You have to kiss Uncle Will!"

Gunner froze and then looked up slowly to the mistletoe hanging innocently from the ceiling. "Uh," he said, and Volly whooped.

"Kiss! Kiss! Kiss!" Several others joined in, clapping and cheering, and Gunner rolled his eyes and leaned sideways to plant a quick kiss on Will's cheek.

The cheering turned to booing.

"That doesn't count!" Cady called from the doorway. "You gotta do it *properly*."

Gunner gave her a filthy look and she beamed at him.

Will cleared his throat. "The people demand it," he said quietly, and Gunner looked up into his eyes. Will was smiling at him, and it was just Will, just his best friend, the man he trusted more than anyone in the world, and who was Gunner even kidding? He'd wanted this for so long, and he was only human.

Gunner went to his knees on the couch, held up a hand to get everyone's attention, and the room went silent as he lowered his head until their lips met.

Will's mouth was soft, and he tasted like eggnog as he opened under Gunner's touch. His breath fluttered warm across Gunner's cheek and he made a soft noise in the back of his throat as their tongues brushed together.

Gunner cupped his face, stroking across his cheekbone, and the world melted away. It was just them, Will yielding so sweetly to him, breath a little ragged as he kissed Gunner like a drowning man. Gunner wanted to shove him down, take him apart, see what kind of noises he could pull from him.

Someone cleared their throat loudly and they startled apart, both of them blinking stupidly.

"*That's* how grownups do it?" Olivia demanded.

"Sometimes," Cady said, her lips twitching. "When they really like each other."

Olivia wrinkled her nose.

Gunner scrambled to his feet, head still spinning. "I hope you vultures are happy," he said with as much dignity as he could muster, and made his escape to catcalls and laughter from the entire team.

Safely locked in Will's bathroom, he sank onto the rim of the bathtub and covered his face. What the *fuck* had he been thinking? His traitorous brain kept replaying the way Will's mouth had felt in glorious Technicolor. All he wanted was to do it again and again. He balled his fists and smacked his temples, rocking back and forth.

Stupid, stupid, *stupid.* Now he had to go back out there and pull his game-face on again, pretend that hadn't meant anything and he'd have done it with anyone. His stomach turned at the thought and he groaned under his breath just as someone knocked on the door.

"Gunny?" Will called softly.

Oh, perfect. Gunner took a deep breath and composed his face as much as possible before opening the door.

Will looked worried. "Are you okay?" he asked.

Gunner summoned a smile that felt almost real. "Of course. Gotta put on a show, right?"

There was a furrow between Will's brows. "That wasn't a show," he said, watching Gunner's face intently. "Don't try and tell me—"

"I won't," Gunner interrupted. "But it changes nothing, Will. I'm sorry, I should have checked before I sat down, I didn't mean to put you in that position—"

"I knew it was there," Will said, and Gunner snapped his mouth shut. "I knew, and I sat down anyway, and I hoped, okay? So if anyone should be apologizing, it's me." He looked ashamed but also faintly defiant. "It won't happen again, I promise. I just wanted to—"

"You wanted to know what it would be like," Gunner said softly, and Will's shoulders slumped as he nodded.

"I'm sorry," he whispered.

God, Gunner loved him. He kept his mouth shut so the words wouldn't escape.

"It *won't* happen again," Will said. He looked up, catching Gunner's eyes. "But I wish it could, because that was the best fucking kiss of my life."

He turned on his heel, leaving Gunner clinging to the doorframe to keep himself upright.

Fuck. He was so absolutely fucked.

Somehow, he found the strength to pull a smile on and go back out to the living room. He was, predictably, met with teasing and catcalls, but he managed to deflect them somewhat by grabbing Cady and dipping her under another clump of mistletoe to kiss her as flamboyantly as possible on the mouth while she flailed and shrieked and pummeled him.

"Girlfriend poaching is off-limits!" Belmont complained loudly.

Gunner set Cady back on her feet. "Gonna do something about it, Belsy?"

Belmont glanced at Will and cleared his throat, shaking his head. "Maybe when there aren't kids present. Wouldn't want your daughter to have to watch you get your ass beat."

"*Language*!"

16

Gunner's mother and sister flew in for Christmas. Olivia was delighted to see Fay, talking a mile a minute from the moment they picked them up from the airport. She also immediately took to Gunner's sister Jessie, who had hair as pale as Gunner's, but as straight as his was curly. Given Jessie's mischievous streak, Gunner had serious doubts about leaving them unsupervised, but he had to admit they were cute together, blonde head bent toward dark as they talked in low, hushed tones about something in the backseat on the way home.

Probably hockey. Gunner just hoped it was hockey and not plans for world domination.

Will came over on Christmas Eve, laden with packages.

"Why aren't you in Toronto?" Fay scolded

after Gunner brought him inside and Fay kissed his cheek. Will smiled down at her, the cold air from outside making his cheeks and nose glow pink.

"Figured Gunny might appreciate the extra support for Olivia's first Christmas," he said. "Plus —" He glanced around to make sure Olivia wasn't in earshot. "I thought… first Christmas, more people might help keep her from being too sad."

Fay patted his cheek. "You're such a good boy. Gunner, isn't he a good boy?"

"He's not a dog, Mom," Gunner said mildly, but he smiled at Will, who returned it. *Thanks*, Gunner mouthed. Will shrugged as if it was no big deal and took off his coat.

Jessie and Olivia came tumbling through and Jessie ran face-first into Will's chest as Olivia hugged his leg.

"Will!" she said, flinging her arms around him. "Do you somehow have *more* muscles than the last time I saw you?"

Will laughed and hugged her back, then bent to greet Olivia. "It's the curse of a professional athlete's life," he said when he straightened. "How're you? How's school? Got all the boys after you?"

Jessie tipped her nose in the air, flicking corn-silk fine hair over her shoulder. "And more than a few girls," she said loftily.

"Oh damn," Will said, blinking.

Gunner tensed. "Jess, are you being safe?"

Jessie gave him a look only a scornful teenager could pull off. "You're not my dad, Gunny." She sighed at the scowl on his face. "Yes, I'm being safe. You don't need to intimidate or threaten anyone."

"Because I will," Gunner said. "You say the word. Someone—*anyone*—treats you wrong, you tell me. They'll never find the body."

Jessie pointed at him. "That right there is why you're never hearing about my love life. C'mon, Livvy, show me your room."

They dashed up the stairs and Will and Gunner were left looking at each other in the hall.

"Hey," Will said quietly, and something in the way he was watching him made Gunner think of the team Christmas party, the eggnog and mistletoe and Will's mouth, so soft and—

Gunner cleared his throat. "Hi. You really didn't have to… you know. Be here."

"Do you not want me here?"

Gunner glared at him but Will looked honestly worried. "You *know* I do, Will, come on. I just didn't want to pull you away from your family."

Will took a quick step closer and leaned into Gunner's space. He was just enough taller to loom over him a little, and Gunner hated how much he loved that.

"You're my family too," Will said, and Gunner wanted to curl up in his arms, drink spiced rum on the couch with the fire burning, lean back against his broad chest and think about nothing at all. "You and Olivia," Will continued.

Gunner was brought back to himself with a thump. Olivia. Of course. The reason he couldn't risk anything with Will anyway, no matter how much he wanted to.

"Will, honey," Fay called from the kitchen. "Come taste-test this for me."

Will smiled at Gunner from only a few inches away. "Duty calls," he said, and his voice was light but his gaze on Gunner felt like an almost physical caress.

Gunner rubbed his arms as Will turned for the kitchen. He could hear Olivia's voice, bright and cheerful floating from her room as Jessie asked questions. The house smelled like spiced oranges, cloves and cinnamon and something else that started with a C, Gunner thought, but he couldn't remember the name of it.

Olivia came bounding down the stairs and collided with Gunner's thighs. She wrapped both arms around one and grinned up at him.

Gunner thumbed her pointed chin. "Is it nice having Gramma Fay and Jessie here?"

"And Uncle Will!" Olivia said. There was cocoa on her cheek. Gunner wiped it off, smiling down at her. Olivia sobered briefly. "I wish Mama was here though."

Gunner bent and swung her into his arms. She looped her arms around his neck and he carried her through into the kitchen. "I know you miss her," he said against her soft hair. "But you know she's here, right? She's watching you. She loves you so much."

Olivia nodded, mouth drooping. "I want to see her, though," she whispered, putting her head on his shoulder.

Will and Fay looked up when they entered but Gunner didn't glance at them. An idea had struck him. He swung left, into the open-plan dining room just off the kitchen. The house had come with a mahogany table and six chairs, which was a little excessive for everyday use, but suited Gunner's needs at the moment.

He hooked a foot around the chair at the far end and pulled it out. "Hey. Liv. Look." He waited until Olivia lifted her head. "You see this chair?" Gunner asked. Olivia nodded, looking confused. "This chair," Gunner told her, "this is your mama's chair. Okay? This is where she sits. This is where she watches you. When *you* sit in this chair, it's like you're in her lap." He lowered her into the chair and pulled up another to sit beside her.

Olivia crossed her legs, smoothing a hand over the polished wood of the seat.

"She will always have a place with us," Gunner said gently. "With you. And maybe you can't see her this Christmas, but that doesn't mean she's not here."

Olivia looked up, past Gunner, and he twisted to see Will in the doorway, watching silently.

"Olivia!" Fay called. "I need your help decorating cookies!"

Olivia lit up and scrambled off the chair. She pressed a quick kiss to Gunner's cheek and then she was gone, running for the kitchen as Will came into the room and sat beside him.

"That was a great idea," he said quietly.

"Don't know if it'll help," Gunner said. He leaned back, stretching his legs and sighing. "I can't imagine Christmas without my mom *now*. Having to go through that before I was even seven years old?" He shook his head and sighed. "It's not right."

Will put a hand on his knee. “Right and wrong isn’t the issue. You’re taking care of her. That’s all that matters. She’ll look back on this and be grateful for how you helped keep Stephanie’s memory alive for her.”

Gunner ached to cover Will’s hand with his own, to lace their fingers together. Instead he cleared his throat and stood.

“I wonder if Mom will let us help decorate cookies too.”

17

Olivia woke Gunner up in the morning by launching herself onto the bed. "Wake up, wake up!" she said, bouncing on her knees as Gunner groaned and rolled over. "Gunner, wake uu-up, it's *Christmas*!"

Gunner pulled a pillow over his head.

Olivia threw herself flat and shoved her head under the pillow so they were nose-to-nose. "Gunner," she whispered. "Wake up."

Gunner peeked at her. Olivia grinned, flashing the gap where she'd lost a tooth the week before.

"Are you 'wake?" she said in a hushed voice.

"No," Gunner said, and closed his eyes again.

"Yes you are, you talked to me! Gunner, c'mooon…."

Gunner snuck a hand out from under the covers and poked her in the ribs. Her squawk was gratifying, so he did it again, and then again, until she was twisting and squirming in helpless giggles and Babe jumped on the bed to join them, drawn by the noise.

Jessie kicked the door open and Gunner and Olivia both froze. Jessie's hair was flat to one side of her head and sticking up on the other. She still had wrinkle-lines on her face from the pillow, and a very unamused expression.

"I think we woke up your Aunt Jessie," Gunner told Olivia in a stage whisper.

Jessie's scowl grew. "*Some* of us need our beauty sleep, even on Christmas morning."

"Hey, you said it, not me," Gunner said, and Jessie flipped him off with both hands before turning to stomp down the stairs. "Whoops." Gunner glanced at Olivia, who looked curious and assessing, and cleared his throat. "That was, uh… a grownup thing. Don't use it, okay?"

"What's it mean?" Olivia asked, rolling upright.

"Something rude," Gunner said. "You want some breakfast? I'll bet you Gramma Fay made something yummy. Race you!"

He let Olivia beat him down the stairs by a scant inch, and they tumbled into the kitchen to find Fay at the counter, putting biscuits into a bowl and wrapping them in a towel.

"Good morning and merry Christmas, princess!" Fay said to Olivia, holding out her arms.

Gunner used the moment to steal a biscuit, dodging Fay's half-hearted swipe and ducking back out of the kitchen with his ill-gotten gains.

Truth be told, he was nervous about how the day would go. Olivia was young and resilient, but it had only been about five months since she'd lost her mother and had her world turned upside down. He wasn't sure how she'd do opening presents without Stephanie there, or how he'd handle it if she did have a meltdown.

He was immensely relieved when Will rang the doorbell, and was the first to answer it.

Will looked cozy and kissable in a cream-colored sweater. His smile was soft and something pulled low in Gunner's gut. Will stepped inside and Gunner moved aside to let him through.

"Merry Christmas," Will said. "Any mistletoe around?"

Gunner looked up sharply and Will's smile widened, clearly unrepentant.

"Asshole," Gunner muttered, fighting his own smile as Olivia burst into the hall and collided with Will's legs.

"It's Christmas, Uncle Will! Are you gonna open presents with us?"

Will stooped and swung her up onto his hip. "You bet I am, kiddo. Did you get me anything good?"

Olivia giggled, grabbing small fistfuls of his sweater. "It's a s'prise!"

"Shall we?" Gunner asked, motioning toward the den.

THEY DECIDED to go around in order of age, opening presents in turn. Not surprisingly, Olivia had the most, making Gunner shake his head despairingly and mutter about spoiling her.

"Which do you want to open first?" he asked.

"*Wait!*" Olivia said, looking suddenly anguished, and jumped to her feet, shedding the pile of gifts in her lap. She pulled on Gunner's arm until he bent so she could whisper in his ear, "Mama, Gunner. You said—"

"Right, of course! I'm sorry." Gunner got up. "Be right back, everyone."

He returned with the chair from the dining room and set it next to Olivia, who beamed up at him and put Ferguson on it.

Somehow the unwrapping went without a hitch, even when Olivia opened the present from her mother. It was a framed picture of Stephanie with Olivia in her arms, their faces turned up to the camera as they smiled, radiant with joy. Everyone stopped what they were doing as Olivia got up and climbed into Gunner's lap, gripping the photograph. She traced Stephanie's face with one finger as Gunner held her. He looked at Stephanie's face, searching for any signs of familiarity. She might as well have been a complete stranger, he thought miserably. Nothing about her sparked a memory—not her lovely, almond-shaped eyes, her satiny dark skin, or her heart-stopping smile.

"Isn't she so pretty?" Olivia asked softly.

Gunner nodded, their cheeks pressed together. "Just like you," he managed.

He caught Will's eyes when he looked up. Will smiled at him, quiet and sympathetic, and Gunner swallowed hard and glanced away.

Olivia kept the photograph next to her the rest of the day, and divided her time between talking to it and to Ferguson.

18

THE TEAM WAS WINNING MORE than they lost, every step inching them closer to the Western Cup playoffs. They were under more scrutiny than ever, their every move dissected and analyzed, and Gunner, along with the rest of the players, curtailed his extracurricular activities, sticking close to home as much as possible. More often than not, Will joined him, with Schulz, Shore, or Belmont often tagging along.

Every spare minute was spent talking strategy, their biggest threats, and what chance they had. Hope warred with exhaustion on everyone's faces as they scraped through January into February. Lane took Olivia to school and hockey practice, and Olivia regaled Gunner with stories of both over the dinner table every day he was able to be home.

They were still winning, still racking up points. Schulz went out for three weeks with an upper body injury. They called up several players, shuffled the lines around, reassessed. Volly hit a hot streak, racking up several goals a game that pushed them up over the hump of Schulz's loss. Gunner made time for the rookies, bringing them to his house for steaks and letting them vent as much as they felt safe, commiserating with the exhaustion.

Everyone asked about Olivia when she wasn't at a game. She still loved Will best besides Gunner, but Lukas was a clear contender for favorite ever since he took her for a skate around the arena after a game, on his shoulders as she held onto his hair and squealed happily and the fans applauded.

Gunner thought they had a shot at the playoffs this year, he really did. Judging from the expressions on the faces around him in the locker room as Will talked them up before a game, the others did too.

He fell into bed and slept the sleep of the dead every night, and if he woke up wishing there was a heavy arm wrapped around his waist in the mornings, well… Gunner had gotten good at not wanting what he couldn't have, or at least telling himself he'd survive without it.

19

GUNNER WOKE up one morning in early February in a cold sweat. *Olivia's birthday was a week away.*

He grabbed his phone in a panic and called Lane.

"What is it?" she asked, sounding worried.

"Olivia's birthday is next week," Gunner blurted. Ty gave him a dirty look for disturbing his sleep.

Lane groaned. "You woke me up for *that*? Do you know what time it is, Gunner?"

"Uh… six?"

"Six. In the goddamn morning. And you're just *now* realizing that maybe we need to do something for your daughter's seventh birthday?"

Gunner clutched the phone tighter. "I'm sorry," he said. "I don't… I'm shit at this, Lane. What do I do?"

Lane sighed. "You're lucky you pay well. Olivia's birthday is all taken care of. It's being catered, the presents are wrapped, her friends are invited. All you have to do is show up."

Gunner collapsed back against the pillows. "I—"

"Yeah, I know. Now hang up so I can get breakfast started, since I'm awake now."

WILL STEPPED in the front door and then froze as a horde of shrieking girls ran past him at top speed, Olivia at the head of the pack.

"Will!" Lane said, holding a tray of cupcakes. There was a smear of icing on her round cheek. "Thank God you're here. Gunner's upstairs and it's almost time to cut the cake. Can you go get him?"

Will took the stairs two at a time. Gunner's door was ajar, so he knocked and then pushed it open a few more inches.

"Gunny?"

Gunner was sitting on the bed, staring at something in his hands. He looked up as Will stepped inside, hurriedly wiping his face.

"Hey," Will said carefully. "You okay?"

"Sure," Gunner said. It sounded automatic, and his voice was raspy, the smile on his face as thin as tissue paper.

"Guns," Will said, sitting on the bed beside him, and Gunner's face crumpled. He tilted sideways until his head was on Will's shoulder, his curls brushing Will's cheek.

"Sorry," he muttered.

Will rubbed Gunner's back. "Don't apologize. What happened?"

Gunner lifted his hand. He was holding a vaguely familiar looking gift. Will took it, turning it to look at the label.

Olivia, it said. *From Mama.*

Oh.

"Liv doesn't deserve this," Gunner managed. "She doesn't—she never wanted to be here with me. She wanted to be with her mother, to grow up w-with her, like she *should* have. And instead she g-gets me. I'm… I'm barely here, I never know what to say to her, I can't give her what Stephanie could—"

"Do you love her, Gunny?" Will interrupted.

Gunner was silent for a long minute.

"Yeah," he finally whispered. He lifted his head, green eyes anxious. "But is it enough?"

Your love will always be enough. Will kept the words behind his teeth with an almighty effort.

"You know she loves you too, right?" he asked instead.

"I—I mean, I hoped, but—"

"Idiot," Will said without heat. "Of course she loves you. She *adores* you. And yeah, it's shitty that she lost her mom. It's *shitty*. But in a lot of ways, she's so, so lucky. She came to you, she didn't end up in foster care or with Stephanie's parents. And now she has not just you, but me and Lane and the whole damn team. Now come on. Your daughter only turns seven once, and you're missing the party."

Gunner caught his wrist before Will could stand. "Will—"

Will waited, Gunner's fingers hot like a brand against his skin. *God*, how he wanted. He wanted to push Gunner back onto the bed, crawl on top of him and see just how far out of his mind he could drive him. It was an ache in his chest, one that never truly went away, the burning need to fill his senses with everything Gunner.

He didn't move. Gunner seemed to be fighting an internal battle, conflict all over his expressive face.

"Thank you," he finally said.

Will lifted a brow. "All those mental gymnastics just to thank me?"

Gunner shoved at his shoulder. "Asshole. I mean it. I'm—I know… you don't have to be here. You have every reason to walk away from me after the way I've jerked you around. But you—you're still here. I don't deserve—"

Will got a hand over his mouth in time to stop him. "Do *not* finish that fucking sentence. I told you, remember? You're my best friend, and you always will be. Non-negotiable."

Gunner's eyes softened and Will could feel his lips curving in a smile.

"If you lick me," Will warned, fighting his own smile, "I'm not above holding you down and wiping your own drool all over your face."

Gunner laughed out loud as Will dropped his hand. "Let's go see what my daughter's doing with all her buddies."

"Oh God," Will said, standing. "There are so many of them, Guns. So *many.* It's terrifying. What if they band together and overthrow the government?"

"Don't be stupid," Gunner said as he headed

for the door. "They'll start smaller than that. Probably aim for the governor first."

DOWNSTAIRS, there were easily twenty children in the den. Someone had organized them into groups and they were playing a party game that involved a lot of shrieking, or maybe that was just seven year olds in general, Will thought, wincing.

Several adults were in the corner, talking and overseeing the absolute cacophony, and they brightened when Gunner stepped inside, Will on his heels.

"Gunner!" Olivia yelled, and broke away from the pack to hurl herself at his knees.

Gunner stooped and swung her up onto his hip. "Hey you. Are you having fun?"

Olivia nodded enthusiastically. "We're gonna have cake and *ice cream.* And I'm gonna open presents and then Lane says we're going swimming!"

Lane appeared in the doorway and Gunner turned, catching her eye.

"Hey, do you think you can keep things running for a few minutes while Liv and I have a little alone time?"

Lane glanced at Olivia, Ferguson tucked into the crook of her elbow, and smiled at Gunner. "Take all the time you need."

Will shifted his feet as Gunner moved for the door, and Gunner glanced at him, jerking his head in a follow-me motion. Will obeyed, faintly grateful for not being left alone with the parents who'd been eyeing him.

They headed for the dining room and Gunner set Olivia down in her mother's chair, pulling another chair up next to her.

"Will," he said, pointing at a third chair, and Will sank into it.

Gunner leaned forward, elbows on his knees, face serious as he gazed at Olivia. "I know you have a lot of presents out there, and I know you're super excited about opening them. But I thought you might want to open this one just with us."

He held out Stephanie's present on the palm of his hand, and Olivia took it, small mouth drooping.

"Is it from Mama?" she asked.

"Yeah," Gunner said softly.

"What is it?" Olivia wanted to know.

Gunner huffed an almost-laugh. "You'll have to open it to find out."

Olivia plucked at the corner of the wrapping paper and then looked up. Her eyes were filling with tears, Will realized with a jolt of dismay.

"I don't want to," she whispered.

Gunner, who was a lot better at the parenting thing than he gave himself credit for, put a hand on Olivia's knee. "You don't have to if you don't want to," he said carefully. "But do you think you can tell me why?"

Olivia shrugged, suddenly mute, and Gunner cast a helpless look at Will, who scooted his chair closer.

"Hey Livvy," he said, smiling when she looked up at him. "Can I tell you a story?"

Olivia immediately scrambled off her chair and into his lap, curling up against his chest. Will held her, gathering his thoughts. Olivia seemed content to wait, holding Ferguson close as Gunner watched them.

"When I was eighteen," Will said, "my father died."

Olivia tipped her head back to look into his face. "I'm sorry, Uncle Will."

Will squeezed her, smiling. "Thank you. But it was a long time ago and I'm okay now, I promise. Anyway, he liked to pick out our Christmas presents before December, sometimes with Mom's help, sometimes on his own.

"So that Christmas, even though he wasn't there with us, there was a present from him under our tree."

He glanced up to Gunner, listening as intently as Olivia. The room was quiet, like they were in a bubble, just the three of them alone.

"Did you open it?" Olivia asked.

"At first, I didn't really want to," Will admitted. "It was like… if I opened it, if I saw what was inside, it would make it real. Like he'd… really be gone."

Olivia put her head on Will's chest and Gunner closed his eyes briefly, hands opening and closing in his lap.

"My mom said something to me," Will continued. "She said he'd bought that present for me, thinking about the way it would make me smile when I opened it. And you know what?" He dipped his head to press his cheek to Olivia's curls briefly. "She was right. It did. It hurt, because he was gone, but somehow it was like he was still there."

Olivia was very still as she processed that. Then she wriggled around so she could go to her knees and wrap her arms around Will's neck.

Will held her, closing his eyes. God help him, he was just as head over heels for this little girl as he was for her father.

After a minute, Olivia let go and hopped off his lap, straightening her dress and then marching over to Gunner.

She lifted her arms in a mute demand, and Gunner immediately lifted her into his lap. Olivia squirmed until she was comfortable and then nodded decisively.

"I can open it now."

Gunner handed her the present and Olivia pulled the wrapping paper off, revealing a small box.

Will leaned forward to see as she opened it. It was a necklace, nestled on a bed of cotton, a silver pendant shaped like a hockey stick. There was something engraved on the stick, but Will couldn't quite read it.

Olivia lifted it out.

"Can you read it?" Gunner asked.

Olivia traced the words. "She… be… bel…"

"Believed," Gunner prompted.

"Believed she… could?" Olivia glanced up at Gunner, who nodded. "So she did." Olivia frowned. "What does it mean?"

"It's about you," Will said, when Gunner didn't immediately speak. "If you believe you can do something, you *can* do it. Anything in the world."

Olivia's smile was like the dawn breaking. "Do you think she knows I like it, Gunner?"

"Yeah." Gunner's voice was unsteady, and Will couldn't blame him. "I know she does."

He helped get the necklace on, and Olivia touched it again.

"I'm gonna go play with my friends now," she announced, wriggled out of Gunner's lap, and dashed away.

Alone, Will and Gunner looked at each other.

"You never told me that story about your dad before," Gunner said.

Will shrugged. "Not really the kind of thing that comes up in casual conversation. How're you doing?"

Gunner rubbed his face. "That was… a lot. But she took it well. I think. Didn't she?"

"Yeah." The need to touch him burned inside Will, hollowing him out, but he didn't move. "You did a great job. Ready to go face the rest of them?"

"Think anyone would notice if we climbed out a window and made a break for it?"

Will ginned at him, relieved when Gunner returned it. "Just remember they can smell fear. You'll be fine."

20

AND THEN IT was the end of March.

Parson called them in for a team meeting in the last week. His face was calm, but his fingers twitched as he spoke, clearly as wired and exhausted as they were.

"We're not a lock yet," he told them. People nodded. They all knew that. "But we're close." Parson looked around. "The points are there. Five more games. You win four of them and we'll be Stanley Cup contenders. Think we can do that?"

"*Fuck yeah,*" they told him and Parson grinned, stepping back to give Will the floor.

THEY TOOK the first two easily. The third, on the Atlanta Spirits' home ground, was a close fought battle that they just barely scraped through, leaving blood on the ice but coming home with a win off Volly's goal in the last five seconds on the clock.

Two more games at home. The team didn't make eye contact much, but they talked in low, determined tones as they geared up to face the Seabirds.

They lost to them in a vicious shutout, a resounding defeat that shook them to their cores and left them bruised and devastated as the Seabirds celebrated on the other side of the ice.

Will and Gunner consoled the rookies, avoiding each other's eyes, talking to the vets, and reassuring everyone. Still one game to go. One more chance. Gunner put on his best reassuring face, talked to reporters blandly, and went home as soon as possible.

THE NIGHT before they faced the Ravens, Gunner couldn't sleep. He lay in bed, tossing and turning so much that Ty finally got up in a huff and joined Babe in his bed on the floor, and still Gunner couldn't settle his brain. He felt like he was buzzing, like if anyone touched him, they'd feel him vibrating. They were *so close*.

At about one a.m., he gave up and got out of bed. He was still so wired he barely felt the floor under his bare feet as he slipped downstairs, left a note for Lane on the refrigerator, and gathered his keys.

He didn't examine what he was doing as he drove to Will's house and punched in the gate code.

He didn't let himself think at all as he unlocked the front door and stepped inside, toeing off his shoes silently. He was coming unspooled, strips of himself peeling away from his core. He *needed*—

"Gunner?" Will sounded half-asleep, appearing in the door of his bedroom. He was wearing nothing but a pair of soft pants that had seen better days, clinging to his hips. His hair was wild and on end, eyes heavy-lidded, and all the longing Gunner had been pushing away for so long, denying and bottling up and ignoring, swamped him in one heavy, drowning wave.

He lunged across the space between them and dragged Will into a bruising kiss. Will made a shocked noise, utterly still for one horrible, frozen moment, and then he was kissing back wildly, mouths sliding together slick and wet as he grabbed Gunner's hips and yanked him close.

Yes. Gunner got a fistful of Will's hair and hooked one leg around his calf, plastering himself against Will's solid frame. He was going to fly apart, shake into pieces from sheer *need,* anchored only by Will's huge hands on his body.

"Please," he gasped when they pulled apart briefly for air.

Will's eyes were huge and dark, looking down into Gunner's. He looked almost as wrecked as Gunner felt, hair wild and mouth swollen with kisses.

The vibrations were still there, in Gunner's core. He wanted to scream, to plead. *Make it stop. Make me feel nothing but you.* He closed his teeth before he begged, pulling Will back into another kiss, but he was trembling, and Will clearly sensed it.

He broke the kiss, looking worried. "What's wrong?" he asked.

They were still standing in the doorway, and Gunner knew if he let Will slow them down, if they stopped and *talked,* it was going to ruin everything. So he pushed Will backward, over the threshold into his bedroom.

Will let him, but his eyes were still shrewd, assessing. Gunner shook his head.

"Don't," he rasped. "We can talk… later." *Or never, never's good too.* "I need—" He was dust scattered by a breeze, a collection of random fragments, and if Will didn't start touching him, *properly* touching him, he was going to be nothing but a vaguely Gunner-shaped lump of molecules on Will's carpet. "*Please,"* he repeated.

Somehow, Will got it. "Bed," he ordered.

Gunner went eagerly as Will turned on a lamp to its lowest setting.

"I'd ask you if you're sure," Will said, but Gunner lost the rest of what he said because he stepped out of his pants and he wasn't wearing underwear.

Gunner had seen Will's cock countless times, of course he had. There was no place for modesty in a locker room. But he'd never been allowed to *look*, certainly never seen it hard, and he forgot the rest of the world existed as he followed the barely curved shape of it where it already strained upward, brushing against Will's belly. His mouth watered. He wanted—

Will snapped his fingers in Gunner's face. "I'm

flattered," he said, sounding equal parts amused and aroused, "but take off your clothes."

Gunner fell over himself trying to obey, kneeling on top of Will's mattress to strip off his shirt as Will hissed appreciatively under his breath, and then yanking his pants off equally fast. Will put a big hand on Gunner's chest and shoved while Gunner was still trying to get them off his feet, and Gunner fell backward with a startled grunt.

There was no time to react before Will was on top of him, and the heavy weight of him pinning Gunner to the bed made a grateful sob tear its way from Gunner's throat. Will froze but Gunner grabbed at him with shaking hands.

"Don't you dare," he snarled, winding a leg around Will's thighs as Will half-laughed against his throat and settled in.

Gunner closed his eyes, letting his hands rove over every inch of Will he could touch as Will nosed along Gunner's collarbone until he found a spot he liked, above the jut of bone, and fastened his mouth to it. Then he sucked, hard and brutal, not shy about using his teeth. Gunner twisted beneath him, the pleasure-pain-pleasure sending jolts through his body. He was only just aware of his erection, despite being so hard it hurt. Will was over him, above him, around him, blanketing him and surrounding him, until Gunner couldn't smell, feel, taste, hear anything that *wasn't* Will sucking his claim into Gunner's skin.

Arousal curled molten hot in his core. He was burning up with it, lit up from the inside out. He'd never felt so safe, Will the walls blocking out the world that so often wanted nothing more than to tear Gunner apart. Will was still busy marking him, and Gunner realized with something like horror that he was going to come untouched.

Words deserted him and he bucked, trying to dislodge Will's mouth—*not yet not yet*—but Will was undeterred. He grabbed Gunner's wrists in both hands without looking, slamming them down onto the mattress as he sank his teeth into Gunner's shoulder and Gunner choked on a scream and spilled between them in a hot, aching rush.

He could hear Will groaning as he came back to himself. His face was buried in Gunner's throat, his breath harsh and ragged, and he was muttering something Gunner couldn't make out, movements frantic and graceless with need.

Gunner got a hand between them but he'd barely brushed the head of Will's cock with his knuckles before Will was stiffening and coming, wet, slippery heat all over Gunner's hand.

He managed to keep himself up on one elbow until he was done, but then he collapsed, driving the air from Gunner's lungs. His breathing was choppy and sharp in Gunner's ear, their bellies slick with mingled come.

Gunner lay quietly, still floating free of his moorings, luxuriating in Will's heat and weight and smell as he slowly, so slowly, settled back into his skin. After a few minutes he stretched as much as he could and took stock.

He felt so good; warm and relaxed and his mind finally, blissfully, still. His shoulder ached, and it was going to bruise like a motherfucker—

Gunner was going to get chirped into eternity for this in the locker room, he knew. *Worth it,* he decided, turning his head just enough to press a kiss against Will's ear.

Will moaned softly. Gunner couldn't help the rush of affection.

"Need to get cleaned up," he whispered.

Will burrowed closer.

"Of course you're clingy after sex," Gunner said, fighting laughter.

"Y'killed me," Will slurred, words muffled in Gunner's skin.

Gunner pushed at his shoulder. "Come on, you weigh a thousand pounds."

Somehow, Will managed to get heavier, and Gunner wheezed a laugh, still shoving at his arm ineffectually.

"I'll do the cleanup," he gasped, "just—*get off*."

Will lifted his head. His hair was sticking up in clumps, lips red and swollen, and he looked so, so pleased with himself. "I did," he pointed out, making Gunner groan, but he heaved himself sideways with a huge moan and collapsed on his back on the bed as Gunner rolled upright and headed for the bathroom and the face towels.

He came back armed with a warm, wet cloth, having cleaned himself up in the bathroom, and settled on the bed beside Will, who already looked halfway back to sleep.

He sighed when Gunner cleaned him up with careful, gentle sweeps, making sure he got as much as possible. Will's cock was soft and spent, nestled in the crease of his hip, and Gunner couldn't help bending to brush a quick kiss against it.

Will made a strangled noise and Gunner looked up to see him staring down at him, eyes dark and mouth half-open.

Gunner grinned wickedly but all he did was resume wiping. When he was satisfied, he threw the cloth toward the bathroom and turned back to Will, unsure for the first time.

But Will just held out an arm.

Gunner went into it gladly, tucking himself up against Will's bulk, one leg thrown over Will's thighs.

Will traced absent circles on Gunner's back with one warm finger.

"What just happened?" he finally said.

"Do you really want a diagram of our play?" Gunner asked, and laughter rumbled through Will's chest. He sounded sleepy and content, all but purring.

"What changed?" he said after a few more minutes.

Gunner pressed his face against Will's shoulder, smelling the sweet spice of leftover cologne. "Nothing's changed," he said.

Will's hand stilled but he said nothing, waiting.

Gunner couldn't figure out what to say next but he knew he needed to say *something,* rescue the situation, make things clear.

"I couldn't sleep," he said. "I—it was like I was… I couldn't hold myself together. Like I was coming right out of my skin. Everything's happening at once and we're so close to the playoffs and *you're* so close, every time I turned around you were there, and I just. I needed you. This."

"Nothing's changed," Will said, his voice flat and unreadable.

"It *can't,"* Gunner said, suddenly desperate for Will to understand. He let go and sat up, cross-legged, next to Will's hip. Will didn't move, watching him silently. In the low light, Gunner couldn't read his expression. Was he angry? Hurt? "I just needed—" He'd said that already. He closed his mouth, cursing himself.

Will propped himself up on his elbows, searching Gunner's face. Gunner met his eyes, bracing for the anger, for Will to push him away. He'd *used* him, Gunner knew, even if Will had enjoyed it just as much as Gunner did, and he was already hunching his shoulders, turning his head and bracing for the fury he knew he deserved when Will opened his mouth.

"Okay, Guns."

"I'm so—what?"

"I said okay," Will repeated. He reached out, covering Gunner's bare knee with one palm. "Whatever you need."

Gunner shook his head, not in denial but to clear it. Will's eyes were clear and open, hand warm.

He opened his mouth and Will's eyes narrowed, something like amusement in them.

"Don't," he warned.

"I wasn't doing anything!" Gunner said, instantly defensive.

"Yes you were." Will sat up. "You were going to try and pick this apart. Overanalyze everything. Talk it to death and decide you're somehow to blame for something. And then you'll feel guilty and you'll pull away and we'll both be miserable again, how am I doing so far?"

Gunner opened and closed his mouth. "That's not playing fair," he said faintly.

"I refuse to apologize for knowing you so well," Will said. "Do you feel better?"

Gunner nodded. "I'm—yeah. Like a thousand percent." He rolled his shoulder and flinched as it pulled on the bite. "You fucker, how am I supposed to explain this tomorrow?"

Will was *far* too pleased with himself. "You know what you'd really never live down? If it were to get out, of course."

Gunner squinted at him.

"The fact that you came from a *hickey*," Will said gleefully. "I hadn't even *touched—*" Gunner got his hand on a pillow and whacked him in the face with it before Will could finish. Will was laughing, pretending to struggle as Gunner hit him again for good measure and then pressed the pillow over his face, breathless with the laughter he was fighting too.

"I will kill you in your sleep," he threatened when he pulled the pillow away.

Will blinked up at him, grinning, and it made something lazy and warm curl through Gunner's belly.

"I'm—I should go home," he said abruptly.

Will just nodded, as if he'd been expecting that. "Alright to kiss you one more time?"

Gunner bent immediately, one hand on the mattress and the other on Will's bare chest, and pressed their mouths together. Will was so solid, warm and reassuring, and he opened sweetly for

Gunner's tongue, a hand coming up to tangle in Gunner's curls.

Gunner wanted nothing more than to curl back up against Will's side, fall asleep cradled by his bulk, but he'd meant what he'd said. Nothing had changed. It *couldn't.* This had been a desperation move on his part, but the fundamental truth remained the same—Gunner couldn't afford to get distracted, not with both the playoffs looming and Olivia needing him.

So he finally eased away, regretfully, and Will let him go.

"Thank you," Gunner managed.

"Well, it's not a service I offer many teammates," Will started, and Gunner hit him with the pillow again, stifling laughter.

21

THEY BLEW the Ravens out of the water, Lukas shutting out their every attempt to score with ruthless efficiency. Gunner and Will played like they were possessed, Gunner scoring on a power-play and then Will on a penalty kill as Belmont seethed in the box. That one had the crowd on its feet, roaring as Gunner hurled himself into Will's arms and the rafters shook with their jubilation. Then it was one for Volly, one for Shore, and another for Gunner, put five-hole on the Ravens' goalie just before the buzzer sounded and the crowd lost their *minds*.

They'd done it. They were in the playoffs for the Stanley Cup.

THEY WERE GIVEN a couple of days to rest and get their feet back under themselves. Gunner spent them with Olivia, knowing they wouldn't see much of each other until they were out of the playoffs or—

He shut that thought down fast. He wasn't as superstitious as some, but he knew better than to tempt fate.

Instead he went with Olivia to her mite league, pleasantly surprised to find that while the other parents were predictably starstruck by his presence, most of them got over it within the first hour. He especially took to a couple around his age. The father was named Kevin, lanky and white, and the mother was Min-Seo, short and Korean. They bickered amiably back and forth over their daughter's skating ability most of the time Gunner was there, Min-Seo occasionally appealing to Gunner to step in when she thought Kevin was being especially egregious, and neither seemed disconcerted by his fame.

Gunner was delighted by them, and stuck around after to sign autographs and pose for selfies with the kids. He was taken aback when Min-Seo hurried after him and Olivia into the parking lot, calling his name.

"Sorry," she panted as she caught up. "Not being a creepy fan, I promise. We were just wondering if you'd like to schedule a playdate for Olivia with Melanie. Might help keep her occupied while y'all are in the playoffs and all."

Gunner glanced down at Olivia, who was bouncing up and down on her toes. "Is that a yes?" he asked her, hiding the smile.

"Yes!" Olivia threw her arms in the air, dropping her gear bag.

Gunner grinned at Min-Seo, who returned it.

"Let me give you Lane's number," Gunner told her. "She'll set it all up with you."

He watched Olivia in the rearview mirror as he drove home. She seemed happy, he thought. She mentioned Stephanie occasionally, but she hadn't had a meltdown in a while. The grief counselor Fay suggested when he'd told her what happened had explained that it could happen again at any time, so Gunner just tried to keep an eye on Olivia's moods and not push when she seemed to be feeling particularly fragile or mutinous.

"Who're you playing first?" Olivia asked, interrupting Gunner's train of thought.

"Seabirds," Gunner said.

Olivia gasped. "You're playing Saint again!"

"I sure am," Gunner said, hiding his smile. "Maybe you can meet him, one of these times."

Olivia clutched her hands together. "*Yes*," she said rapturously. "And Carmine?"

"I'll see what I can do," Gunner told her. "First two games will be here. Lane will bring you to those. But then we'll go to them, so you'll have to watch on TV like everyone else."

Olivia's sigh indicated she'd made her peace with the world being a cruel and unjust place. Gunner turned his head so she wouldn't see the smile he couldn't fight.

"Do you like it here?" he asked her abruptly.

Olivia brightened. "I like the mountains. It was hard to breathe at first but it's so pretty."

"Yeah, the altitude takes some getting used to.

Gives us a bit of an advantage during home games, too. Hey, one more night off. Would you like to go out? Anywhere you want."

Olivia bounced in her seat. "Korean? And can Uncle Will come too?"

Uncle Will could indeed come, as it turned out, and met them at Gunner's favorite Korean restaurant. Gunner was struck dumb when he appeared. Will was wearing a sports jacket over a plain T-shirt, and his hair was styled in perfect, messy waves off his forehead, no gel in sight.

Olivia waved wildly when she saw him. Will threaded his way through the tables and bent to hug her. Olivia stood on the seat so she could get her arms around his neck as Gunner watched. Will whispered something in Olivia's ear and grinned at Gunner over her shoulder, then he was sitting down across from him and Gunner told himself he wasn't disappointed they weren't side by side.

"Hi," he said, dopey like he hadn't seen Will the day before. "You look nice."

Will grimaced. "Had to do a photo shoot."

"I like your hair," Gunner said before he could stop himself.

Will's eyes narrowed and then heated. "Yeah?" His voice was low.

Gunner cleared his throat as the server arrived. *No flirting,* he told himself sternly. They placed their orders, and Will leaned over to Olivia and asked her how hockey was going. Gunner watched the serious way Will asked questions and really listened to the answers, commiserating over the drills her coach made them do and occasionally glancing up at Gunner, a smile in his eyes.

Gunner was enjoying watching them interact so much that it took awhile for him to realize something else was going on with Will. But then the penny dropped and he frowned. Will was tense, fiddling with the hem of his napkin, his eyes soft on Olivia but his shoulders a rigid line. Gunner reached under the table and nudged him with a shoe.

Will glanced up and Gunner raised an eyebrow at him. *You okay?*

Will hesitated briefly, then nodded, summoning a smile. Gunner narrowed his eyes and Will's smile turned briefly genuine.

Later, he mouthed.

After dinner, Gunner got Olivia into the car and told her he'd be right back.

Will was waiting, hands in his pockets.

Gunner leaned a hip against the bumper. "What's going on?"

Will shifted his weight, not looking at him.

Alarm seized Gunner. "Is it—us?"

"No!" Will said. He sounded honestly startled and Gunner relaxed a fraction. Will ran a hand through his hair and sighed. "I'm just—" He shrugged. "Been a long week."

Gunner glanced around the parking lot. They were collecting enough curious glances that it was only a matter of time before someone asked for an autograph or selfie.

"Come over tomorrow," he said abruptly.

"The game—" Will protested.

"Before our naps," Gunner said. "It's a three minute drive to your house. You can go nap after. You obviously need to get something off your chest."

Will hesitated but finally nodded. "Okay," he said, and there was something like relief in his eyes. "See you then."

He was on Gunner's doorstep the next day at one p.m. sharp. If anything, he looked *more* jittery, eyes flickering around the room, feet unable to stay still. He greeted the dogs with genuine, if distracted, affection, and Gunner led him through into the den.

"Thirsty?" he asked as an afterthought.

Will shook his head. He sat stiffly on the couch, and Gunner flopped down on the other end.

"What's going on inside that giant head of yours?" Gunner prodded gently.

Will gave him an offended look. "It's not *that* big."

Gunner snickered. "Said that a lot, eh?"

"Oh fuck off," Will snapped, but some of the tension bled from his frame. "Where's Olivia?"

"School," Gunner said, stretching until his shirt rode up and then settling back with a pleased sigh. "Lane goes back to her place during the day.

They won't be back until after I leave for the rink." He nudged Will's thigh with a toe. "Will. Hey."

Will folded forward, sighing, and braced his elbows on his knees, staring at the carpet.

Gunner was becoming alarmed. He sat up and scooted nearer, until their thighs were pressed together. Will said nothing for a few long moments, but he leaned into Gunner's side.

"It's a lot," Gunner said carefully. "A lot of pressure on you."

Will nodded silently. "I have to keep everyone together, convince them we can do this, when I'm not sure we *can.*"

"What do you mean?" Gunner asked. "We're ready, Will. We bled to get here and we're going to do this, okay? The rookies are getting a lot of ice time, no one's out with any serious injuries right now, our lines are solid and our powerplay unit is kicking *ass.* Why do you think we can't do it?"

Will shook his head. "Maybe it's me that can't do it," he mumbled, still staring at the carpet.

"That's bullshit," Gunner said sharply. He pushed Will's shoulder with his own. "We're here because of you. We go where you lead. Where's this self-doubt coming from?"

"I'm being stupid," Will said. He lifted his head and gave Gunner a shadow of a smile. "Just… tired, I guess." There were dark circles under his eyes, almost bruises.

"When's the last time you got decent sleep?" Gunner asked.

Will shrugged again.

Gunner stood and held out a hand. When

Will hesitantly took it, he hauled him to his feet. "Come on."

Will followed him upstairs without protesting, which spoke to how tired he really was, and worry spiked in Gunner's gut. He had to get Will's head on straight before they faced the Seabirds tonight, or this would bleed over and infect the team.

In his room, he pulled his shirt off and tossed it in the hamper, then set an alarm on his phone. "Get in bed," he ordered.

Will balked briefly.

"We're not having sex," Gunner told him, rolling his eyes. "You need sleep, and you're a cuddler. So we're going to cuddle. Get your ass in the bed."

Will scowled but took off his shoes. He stripped to his boxers and climbed under the covers as Gunner hummed approval and snugged himself up tight against Will's back. Will ran so warm that they were almost immediately overheated under the blanket, and Gunner pushed it back, leaving the sheet up over their shoulders and wrapping an arm around Will's waist. He buried his nose in the hair on the nape of Will's neck, smelling piney shampoo.

The last of the tension drained from Will's body and he took a shaky breath. "How do you always know?" he whispered, voice wondering.

Gunner flattened his palm over Will's chest, feeling his heart thumping steadily beneath his hand. "Remember the first time we went to Indy?" he asked finally.

Will grunted softly.

"The win was good, but seeing them—it

brought it all back. And you… you knew, somehow. You knew what to say, what *not* to say. What to do, to keep me together. Don't think I didn't notice someone was with me at all times. I know that was you."

Will huffed a quiet laugh, circling Gunner's wrist with his fingers. "Guilty."

"Maybe we rescue each other," Gunner said, and Will squeezed his wrist silently.

Gunner held on until Will's breathing evened out into sleep. Then he closed his eyes and followed him over the edge.

GUNNER WOKE up on his side. Will had rolled to face him, tangling one leg between his. His eyes were soft, searching Gunner's with peculiar intensity, and Gunner, still half-asleep, reached out without thinking and pulled him in until their mouths met.

Will made a startled noise that morphed into a pleased hum. He opened his mouth, tasting Gunner's lips, and Gunner sighed against him, warm and comfortable. They kissed slowly, languidly, for several minutes, and Will was smiling when he eased away.

"Let's go win a hockey game," he murmured.

22

THE LOCKER ROOM was filled with chatter and bravado, and Gunner had to duck more than one flying roll of tape or balled up sock, but he couldn't help his grin as he put on his pads. He liked their chances, and he liked the mood in the room.

Parson got up to address them, reminding them of the drills they'd practiced and warning them not to take stupid penalties. When he was done and Will had had his turn, Gunner, on impulse, jumped up on his locker. Everyone swiveled to look at him, curious.

Gunner cleared his throat. "My daughter's in the crowd tonight. She's never seen her father win a playoff game. Can you guys help me out with that?"

The roars and cheers from the men made Gunner's ears ring, but he was grinning fiercely as he hopped down and grabbed his skates.

When they filed onto the ice, every single

player lifted his stick and tapped the glass in front of Olivia where she was pressed up against it, waving at them as they passed below. Gunner tilted his head back and pulled a face at her and then blew her a kiss. Somehow, Olivia's smile got even wider.

THEY BLEW the Seabirds out of the water, establishing a three point lead in the first period that they never lost. It felt like redemption for the last time they'd faced off, like a cleansing of the beating they'd taken before.

WILL SHOWED up on Gunner's doorstep the next day, the smile on his face shy and a little bit heartbreaking. Gunner grabbed his wrist and pulled him up the stairs.

They woke up the same way, almost nose-to-nose, and Gunner kissed Will, once again muzzy with sleep and thinking of nothing but tasting his mouth. Will sighed appreciatively against him and kissed back but allowed Gunner to draw away when he was done.

The second game was bloodier, the Seabirds clearly determined not to let the Direwolves pull too far ahead, but they still came away victorious. On the east coast, the Boston Otters faced off against the Riptide.

Game three was in Portland, deep in enemy territory. Gunner said goodbye to Olivia at the house, swinging her and Ferguson up into his arms and hugging her close.

Olivia clung to him, smelling like strawberries. “Play good,” she whispered in his ear. When she sat back, she was holding Ferguson between them, offering him to Gunner. “He’ll help you, ‘cuz I can’t be there.”

Gunner looked at the disheveled not-an-anteater and at his daughter again and wondered how he’d ever gone without this. He accepted custody of Ferguson with appropriate gravity, promising to take extra special care of him, and then crushed Olivia against him and peppered kisses to her face until she was giggling and squirming.

In Oregon the next day, Gunner got ready for his pregame nap wondering if Will would come to him or if he’d decide it was safer to stay in his own room.

A soft knock on the door answered that question and Gunner opened it to Will, looking sheepish but determined.

“No one saw,” he said when he was safely inside. “I just—I think it’s helping?”

“Get your ass in the bed already,” Gunner said.

This time he woke up with his head on Will’s chest, Will wrapped around him like an octopus. He lay quietly, unwilling to break the spell, and he knew when Will woke up, his breathing changing just a fraction. Gunner tipped his head back silently and let Will claim his mouth.

Gunner put Ferguson on the locker by the door in the guests' dressing room, and one by one, the men tapped him gently with their sticks as they filed out.

They swept the Seabirds. Four games, a crushing blow that rocked Portland and left the Direwolves the victors. In Arizona, the Wildfire took down the Austin Spurs in five games. They'd face the Direwolves in Denver in a week's time. On the east coast, the Riptide and the Toronto Wolverines were going head-to-head.

Gunner, Will, and the team flew home, drunk with victory and a lot of alcohol. Gunner thought this would be one of his best memories yet—Will flushed and tipsy, unsteady on his feet as he toasted the team and told them all what a great job they'd been doing, his smile softening when he looked at Gunner.

"Jesus Christ," Belmont said, "get a fucking room."

How do you think we got here? Gunner wanted to retort, but he kept his mouth shut and grinned back at Will before taking another swig of champagne.

He was wrung-out and exhausted when he got home, but Olivia was beside herself with joy when he came through the door, clearly relieved to see Ferguson was still in one piece but not even giving him a cursory inspection before hurling herself at Gunner, who caught her and laughed, kneeling in the hallway as the dogs danced around them.

The doorbell rang early the next morning. Lane and Olivia were already gone, so Gunner dragged himself out of bed and down the stairs, wondering fuzzily if it was Will.

The door swung open to reveal Clancy. He wasn't smiling.

"Hi!" Gunner said stupidly.

"Hi," Clancy said, and punched him.

23

Gunner stumbled backward, face blooming with sudden, shocking pain. He lost his balance and sat down hard as Clancy stepped through the door, rubbing his knuckles.

"What t'*fuck,"* Gunner managed, staring up at him with one hand cupping his jaw.

"We're talking," Clancy informed him, stepped around him, and stalked down the hall toward the kitchen.

Gunner's face *really* hurt, but he scrambled upright and went after him. He found Clancy rummaging in the refrigerator, muttering to himself.

"You have shit taste," Clancy said over his shoulder. He grabbed the orange juice and pulled a glass from the cupboard.

"Where's Will?"

"Will won't be joining us."

Gunner rubbed his jaw gingerly. He sat down at the table, keeping a wary eye on Clancy, who was pouring juice and scowling at the glass ferociously.

"What are you even doing here?" Gunner asked.

Clancy flicked him a glance. "Snowcaps went out in the regular season, so I'm here to support my brother and former team." He drained the glass like he wished it was alcohol and poured another. "Imagine my surprise when I show up to find Will *not* an absolute fucking wreck the way he usually is in the playoffs—even if he does hide it well—but instead he's *happy*. Fucking… *humming* while he washes dishes. So I think 'oh my god they did it, they finally got their heads out of their asses and admitted how they feel to each other'."

Gunner squirmed and Clancy pinned him with a searing look.

"I asked him what had happened. He told me everything."

"Everything?" Gunner kind of wanted the floor to open up and swallow him.

"*Everything*," Clancy hissed. "Up to and including you telling him there would be no relationship and then coming over for sex right before the playoffs and then telling him there would *still* be no relationship because apparently that was just you getting your rocks off."

Gunner put his head in his hands.

"But he's okay with that, he told me," Clancy continued. "Because he just wants *you* to be happy, and he'll do whatever he needs to do to make that happen."

Gunner wanted to *die.*

Clancy smacked the glass down hard on the

counter, making Gunner jerk. "You stupid son of a bitch," he snarled.

"Hey," Gunner protested, but it was weak and lacked conviction. "I'm just looking out for Olivia, okay?"

"Bullshit." Clancy's eyes were angrier than Gunner had ever seen them. "You're scared. And I get that, because this shit is scary. But you're being a *fucking dumbass* and you're hurting *my brother* in the process." He straightened and Gunner was forcibly reminded just how big he was. "I love you, Gunner," Clancy said. "But I love my brother more. And if you break his heart, I will *fuck. You. Up.* Are we clear?"

Gunner swallowed hard. "You make it sound like I'm toying with him," he said, his throat tight.

"Aren't you?"

"No!" Gunner shifted his weight on the hard chair. "It—look, the first time—the *only* time, I was freaking out. I didn't know where else to go, and Will—" He dragged in air. He wanted, desperately, to be *with* Will, to let his steady presence settle Gunner's jagged nerves. "He… understood. He helped."

"With sex." Clancy's voice was flat.

"I mean, it's a time-honored method?" Gunner tried.

Clancy looked even less amused, somehow.

Gunner deflated, plucking at the tablecloth that was puddled over his knees. Silence blanketed the kitchen.

"I think I was having a panic attack," he finally said to the table. "So I went… to the only place I felt safe." He couldn't look at Clancy while he was talking, but at least the tablecloth wasn't judging him. Probably. "After we—it's complicated, okay?"

Clancy snorted rudely.

"I didn't mean to, I don't know… lead him on or anything like that," Gunner said, finally managing to look up. Whatever Clancy saw in his face made his eyes soften a fraction but he said nothing, waiting for Gunner to continue. "I just —Olivia needs things to be as normal as possible. And… throwing in a possible romantic relationship would be bad enough, upsetting her routine and whatever, but then when it goes bad? What happens when he gets sick of me? What happens when he remembers how immature and wild I am?" The words caught and clogged in Gunner's throat. "When he l-leaves me, I'll have to—" He couldn't breathe. He dug his fingers into his thigh muscles, struggling for composure.

Clancy sighed, set the glass in the sink, and crossed the kitchen to drop into the chair opposite him. "God, Guns," he said quietly. "Just how little do you think of yourself?"

Gunner didn't see the point in answering that.

"I can't fix your self-esteem," Clancy said, resting his forearms on the table. "But I'm going to tell you exactly what I told Will back in October. Shit or get off the pot, bro."

Gunner huffed an almost-laugh. "So classy," he mumbled.

"You don't come to me for class," Clancy said.

"I don't come to you for anything," Gunner retorted. "You're the one who showed up on *my* doorstep and oh yeah, fucking *suckerpunched* me, thanks for that."

Clancy looked only mildly apologetic. "To be fair, you're setting my brother up to break his heart. I think that deserves at least one punch."

Gunner sagged. "Yeah." He rubbed his face, careful of the bruise forming.

"I mean it," Clancy said, leaning forward. "You either step up, tell him how you feel and that you want to be with him, or you cut him loose. Which, by the way, is literally word for word what I said to him and I am *tired* of repeating myself. You can't have it both ways. No more napping together, which—Jesus, what *is* that, anyway?"

"It…" Gunner squirmed. "I don't *know,* okay? It helped. He was freaking out about the first game, I did what felt right. It worked, it calmed him down. I just… I just wanted to help him like he's helped me."

"By cuddling him."

"Oh, fuck off," Gunner snapped. "Men like to cuddle too."

Clancy's grin lit his face. "Step up, Gunner. Tell him the truth. But if you're not willing to go all in, you need to let him go so he can find someone else. He's never going to be able to do that if he's still hung up on you. Don't you think he deserves at least that much?"

Gunner put his head down on his arms. "I hate you a lot," he said to the table.

"I know, buddy." Clancy sounded sympathetic. "I'm going back to Will's now. Don't tell him I punched you; he'll try to defend your honor and I'll have to kick his ass and it won't be fun for anyone."

Gunner sighed. "Please go away."

The house was quiet when Clancy left. Finally, Gunner sat up and called the dogs. Maybe a run would clear his head.

It was chilly under the trees, mist rising from the fields he caught glimpses of in flashes as he pushed himself until he broke a sweat.

Tell him the truth.

Step up.

Might as well ask Gunner to sprout wings and fly to the moon.

He ran faster, until all he could feel was the pounding of his feet on the dirt, the burn of his lungs. When he finally slowed, only Babe was still with him, looking bright eyed and eager for more.

"Energizer—Bunny," Gunner wheezed, doubling over and putting his hands on his knees. Babe danced around him, trying to lick his face as Gunner pushed him weakly away.

Eventually he had to go home, nothing settled in his head. He loved Will—of course he did. And he was pretty sure Will loved him back the exact same way. That hadn't been a pity fuck.

"What are you so afraid of?" he said out loud, and Babe gave him an inquisitive look.

Myself.

It came down to that, didn't it? Because no matter what he wanted, he was going to find a way to fuck it up. It was what he did, what he was best at.

What was the alternative?

He couldn't keep Will in this state of limbo

for himself. It was selfish and unfair and Clancy was right, much as it galled Gunner to admit it.

Gunner braced his hands on his knees again, breathless for an entirely different reason. “Fuck, Babe, I have to tell him.”

Babe tried to lick Gunner’s face again.

Gunner collected Ty, who’d wandered his way slowly homeward, and they went back to the house, where he showered and tried to figure out how he was going to do what he knew he had to do.

24

He didn't get a chance to even catch Will alone for several days. Every hour was scheduled—press interviews, photoshoots with extra makeup for the black eye he refused to explain to anyone, sound bites for the media in between practice and strategy sessions. Gunner was rushed off his feet, unable to find a space to breathe, let alone get Will by himself. He'd tell him before the first Wildfire game, he promised himself, but game day rolled around and Gunner was still stuck in limbo.

He got ready for his nap with his heart in his throat. Would Will come to him? Would Clancy *let* him? That made Gunner snort in spite of his nerves. As if Will would ask Clancy's permission.

The front door opened and softly closed and Gunner sat down on the bed, hiding the rush of relief by shoving his suddenly trembling hands under his thighs.

Will appeared in the doorway, looking uncertain. There were dark circles under his eyes. He shifted his weight.

"Guns?"

Gunner held out a hand and Will went to him gladly, crawling onto the mattress and pulling Gunner into his arms.

"How're you doing?" Gunner asked, praying his voice sounded normal. Will felt so good snugged up tight against him, one heavy arm draped over Gunner's waist.

"Stressed," Will murmured. "But we're gonna do this."

Gunner huffed agreement.

"Is this gonna be a problem for you?"

"What?"

"You said your ex is on the Wildfire," Will said. "I don't know—who or anything, and I know we've played them before, but we've never gone up against them in the playoffs before, so I just wanted to make sure. Are you okay?"

Will, always looking out for him. Making sure he was safe.

"Yeah," Gunner said softly. "I mean—I don't think it'll be an issue." It wasn't like Mateo had ever so much as acknowledged his existence after the breakup and the trades anyway.

He drew a breath—*now, do it now before you lose your nerve*—and Will squeezed him.

"Don't," he said quietly.

Gunner deflated. "I didn't—"

"You want to say something," Will said. "And I'm asking you not to."

Gunner wriggled around until they were face

to face. "You don't know *what* I was gonna say," he points out.

Will's eyes were soft and full of affection. "We've got a good thing going," he said. "Helped us sweep the Birds, didn't it? So let's just… *keep* it going for now. Don't rock the boat."

Gunner narrowed his eyes. "Clancy's not gonna like it."

Will's smile was wide and unabashed and Gunner fought the urge to kiss it off his face as Will laced their fingers together between them on the bed. "Clancy can kiss my ass. Go to sleep."

Gunner sighed, accepting the inevitable. "After," he said instead.

Will smiled at him and closed his eyes. He was asleep in under a minute but Gunner lay awake for a while longer, watching his face.

THEY LOST the first game by a three point margin. Gunner couldn't seem to get his hands to cooperate with his stick, losing puck after puck until he was clenching his teeth in frustration and making stupid mistakes in an attempt to get his mojo back. He could *feel* Mateo's eyes on him from the bench—he was sitting out the first game due to a mild lower body injury—but they didn't speak and Gunner didn't do more than nod at him before puck drop.

He couldn't meet Will's eyes in the locker room, after. Will was upset, of course, just like he always was after a loss, but it didn't seem directed at Gunner specifically. Still, Gunner didn't want to look at him and see disappointment on Will's face, so he cooled down and showered quickly before heading home to lick his wounds.

THEY HAD a day off to rest, and then Will showed up on game day. This time, Gunner met him at the door.

They regarded each other for a long moment before Will quirked a smile at him. "Nobody's luck is perfect every time," he offered.

Gunner sighed and let him in.

THE WILDFIRE CAME TO WIN, bolstered by their victory and determined to repeat it. Gunner got knocked into the boards in the second period and play was halted as he tried and failed to get back up, vision fuzzing around the edges. He was aware of a hand on his back and someone shouting in his ear but he couldn't *focus,* everything blurry. Finally the world stopped spinning enough that he managed to grab hold of the boards and someone's arm and drag himself to his skates.

He refused help getting off the ice, and was escorted down the tunnel to go through concussion protocol. It wasn't a concussion, he told the medical personnel, but they ignored that and kept checking him over.

Finally, they agreed that it was nothing but a bruise, and released him to dash back up. Parson was clearly relieved to see him, gesturing for him to get ready for a shift.

There was a roar when he stepped out on the ice—whatever else was going on, Gunner was a hometown favorite and no one liked seeing him knocked around.

The score was tied late in the third, and no one wanted to go to overtime. Gunner stole the puck with less than a minute on the clock and raced down the ice on a breakaway, three Wildfire hot on his heels. He dropped the puck between his skates, reaching after it with his stick and scooping it up and over the goalie's knee.

The goal horn went off and Gunner whooped as his line converged on him, Will in the lead. Then it was a matter of keeping the puck away from the increasingly desperate Wildfire until the clock ticked down.

The buzzer sounded—the games were tied 1-1 and the Direwolves were heading to Arizona.

Gunner spent the time before they left studiously avoiding Clancy, who alternated between significant looks at Will and death glares at Gunner, who pretended not to notice.

Luckily, Parson had more than enough to keep them busy before they got on the jet, and Gunner left Denver with Ferguson safely tucked away in his bag and Olivia waving goodbye to him as Lane held her hand.

He'd tell Will if they won the third game, Gunner decided. It was the perfect time—they'd be high on the win and it would make Gunner's chances of being rejected much lower.

They lost.

It wasn't even close—the Wildfire shut them out ruthlessly, denying every attempt at a goal. The Direwolves left the ice dejected, no one looking at each other. The room was subdued as they went through their usual media obligations and headed back to the hotel.

Gunner called Lane that evening and talked to Olivia, consoling her over the loss. He forced cheer he didn't feel into his voice until he could hear the smile in hers again, and then he told her goodnight and went to bed.

Next win, he told himself, staring at the ceiling. All they had to do was win and he'd tell Will he loved him and wanted to be with him for real. That settled in his mind, he rolled over and fell asleep immediately.

Will didn't come to him for their pregame nap the next day. Gunner waited, checking his phone over and over, but there was nothing. No messages, no missed calls. Finally, Gunner crawled into the bed that suddenly felt much too big and pulled the sheet up. It took him far too long to fall asleep and he was muzzy-headed and tired when his alarm went off. Maybe Will had come to his senses and he was cutting things off before Gunner had a chance to fuck it up.

But Will greeted him with a smile in the locker room, wide and uncomplicatedly happy to see him, and Gunner returned it hesitantly before turning to get changed.

Still, he was off-balance now, unsure of himself on the ice, caught up in whatever was going on between him and Will, and it was making him slower to react, easier for the Wildfire to get past. They scored within the first two minutes of puck drop and Gunner got a sick feeling in the pit of his stomach.

Parson pulled him off a shift and yelled at him for a solid three minutes as Gunner sat with his shoulders up around his ears, nodding every time Parson paused for breath. Finally, Parson was distracted by Volly pulling a stupid move and spun to ream him out.

Will scooted closer and bumped their shoulders together. "Okay, bud?"

"Yeah." Gunner watched the play, not wanting to see the concern on Will's face.

"Sorry I didn't come by earlier," Will said, keeping his voice pitched for Gunner's ears alone. "Couple of the rookies came up and we were talking about some stuff. My phone died and I forgot my fucking charger, so I couldn't text you."

Gunner nodded, gripping his stick, eyes still on the ice, but it was a little easier to breathe. "Fine by me," he said, keeping his tone light. "I sleep better without you snoring in my ear anyway."

Will snorted a laugh and shoved him gently.

GUNNER FACED off with Tanaka for the next puck drop. He liked Tanaka, respected him as a person and an up-and-coming player, and felt not an ounce of guilt for winning the drop and dodging Tanaka's attempted check on him as he rushed for the net. He was so focused on getting there that he didn't see Mateo coming until it was too late to brace.

He was on the ice, blinking stupidly up at the rafters and trying to remember how to breathe. Someone in gray and white collided with a red and orange jersey in the periphery of his vision but Gunner was still concerned with the fact that there was no air in his lungs.

Volly bent over him, face scrunched with worry. "Okay?"

Gunner flapped a hand, meaning to signify *no air,* and Volly patted his shoulder.

"That was a hard hit. What'd you do to piss him off so much?"

Gunner squeezed his eyes shut as the first blessed trickle of oxygen reached his lungs and he was finally able to draw a breath.

Volly helped him up and Gunner skated slowly for the bench.

"I'm fine," he told Parson and the medic who was hovering behind him. "Got the wind knocked out of me. Everything's fine."

Will had taken a penalty for fighting and Mateo one for the check on Gunner. Almost off the penalty kill for Will, Tanaka delivered a neat wrister past Lukas's blocker and they were up by two.

This was the universe's way of telling him to keep his mouth shut, Gunner decided as he waited for his next shift.

But then Schulz delivered a beauty of a goal on the Wildfire goalie, sniping it five-hole, and less than a minute later, Volly scooped up a rebound and sank it on him.

Just like that, the tide of the game turned. Invigorated, Gunner managed to get the puck from Tanaka and sent it to Will, who slammed it home under the goalie's desperately reaching glove.

They hung onto the lead by their fingernails, keeping the puck away from every attempt by the Wildfire to regain it. Then the buzzer sounded and Will slammed into Gunner, shouting in his ear as the rest of the team tumbled out to surround them.

Gunner held onto Will's waist, laughing and dizzy in the crush of bodies.

"I want to tell you something," he shouted and Will pulled back enough to meet his eyes.

"Hotel?" he asked, and Gunner nodded, grinning at him, victory setting his veins on fire.

He couldn't wait to get through the media scrum and cooldown, but he kept his patience, aware of Will a few feet away in his own knot of reporters. Gunner answered the usual questions with his standard non-answers, careful to keep personal feelings out of his voice.

Then he was finally free to shower and change, which he did with a sense of dread and hope mixing under his ribs, making it hard to breathe. He was going to ask Will to be *with* him. He was going to go for it. Gunner had to brace his hands on the cold tile and take deep gulps of air for a minute. He didn't think he'd ever been this terrified in his life.

When he got out of the locker room, Will was waiting for him in the hall, back to him as he talked to someone. Gunner couldn't help the goofy grin as he joined him.

It slid off his face in a hurry when he realized Will was talking to Mateo.

"Hey!" Will greeted him. "Look who dropped by to say hi."

Gunner forced himself to look Mateo in the face. He looked good, perfect cheekbones and dark eyes, one slightly marred by the shiner rapidly developing, and as big and muscular as ever, but there was a tightness around his mouth.

"Hi," Gunner said.

"I was hoping to have a minute alone with Gunner," Mateo said to Will, who nodded easily.

"See you at the hotel, Guns." His fingers brushed Gunner's wrist, feathersoft and barely there, and then he strode away down the hall, and Gunner was alone with Mateo, who wasn't looking at him.

He cleared his throat. "Um—"

Mateo shook his head. "Don't," he said. He looked up and Gunner flinched from the anger in his eyes. "My therapist said I have to forgive you."

That was so far from what Gunner expected him to say that he was left gaping.

Mateo turned away, digging the heels of his hands into his eyes. "*Fuck*," he spat. "I shouldn't have done this."

Gunner found his voice. "Just… say it," he managed. "Get it out. I deserve it."

"You *deserve*—" Mateo cut himself off. "I hated you, for a long time. I think I still do, a bit."

Gunner willed himself not to react, waiting.

When Mateo looked up, his eyes were wet. "I thought I loved you," he said, and his voice was small, broken and confused. "I—and you—"

Gunner held himself very still. There was a distant roaring in his ears.

"You *laughed* when I told you," Mateo whispered. He shook his head again as if trying to clear it. “Like I was some stupid kid with a crush. Like you couldn’t *fathom* returning my feelings. Do you even remember?”

Gunner remembered, all too clearly. Mateo with that naked hope in his soft brown eyes. It had shaken Gunner to his core, scared him down to his toes at the thought of someone seeing him clearly and wanting to be with him anyway.

He cleared his throat, groping for words, but Mateo beat him there.

“Did you even know him, that guy in the bar?”

Hot shame rushed over Gunner. He shook his head wordlessly. Mateo’s mouth tightened as if he wasn’t surprised.

“Just couldn’t wait to rub in my face how extremely not-special I was,” he said quietly. “I hope he was everything you were looking for.”

Be angry with me, Gunner wanted to plead. *Scream at me. Punish me for what I did to you.* He deserved to bleed for his sins, but Mateo was turning away.

“Wait,” Gunner croaked.

Mateo paused but didn’t look at him.

“I’m sorry,” Gunner whispered.

Mateo hunched his shoulders.

“It wasn’t you,” Gunner said, willing Mateo to believe him. “It was—I fucked up. I was—it was never you. I know you don’t believe me, I don’t blame you. I wouldn’t either. But—” Mateo still wasn’t looking at him. “You deserved—*deserve*—someone good enough for you, and I knew that wasn’t me but I didn’t know how to tell you.”

Gunner thought he'd maybe never hated himself as much as he did in that moment.

"So you decided to show me." Mateo's voice was flat.

Gunner said nothing. Silence fell, cold and awful.

Finally, Mateo nodded. "Alright." He took a step away.

"That's it?" Gunner didn't even know what he was asking for.

Mateo lifted a shoulder. "What else is there?"

"You could—" Gunner floundered. "You could hit me. I deserve it."

Mateo regarded him steadily. "Would that make you feel better?"

Yes. Gunner shrugged wordlessly.

"I'm not going to hit you," Mateo said. "I didn't even mean to check you that hard during the game." His mouth worked silently for a minute. "I don't hate you," he finally said. "I feel sorry for you." And he turned and walked away, leaving Gunner alone in the cold concrete hall.

Gunner didn't go back to the Direwolves' hotel. He walked aimlessly through Scottsdale until his feet ached and his face was numb from the cold, then he called a cab and asked for the hotel nearest the airport. The driver wanted to talk, but Gunner couldn't summon the spirit for friendly conversation. He stared out the window and answered in monosyllables until she took the hint and shut up.

Gunner made sure to tip her well when she dropped him off, and then he dragged himself into the hotel and booked a room for the night.

He had about a dozen texts and several missed calls on his phone from Will when he was able to look at it. Gunner didn't read the texts or listen to the voicemails. He typed out a short message instead: *Something came up, see you on plane* and turned off the phone.

He spent the night sitting in the dark on top of the covers, arms around his knees, staring into the shadows.

25

Seven years ago

"THAT'S IT?" Mateo sat up and Gunner rolled over to put room between them and sat up too. "I tell you I love you, and—"

Panic clawed at Gunner's throat. *You can't love me,* he wanted to say. *I'm not worth loving. You're going to realize that soon enough.* But he couldn't get the words out, staring dumbly at Mateo, who had the back of one hand pressed to his mouth.

"Look—" Gunner stopped to clear his throat. "This was just some fun. Okay? I never meant to —you weren't supposed to fall in *love.* I'm—we've got too much to do. Hockey's more important—"

"More important?" Mateo interrupted. "More important than *love?* How can you even say that?"

Gunner shook his head and slid backward off the bed. "I'm—I can't—"

"Don't you dare leave this room," Mateo shouted, but Gunner was already gone, letting the door close behind him and almost running down the hall.

He couldn't even remember what city they were in. The games blurred together on away trips, although the alcohol probably helped with that. Somewhere in the midwest, he thought vaguely, and got in the elevator, listening for Mateo's footsteps. But there was silence except for the humming of the ice machine as the elevator doors whisked closed and he descended to the ground floor.

The bar was still open, and he headed that way blindly, thinking very hard about nothing at all.

Despite that, he could still hear Dean's voice in his head. "You're a fucking anchor around our necks, aren't you? When are you going to get it through your thick skull; you're nothing without us. You need us. We don't need you."

"What can I get you?" the bartender asked, and Gunner jerked.

"I—uh. Whisky, neat."

"Preference on brand?"

"The kind that gets you drunk," Gunner snapped, and the bartender rolled her eyes and reached for a bottle as Gunner slid onto a stool.

"Can't believe you went second," Dean said. "You." He made a disbelieving noise. "But I guess you just hadn't fucked up enough by then for them to realize."

Gunner knocked the first shot back and gestured for another one.

Dean was right. That was the real kick in the nuts. He was deadweight. All he did was drink and party and sleep around. Just because he hadn't slept with anyone but Mateo since they got together didn't change that he was taking up space on a team that didn't like him and had every reason not to.

His point production wasn't good enough to make up for his personality, after all. He was too loud, too reckless, too… much.

He downed another shot. The only chance Mateo had was to get as far away from him as possible.

"You look like a man on a mission," someone said.

Gunner glanced up. The man standing beside him was wearing a suit with the tie pulled loose around his neck. He had spiky blond hair and friendly blue eyes that were assessing Gunner with keen interest.

Gunner saluted him with his glass, frowning when he realized it was empty. "Have a seat and join me."

"I'm Rod," the man said. He sat on the stool beside him. "What are we drinking?"

"Whisky, I'm pretty sure," Gunner said.

"What's your name?" Rod asked.

Gunner squinted at him. "What's your opinion of professional sports, Rod?"

"Hate 'em," Rod said promptly. "Whole lotta brainless jocks running around in tight clothes, posturing for their fans and their own fragile masculinities."

Gunner laughed without humor. "That sounds about right. You can call me Josh." His father's name. He'd left when Gunner was eight—he wouldn't care if Gunner used his name for a night.

Rod's smile widened. "Josh. Nice to meet you."

They talked for an hour, until the alcohol had burned off the worst of the panic buzzing in Gunner's head. He could still feel it, battering moth-soft wings against his skull, but it was dimmed, muted by Rod's easy smile, the way he seemed to be interested in Gunner's opinions. He was a businessman, in town selling something to someone, and he was sharply funny, acerbic in his observations of things he didn't like, wielding his malicious wit like a scalpel.

Gunner didn't particularly like *him*, but he was the perfect antidote to hearing Dean's voice in his head.

Finally, Rod had drained his glass and set it back on the bar. He pinned Gunner with a look. "What do you say we have a nightcap in my room?"

Even though he'd known it was coming, Gunner hedged, floundering for something to say. "It's pretty late," he said after a minute.

"Come on," Rod wheedled, sliding off his stool and stepping between Gunner's knees. "Why do you think I'm here?" He put a hand on Gunner's thigh, sliding it upward. "If you come upstairs with me, I'll give you the best fuck of your life." He was leaning forward, eyes hot, and Gunner was opening his mouth to tell him no when Rod kissed him.

Fuck. The whisky had slowed Gunner's reflexes so much that it took him a long second to find the coordination to break away. He looked up as he did and turned to stone at the sight of Mateo standing in the door of the bar, arms wrapped around his ribs. Unshed tears stood bright in his eyes.

Rod leaned in again and Gunner shoved him back so hard he stumbled, but it was too late—Mateo had already bolted.

"What the fuck?" Rod complained. "You fucking cocktease, you made me spend an *hour* on you just for you to turn me down?"

Gunner shot to his feet, head spinning. "Get the fuck away from me," he said, and went after Mateo.

But he couldn't find him. The room was empty, he didn't answer his phone, and he didn't come back for the rest of the night, as Gunner paced and fought the tears and Dean's voice echoed in his head, sharp with fury.

Mateo asked for a trade the next morning.

26

Present day

Gunner was the first to the airplane and managed to sweet-talk the crew into letting him board early by tipping them handsomely and promising to stay out of their way. He tucked himself into a seat at the back and kept his word, staying quiet as the crew bustled around getting everything ready.

Will was the next to board and he made a beeline for Gunner, dropping his bag in the aisle to lean over the seat and inspect Gunner from head to toe.

"What happened?" he demanded, and Gunner twitched away from his intent gaze.

"Put your bag away before someone trips over it," he said.

Will looked blank, like he'd forgotten he even had luggage, then turned and shoved it in the overhead compartment with no regard for the contents. Then he sat down beside Gunner.

"What the fuck happened?" he said. "Are you okay?"

"I'm fine." Gunner resisted the urge to draw his knees to his chest and instead pushed his hands under his thighs. "Nothing… happened. I just—"

"Did you go out with Mateo?"

Gunner shook his head unthinkingly, then cursed himself. He should have lied, said he'd gone out. Maybe then Will would stop *digging*.

He was saved by the rest of the team filing into the plane, cheerfully chirping each other.

"Guns!" Belmont said. "Where the hell were you this morning? Will said you left for the airport early."

Gunner glanced at Will, who shrugged.

"I packed your bag for you," he said in a low voice.

Gunner didn't deserve him.

Thankfully, Belmont didn't seem overly invested in Gunner's answer, settling in the row opposite and insulting Schulz as he got comfortable.

"You wanted to tell me something," Will said.

Gunner flinched and tried to cover it. From the way Will's eyes were narrowed, he didn't miss it.

"I, uh—" Gunner fumbled. "It was nothing important."

Will said nothing, watching Gunner's face.

He wasn't going to get out of it that easily, Gunner knew. "After the finals," he said.

Will's brow drew down.

Gunner forced himself to be still. "There's too much riding on this," he said quietly, for Will's ears alone. "I'm not saying no, just—wait. The team needs us."

Will didn't like it, it was clear, but he finally nodded sharply, just once.

They didn't speak the rest of the way home.

GUNNER WAS GREETED by Olivia and the dogs, all of them ecstatic to see him, and Olivia demanded they go over game tape and discuss his plays. Gunner, willing to do just about anything to get the dual images of Mateo's betrayed face and Will's worried one out of his head, agreed, and they curled up on the couch together as Lane ran errands.

Olivia nestled trustingly against Gunner's side, watching the plays intently. She had a sharp eye for where the puck was going, Gunner thought. He resolved to take her to the arena and play some one-on-one games with her after the finals, to hone her puck handling skills.

She flinched when Gunner went down, pressing into his side a little bit harder.

"I wasn't hurt," Gunner told her.

Olivia tipped her head back to look up at him. "You stayed down a long time."

"Got the wind knocked out of me," Gunner said ruefully. "Ever had that happen?"

Olivia shook her head.

"You feel like you can't breathe. You can't get air in your lungs. It can take a minute or two before you really start to function again. But it was a clean hit, and I'm fine, I promise."

Olivia sighed. "I don't like it when you get hurt."

"Part of the game," Gunner said. "Besides, I'm still young and healthy, no major injuries—I really am okay. Look—" He tapped the screen. "Watch this footwork by Uncle Will. Isn't that something?"

Just like that, the hit was forgotten and Olivia was absorbed in the action again.

"How many more games?" she asked after a few minutes.

"Three, unless we can win the next two," Gunner said. "We're tied right now—if either team wins two games, they'll advance."

"You can do it," Olivia announced, and Gunner smiled, rubbing his cheek against her soft curls. "Ferguson helped, didn't he?"

"Yeah," Gunner said. "But not as much as you."

Olivia's smile was heartstopping, and Gunner smiled back at her.

As glad as he was to be home, Gunner couldn't help the nausea that swamped him at every turn. He knew what he had to do, and he couldn't bear the thought of it. He was restless, twitchy, and couldn't stop pacing, trying to shake the unsettled feeling under his skin, but nothing helped. He had to cut Will loose, and it was going to break him.

Doesn't matter, he told himself. Olivia had

gone to bed and the house was quiet. *This is for Will.*

He wanted to cry. He wanted to punch something. He wanted to run and never stop. He stood stockstill in his kitchen and called Clancy.

CLANCY WALKED INTO THE HOUSE, took one look at him, and swore under his breath as he reached out to pull him into a rough hug. "Jesus fuck, Guns," he said in his ear.

Gunner clutched at him, blinking back tears. "I'm s-sorry," he managed.

Clancy tightened his grip. "So am I. Come on, let's get hammered. What do you have here?" He released Gunner and headed for the alcohol cupboard, where he started pulling out bottles.

Gunner sat on the couch, curling his legs beneath him as Clancy poured shots and handed him one. "You're not going to talk me out of it?"

"Can I?"

Gunner shook his head wordlessly and downed the shot, handing the glass back as the whiskey burned a path to his stomach.

"Then I'm not gonna try." Clancy pinned him with a look. "You're making the wrong decision and I think you know it, but you're still my friend and I love you. And at least you're doing *something.*"

"I don't deserve you," Gunner said, accepting another shot.

Clancy snorted. "Less talking, more drinking."

Gunner woke up with only a minor hangover on game day and a sense of peace, or maybe simple fatality, clinging to his shoulders. He was going to give Will a chance at finding someone good enough for him, who could make him truly happy the way he deserved. That was all that mattered.

He went to practice that morning and was somehow able to joke with the team as they warmed up, waiting for Parson. Gunner worked on the drills he'd promised to show Foster until they were both sweaty and panting, then made his way around the team, checking in on everyone with a touch or a look, gauging moods and states of mind. They seemed upbeat and determined, focused on what they had to do to win the next two games.

Will was doing the same thing, eyes crinkling with the smile he reserved for Gunner when they crossed paths, but they didn't speak much.

Gunner found a moment just before practice to pull him aside, though. "No nap today," he said under his breath.

Will's face fell.

"I'm sorry," Gunner said, hating himself. "It's just—I need to—" He cursed himself when he couldn't find the words, but Will just nodded.

"See you there, Guns." There was nothing but affection in his smile, and Gunner hated himself just a little more.

27

They were playing to a sold-out crowd of gray and red jerseys. The roar when they took the ice shook the rafters, and Gunner let the familiar feel of it soak through him, grounding him and sharpening his focus as he warmed up and batted pucks at Lukas. He didn't look at the white and orange-red jerseys on the other side of the arena, intent on finding his groove.

They lined up for the opening and Will bumped his shoulder briefly. Gunner slanted a glance at him but Will wasn't looking at him, watching the singer belting out the anthem as if he hadn't heard it several hundred times and more. Something settled into place in Gunner's chest. This was what he was here for. They were going to win, and advance to the Cup playoffs. He could *feel* it. He jostled Will back without looking at him, but he caught the flicker of Will's smile out of the corner of his eye.

The Wildfire weren't going to make it easy for

them, though. The captain had his team fired up and they were out for blood, taking no prisoners. Schulz took a nasty shot to the head and was escorted down the tunnel for concussion protocol. Shore twisted his knee in the first period, and the Wildfire were up by two when the buzzer sounded.

Everything else fell away when they took the ice for the second period—doubts, fears, worries were swept aside until all Gunner saw was the puck, the net, the path it would take. He aimed, a defenseman hot on his heels, fired, and watched as it sailed cleanly between the goalie's knees and hit the back of the net.

He didn't see who crashed into him from behind. Gunner hit the boards in a confused tangle of arms and legs. Even over the roar of the crowd he could hear the sickening *snap* of his left leg and he couldn't help the scream that wrenched from him.

The other player dragged himself free and got clear as Gunner curled in a ball, gasping for air. All he could feel was the pain in his leg, nauseatingly sharp and radiating outward in vicious corkscrews, twisting his stomach and crowding out all thought. He had to get up. Had to get off the ice by himself. He rolled to his side, sobbing a breath, and then Will was there, hand on Gunner's shoulder, mouth to his ear.

"What is it?" he asked tautly, fingers tight on Gunner's jersey.

"Leg," Gunner managed. "Feels—broken."

"Shit. Don't move," Will ordered him.

"I don't want to be carried," Gunner said—

begged, groping for Will's hand, and Will swore thickly above him and grabbed him.

"Alright," he said. "I've got you. No, I've got him!" This to the medics who were approaching with a stretcher. "Guns, arm over my shoulder. Left leg?"

Gunner nodded, gritting his teeth against another wave of nausea.

"Left arm over my shoulder, then," Will said, and bent so Gunner could obey. "I'm going to stand up, you just hold on."

He got to his feet in a slow, controlled rise, lifting Gunner like he weighed nothing. Gunner choked back another noise as his left foot hit the ice and he couldn't help curling against Will's shoulder, blindly seeking comfort.

Will wrapped an arm around his waist. "Breathe," he murmured. "Taking you to the bench now, hang onto me."

Gunner closed his eyes. The crowd had fallen silent but they began to cheer again, waves of sound overlapping and buffeting Gunner's ears as Will guided him to the bench and the waiting stretcher.

He grabbed wildly for Will when the medics had him strapped down though. "Will—"

Will took his hand again, bending so Gunner could speak without shouting.

He wanted to tell him he loved him. That he was sorry for fucking up so much. That he didn't deserve him but still *wanted* him. The words clogged in his throat, choking him. There was so much to say and not enough time.

"Kick their asses," he finally managed.

Will squeezed his hand and let go, watching the stretcher until Gunner was wheeled out of sight down the hall.

THE PARAMEDICS GAVE him a shot of something that numbed the worst of the pain and left Gunner in better control of his faculties by the time they reached the hospital. He flatly refused to be put under when the X-ray came back and the doctor said he needed surgery, though.

"Give me a local," he told him. The doctor looked baffled. "And turn on the TV, I need to know what's happening."

The doctor opened his mouth to argue and a nurse grabbed his sleeve, leading him a few feet away. Whatever she said worked—the doctor scowled thunderously but ordered a small television set to be wheeled in and put in place by Gunner's head as they prepped him for surgery.

Gunner didn't even look at what they were doing, eyes glued to the set. It felt like he'd already been gone for an eternity, but the third period was only half done when the nurse found the right channel.

They were still down by one, but Gunner could see that wasn't going to last. The Direwolves were galvanized, stealing the puck and keeping it away in a perfect flow of give and take down the ice. The Wildfire were scrambling to catch up but it was useless. Volly took a perfect snipe between the goalie's knees and the goal light went on.

Gunner couldn't breathe, watching spellbound

as Will grabbed it next. He was pushed out of the offensive zone by the Wildfire, so he dropped back to the neutral zone, buying time.

Will had always been good on the ice. It was where he communicated best, where he was most comfortable. But his playing now was like nothing Gunner has seen before. He was fast and deadly, unhesitatingly slamming an unlucky forward into the boards without losing the puck, then spinning and dropping it to Foster, who rushed the net. Will was already in position when Foster got there, covered in defensemen, and there was no way Will could even *see* the puck when Foster slammed it across to him, but somehow, somehow he caught it on his tape and tipped it in.

"*Yes!*" Gunner shouted, punching the air, and the doctor swore.

"Put him under," he ordered. "I can't work like this."

"What—no, I need—"

But it was too late—the nurse gave him an apologetic look as she slipped a needle into Gunner's IV, and Gunner was pulled under before he could finish.

THE ROOM WAS quiet when he woke up. He could hear muted beeping and soft conversation outside, and he rolled his head on the pillow, struggling to bring his brain online. His leg didn't hurt—he couldn't feel it at all, in fact. Had they amputated? Suddenly terrified, Gunner struggled to one elbow, blinking gritty eyes that refused to focus. He was immeasurably relieved to see both his feet beneath the blanket, blurry but definitely there.

He collapsed back on the pillows, out of breath, and passed out before he could call the nurse.

THE NEXT TIME he came to, he was already thinking more clearly, his brain no longer the foggy mess it was before. He opened his eyes. The room was dim, but he could see a shape on the couch at the end of the bed.

"Did we win," he rasped.

"Yeah," Will said quietly. He stood and stepped into the light, putting his phone away. Gunner drank in the sight of him greedily as Will smiled. He looked exhausted, pale and washed out. "How are you feeling?"

"Olivia," Gunner blurted, suddenly horrified. "Oh God, where is she? Is she okay?"

"She's fine," Will said soothingly. He drew up the chair beside Gunner and dropped into it. "I just texted Lane. They're on their way." He found the call button on the bed and pressed it before Gunner could protest.

The nurse came in, checked Gunner's vitals, and declared him doing well.

Gunner barely noticed her, eyes on Will, who was leaning back in the chair. He looked on the verge of sleep, exhaustion in every line of his body.

"You shouldn't be here," Gunner's mouth said with no input from his brain as the nurse left.

Will flinched and hurt crossed his face.

"No," Gunner said, cursing himself. "I mean you should be resting, Will, you have to go back to Denver and—fuck, I won't be with you. *Fuck.*"

Will's expression eased but the door opened before he could answer and Olivia burst through.

"*Daddy,*" she sobbed, and hurled herself at the bed.

Gunner reached for her, forgetting everything else to gather her into his arms as she twined both arms around his neck and wept against his shoulder.

"I'm okay," Gunner said, tears spilling from his own eyes. "I'm here, Livvy, I'm okay, I promise—"

Olivia's small body shook with her hiccuping sobs, and Gunner held her as Lane stepped up to the bed, face drawn with concern.

"I told her you'd be okay," she said, rubbing Olivia's back gently. "But she needed to see for herself."

"I'm sorry," Gunner told Olivia, brushing her hair off her forehead. "That must have been so scary for you."

Olivia nodded into his throat, but the worst of the tears had eased. She refused to let go, though, and Gunner shook his head at Lane when she suggested it.

Will cleared his throat. "I should… go."

Gunner eased Olivia to the side, tucking her close, and looked up at him. "Will—"

"I'll tell the guys you're okay. They'll want to come see you before we leave."

Gunner nodded, wordless, and watched him as he leaned over the bed and pressed a gentle kiss to

Olivia's forehead. Olivia smiled at him and Will returned it. When he straightened, his hand trailed down Gunner's arm but he stepped away before Gunner could react.

"See you tomorrow," he said, and left.

28

It took a while before Olivia was willing to let Gunner out of her sight. At first she demanded to sleep in the room with him, and Gunner had to call in backup in the form of the nurse, who was clearly sympathetic but still firm as she explained Olivia couldn't stay once visiting hours were over.

Gunner squeezed her when she drooped. "The dogs will be worried," he pointed out. "Do you think you can take care of them for me until I get home?"

Olivia sighed but nodded, accepting the inevitable. Before they went, she flung her arms around Gunner's neck and kissed his cheek messily.

Gunner managed to hide the wince at the jostling of his leg and held her tight.

"I love you," Olivia whispered in his ear, and Gunner had to squeeze his eyes shut briefly.

"I love you too," he told her, matching her tone, and her smile lit up the room.

THE NEXT MORNING, the doctor told him his tests had all come back and other than his leg, he was in excellent health. "I see no reason for you to not be able to rejoin your team next season, as long as you take the time to heal and rehab it properly over this summer," he said.

The team descended on him immediately after, coming in pairs that started with Will and Arseni. Every single one of them had a giant stuffed teddy bear or balloons or massive bouquet of flowers, and soon Gunner's room was overflowing with get well messages as all his teammates told him how the game ended, how Will scored the final two goals that put them ahead, the fight Belmont got in, how Lukas made an incredible save.

The nurses were looking a little frazzled by the time the last of the players left, but Gunner was happy, relaxing against his pillows with a sigh.

There was a knock on the door and Gunner looked up to see Clancy smiling at him.

"Hey, Clance," Gunner said, lifting his bed again.

"Hey, dumbass," Clancy returned. He was holding yet another stuffed animal, a panda this time, and Gunner couldn't help his laugh.

"I'm giving every single one of those to Olivia," he warned.

"Oh, you think I bought it for you?" Clancy retorted. "That's adorable. Your daughter's way cuter than you." He set the panda down and flopped into the chair. "How are you feeling?"

"Like I fell off a roof," Gunner said. He shifted in the bed and winced.

"What's the doctor saying?"

"Clean break. Should heal with no problems. But I'm out for at least six weeks."

Clancy grimaced. "Sucks, man. I'm sorry."

Gunner lifted a shoulder. "It is what it is, right? I can't change it."

"They wouldn't be here if it weren't for you," Clancy said. "Whatever else has been going on with you, you've been playing great."

"Well, they're gonna have to finish without me," Gunner said. He couldn't help the bitterness in his voice but if anyone could understand, it was Clancy. He glanced up. "Will played well last night, didn't he?"

"God, yeah," Clancy said. "Don't tell him I said so, of course, but he was incredible."

Gunner almost smiled. "He's always incredible."

"And you're biased." Clancy snickered. "You make him better, you know."

"What?"

Clancy leveled a look at him. "You think you're the only one who gets anything out of your friendship? He was a decent player before you came along, but he was so painfully, horribly introverted and awkward that he couldn't get out of his own way. You pulled him out of his shell, Guns. You made him a better player, a better *person,* to be honest."

Gunner's face was burning. He stared at his lap, unsure what to say.

"I'm just saying, it goes both ways." Clancy's

voice was gentle. "I know you think you don't deserve him or some shit like that, but I don't think you've ever really *seen* the difference you've made in his life." He reached in his bag and pulled out a tablet. "I want you to do something for me." He put the tablet and a charger on the bed next to Gunner's leg. "Watch some more game tape for me. Of Will before and after you got here. Okay?"

"I don't understand," Gunner said.

"I think you will," Clancy said cryptically. "I gotta get going. Will's gonna need you in the box for the Cup playoffs, so you focus on getting better." He winked and left before Gunner could say anything else.

GUNNER SPENT the rest of the day watching game tape. He found a selection of Will's old games cued up and waiting for him, and he worked his way through each one, watching everything Will did with an eagle eye.

It was true, he realized after a few hours. Will's play was good before Gunner came to Denver, but not inspired. He hadn't really made any waves—he'd played a solid but not exciting game.

Gunner went through the files until he found a recent game, one of the playoffs against the Wildfire. The difference was electrifying. Will was faster, more confident, a playmaker instead of just doing what he was told. He had a sixth sense for his teammates and where the puck would be, able to put himself in position three and four moves ahead of it.

I helped him. The concept was staggering, so revolutionary that Gunner had to close his eyes and breathe for a minute. *I make him… better.* He opened his eyes and hit play on the game again. He watched Mateo's hit on him and Will barreling across the ice to collide with him. He threw punches with single-minded intensity, clearly furious but channeling the rage into sharp, hard jabs that had Mateo's head rocking back with the force of them.

He really does love me, Gunner thought, and pressed his hands to his mouth helplessly. *He loves me and I'm…* good *for him.*

He fumbled for his phone, swearing as his suddenly clumsy hand knocked it off the table. He strained to reach it but it was on the floor out of his grasp, and he finally gave up and called a nurse, who handed it back to him with an indulgent smile.

Will answered on the first ring. "Guns?" There was a lot of background noise and Gunner had to strain to hear him.

"Hey—are you on the plane?"

It got quieter suddenly. "Yeah," Will said. He sounded worried. "I went in the bathroom. Are you okay?"

"Yeah," Gunner said. He clutched the bedspread. "I just—" His courage deserted him, his throat suddenly dry as dust. "Good luck," he finally said weakly.

"It's not the same without you," Will murmured.

The nurse chose then to walk in the room, and Gunner jolted.

"Fuck, I gotta go. Um—"

"I'll call you when I land, if you want," Will said.

"Okay," Gunner said, unwilling to hang up.

Will laughed quietly. "Bye, Guns."

An itch was forming under Gunner's skin as the day crawled on. He was restless, wanting to move, like his entire being was being pulled toward something, but he didn't know *what.*

It wasn't right, that Will and his team—*their* team—were in Arizona and Gunner wasn't.

"Oh, *fuck it,"* he said out loud, and grabbed his phone again. He dialed quickly. "Lane? I need you to do a few things for me."

29

"Are you sure this is a good idea?" Lane said when she showed up the next morning with a wheelchair and a pair of crutches. Olivia was by her side, fizzing with excitement.

"Nothing I do is ever a good idea," Gunner said through his teeth as he zipped up his pants. He had to use scissors to cut the left leg open so his cast would fit, and he shoved his right shoe on with shaky hands, dizzy with medication and pain.

"Yeah, but—"

"You don't have to come with us," Gunner said. "We won't be gone that long."

"Oh, don't be stupid," Lane retorted. "You think I'd miss this?"

Olivia was bouncing on her toes. "Are we really going to Arizona?"

Gunner grinned at her. "We sure are. Got your bag packed?"

"Yeah! Ferguson's comin' too!"

"Good," Gunner said, and eased himself into the wheelchair.

THE NURSES WERE, predictably, very displeased when Gunner checked himself out. He stopped to sign as many autographs as he could, thanking them for taking such good care of him and promising not to overdo it and make things worse.

He was trembling by the time they made it downstairs and into the car. Olivia helped him buckle and patted his good leg gingerly.

"Plane leaves in an hour," Lane said, checking her watch. "We'll have to hurry. But I got first class tickets, like you asked. There should be room for your leg."

Gunner smiled at her faintly. "You're getting a serious bonus," he said, and closed his eyes to her laugh.

THE FLIGHT TOOK FOREVER and no time at all. Lane did a good job of distracting Olivia, and Gunner was free to think about what he was going to do when they landed. He was *terrified,* his mouth dry and palms sweaty, but he was seeing this through, one way or the other.

Lane had ordered a car with significant leg room that was waiting for them at the Denver airport, and she shrugged when Gunner gave her an appreciative look.

"Amazing what gets done with money. Thanks for the credit card, by the way."

Olivia was bouncing on the seat as Gunner eased himself inside, jaw clenched.

"Let's go, let's *go*," she urged, and Gunner couldn't help his smile, even through the pain.

The drive didn't take long, and Lane took the wheelchair at the rink, stopping to ask for directions and then pushing Gunner through the halls as Olivia danced alongside.

Luckily, the Direwolves staff recognized Gunner and let them through, with a few puzzled looks but no questions asked.

Lane stopped outside the guests' locker room. "Okay, Liv, this is as far as we go."

Gunner took the crutches from her and levered himself upright. His chest was tight and he couldn't get his breath.

"You've got this," Lane said quietly.

"Serious bonus," Gunner told her, and opened the locker room door.

It took a minute for the team to realize he was there. Belmont saw him first, his mouth dropping open, and Gunner put a finger over his lips. Lukas was next, eyes going wide and a smile creeping across his face. The room went silent in a wave as more and more people saw him standing there.

Will was on the far side, head down as he strapped his pads in place, and he looked up, frowning, at the sudden silence. He froze in place when he saw Gunner balancing on the crutches just inside the door.

"Gunny?"

Gunner swallowed the butterflies, the terror, pushing it all down and away to focus on Will's beautiful face. His voice shook only a little when he said, "I need to tell you something."

Will crossed the room to him, worry carving lines around his eyes. "What are you doing here?" he said urgently. "You should be in the hospital. Why—here, sit down."

Gunner batted at him as Will tried to help him sit on the nearest locker. "Will, stop. *Listen* to me."

Will stopped, drawing back enough to look him in the eyes.

"I love you," Gunner said, and it was too loud, a little defiant and unsteady.

Will stared at him. The locker room was dead silent.

Gunner tipped his chin up. "You make me better," he said. "You make me want to *be* better. A-and I make *you* better. I know that now. I do. So." He was going to die of oxygen deprivation, he thought faintly. "Um. That's all."

Will was rooted in place, and terrible doubt seized Gunner. He was wrong, he'd gambled and lost, Will didn't love him after all—

He opened his mouth, no idea what he was going to say, and Will took a quick step forward into his space, cupping his jaw in both hands and covering Gunner's lips with his own.

Gunner nearly sobbed with relief, sagging

against him as the locker room erupted behind them with roars and cheers and wolf whistles.

"I'm so sorry," Gunner tried to say against Will's mouth, but Will wouldn't pull back enough to let him talk. "I love—mmf—I'm sorry, I—"

"Shut *up*," Will said, and kissed him again.

The team crowded around them, slapping them both on the back, knocking Gunner off-balance and making him flinch with pain until Will growled at the press of hands and made them back off.

"Fuckin' *finally*, Guns!" someone shouted, and Gunner hiccuped a laugh and hid his face in Will's throat.

There were tears on his cheeks when he lifted his head, but Will was smiling down at him, warm and steady and solid, and his team was surrounding him, and he was loved, he was wanted, he was *needed*.

"I can't believe it took you six years to figure out that you're good for me," Will said, their foreheads pressed together. "I knew that by the second *month*."

Gunner's laugh was shaky. "I've never been swift on the uptake." He looked around the room, at the players surrounding them, still grinning like maniacs, and cleared his throat. "Win this one for me, eh, boys?"

The team roared again and Will pulled him into another kiss.

30

Gunner woke up first, stretching luxuriously with a yawn. Beside him, Will mumbled something and rolled over, reaching for Gunner in his sleep. Gunner let him pull him close, nuzzling the nape of his neck, and smiled to himself, lacing their fingers together where Will's hand rested on Gunner's stomach.

Will rumbled contentedly, deep in his chest, and his hand slid down over the cut of Gunner's hip. His breath was hot on Gunner's skin when he scraped his teeth lightly across the bumps of Gunner's vertebrae, making him shudder and arch into it.

Gunner was hardening rapidly as Will continued to explore, but he made no effort to touch himself or hurry things up as Will's touch lit trails of heat along his body.

"Hey," Will said after a few minutes, hand stilling.

Blinking, Gunner resurfaced. He looked over his shoulder into Will's face, warm with love.

"Hey, Western Conference winner," Gunner said, just to see the smile spread across Will's face.

It worked. Will tugged Gunner into a kiss, the angle awkward, and after a minute, made a dissatisfied noise with his access and rolled Gunner to his back, careful as ever with his leg in its bulky cast.

"What time is it?" he asked, voice rough with sleep.

Gunner checked the clock. "Not even five. You can go back to sleep."

Instead, Will propped himself on one elbow above him. He bent to kiss him again as Gunner smoothed his palms across Will's freckled shoulders, smiling into it.

It had been a week since the Direwolves beat the Wildfire in a resounding victory, returning home triumphant as the Western Conference champions. Tomorrow, they went up against the Riptide and it would be no easy win, Gunner knew.

Will growled against Gunner's mouth. "Am I boring you?"

"Sorry," Gunner said hastily. He looped his arms around Will's neck. "Just… wish I was gonna be out there with you."

Will's eyes softened and he took another quick kiss. "Me too," he murmured. "I'm gonna win it for you."

Gunner surged up and caught Will's mouth in something like desperation, hot and wordless. Will kissed him back just as hard, hands beginning to rove Gunner's body again.

He skimmed fingers over Gunner's ribs, making him twitch and laugh breathlessly.

"You've lost weight," Will said, pulling away briefly.

"You know how playoffs can be," Gunner said, trying to drag him back down.

Will seemed not to notice, tracing the line of Gunner's hip. Gunner couldn't help the whine as Will dipped lower, knuckles brushing the head of Gunner's cock where it was flushed and hard against his belly.

Gunner bucked up against him and Will pinned his hips with one hand.

"Careful," he chided, then dropped his head to close his mouth around Gunner's nipple.

Gunner choked on air, back arching. Will's tongue was hot and wet and he wasn't shy about using his teeth, scraping them across sensitive skin and then sucking until Gunner was writhing, unable to think.

"Please, *please*," he chanted, one hand tangled in Will's soft hair, but Will seemed not to notice, taking his time with the first nipple before moving to the other. This put more of his weight across Gunner's chest, and he sighed, letting Will pin him to the mattress. "I love you," he whispered and Will lifted his head.

His eyes were dark, lips red, and he looked wrecked already, but he smiled, bright and mischievous. "Took you long enough to figure it out."

Gunner shoved weakly at his shoulder. Will

didn't even sway, smile widening. "I've known it for years," Gunner pointed out.

Will's smile turned tender. "I'm glad you finally found the balls to tell me, then."

Gunner laughed out loud. "Oh, shut up and kiss me."

Will was only too happy to obey, and they made out languidly for a while, hands roaming across each other's skin. Gunner's arousal was a warm glow in the pit of his stomach, but he felt no need to chase it, content to lose himself in Will's touch and smell and feel.

He had no idea how long it was before Will pulled away and leaned across him to fumble in the bedside drawer.

"Can I fuck you?" he asked.

"Oh *God* yes," Gunner said, already pulling off his pants, then hesitated. "How, though? I mean —" He gestured at his leg.

"Let's try with you on your left side," Will said, and Gunner rolled over obediently. Will made sure he was comfortable, grabbed the lube, then tucked himself up against his back, smoothing a hand down Gunner's flank. His hand dipped below the curve of Gunner's hip and urged his leg up.

Slick fingers probed his entrance and Gunner let his head fall back against Will's shoulder as Will stretched him open, slow and relentless.

"*God*," he panted, eyes squeezed shut. "W-Will, I—"

"I've got you," Will soothed, their cheeks pressed together. "Just hang on, baby."

Gunner whimpered as Will added another

finger and twisted, his knuckles dragging against his rim. At that angle, Will couldn't get very deep, but it didn't seem to matter. Gunner could already feel the pressure building in his chest, and he knew it wasn't going to take much.

Will took his time here too, pushing in and retreating in what felt like slow motion, until the world dropped away, narrowed down to the slick slide of fingers stretching him wide. Gunner was panting, shaking with the effort of being still when Will finally pulled out, and he couldn't help the whine.

"Shh," Will said, slipping his left arm under Gunner's body to pin him against his chest. Gunner relaxed into him and then there was a blunt pressure at his hole, crowding all coherent thought from Gunner's mind.

He cried out and Will clapped his free hand over Gunner's mouth, not stopping his forward motion. "You'll wake Olivia," he said, suppressed laughter in his voice.

Gunner groaned deep in his chest and shoved his hips backward, taking Will in another inch. He delighted in the hitch in Will's breath and then Will was suddenly sliding out and pushing at his shoulder, rolling him over onto his stomach.

"Can't get deep enough. This okay?" he asked, and Gunner shifted until it was comfortable, spreading both legs and canting his hips invitingly. Will swore thickly at that, settled between his legs, and slid back in, one smooth, strong thrust that punched the air from Gunner's lungs.

He gasped into the pillow as Will lowered himself down until he was blanketing Gunner from head to toe, their cheeks pressed together and Gunner's hips molded against Will's pelvis. Will's breathing was harsh in his ear and Gunner reached up behind himself blindly to cup Will's skull.

Will kissed his cheek and began to move. He fucked Gunner in sharp, hard thrusts, grunting under his breath with the effort, elbows braced on either side of Gunner's head. Every movement dragged Gunner's cock over the sheets, the high thread count cotton feeling like sandpaper against his over-sensitive skin. It was rough and dry and perfect and Gunner wanted it to last forever, for Will to fill all his senses and consume him. He was a forest fire, a conflagration, flames roaring through his nerves and setting him alight from the inside out.

Will's hips were speeding up, losing their rhythm, his breath jagged. He pressed his face to the curve of Gunner's neck, then sank his teeth into the muscle and Gunner came with a helpless wail that was muffled by the pillow as Will drove deep and froze, body shaking minutely as he spilled into Gunner's core.

He collapsed on top of him, making him grunt, and pressed sloppy kisses to the nape of his neck. Gunner lay there and enjoyed it until the wet spot started getting uncomfortable, and then he pushed and shoved until Will rolled to the side with an aggrieved moan. Gunner twisted and poked him in the side.

"I'm crippled," he said. "You have to clean us up."

Will moaned again, reaching out blindly to try

and pull Gunner against him, but Gunner avoided his groping hand and poked him again.

"Stop," Will protested on a laugh, and Gunner grinned. He leaned in and pressed a kiss to Will's mouth.

"Clean us up so we can go back to sleep," he ordered.

"Ugh, fine." Will rolled out of bed and padded into the bathroom, returning with a warm wet cloth and wiping Gunner down with careful strokes. He got dressed and then helped Gunner pull his pants back on over the cast, putting a dry towel over the wet spot before crawling back into the bed. "Is this going to be a thing?" he teased. "This whole coming untouched business?"

Gunner pinched Will's forearm, no force behind it. "Only ever happens with you," he mumbled, and Will laughed against him, body shaking silently.

"You're good for my ego," he said.

Gunner hummed, relaxing into his arms. He wasn't sure he'd be able to sleep again, but he felt *good,* floating on a sea of endorphins and pleasure that had drowned out the pain of his leg, and he thought vaguely he could stay like this all day.

Will kissed the curve of his ear. "I love you too," he whispered.

The bedroom door creaked open and they both froze.

"Daddy?" Olivia's voice quavered just slightly, and Gunner sat up.

"What's wrong?"

Olivia knuckled at her eyes with the hand not gripping Ferguson. "I had a bad d-dream."

"Come here," Will said before Gunner could, holding out a hand, and Olivia scrambled onto the bed to settle between them.

Gunner met Will's eyes in the dark over Olivia's head. Will smiled at him and stroked Olivia's hair off her forehead.

"Better?" Gunner asked.

"Better," Olivia said, already sounding drowsy. She nestled into Gunner's warmth, smelling like strawberries and coconut, and Gunner reached across her small body to lace his fingers between Will's again.

"What was the dream about?" Will asked gently.

"Ferguson ran away from home," Olivia said in a small voice.

"Well, that's just silly," Will said. "Everyone knows anteaters need their Olivias to survive."

Olivia's frame vibrated with her soft laugh, and Gunner smiled against her hair.

Thank you, he thought. *Thank you for giving me this, Stephanie. I promise I'll take care of our girl.*

He fell asleep in a tangle of arms and legs, still smiling.

CODA

"Message received, 10:01 AM."

Beep.

"Liv," Stephanie said clearly. "Livvy, Olivia, sweetest baby girl. You are my favorite person in the whole world, did you know that? I love you to the moon and the stars and back again. You're going to do so many things, sweetheart. You're going to go to all the places we wanted to visit together. You're going to play hockey. You're going to get into a good college and be such an amazing woman, and you know what I love most about you? It's that you're going to fight for good, every day of your life. You're going to make a difference. You believed you could, and you will. And I promise I'll be there watching you, every step of the way."

"I love you, Olivia." Stephanie sounded tired now, weaker. "Take care of your daddy, okay? I know he's going to love you every bit as much as I do."

Beep.

"End of message."

ACKNOWLEDGMENTS

This book, like all my books, took a village to create. Aaliya, first and best beta and platonic soulmate. Your endless enthusiasm for everything I write keeps me going more than you'll ever know.

Sarah, artist *and* wordsmith, your talents amaze me and I'm so glad we're friends and I have you to help me with all of this. I'd be completely lost without you.

Em, thank you for your enthusiastic speed-read (seriously girl, you read the whole thing in a day? Respect) and your wonderful comments.

And last (but not least, etc.), Other Sarah, or as I affectionately refer to you when I'm talking to Aaliya, Tumblr Sarah. Your eagle-eye caught so many tense slips that I missed, and I'm so, so grateful to you for your hard work (and also your friendship, I seriously adore you).

And to my readers, thank you so much for picking up this book. Whether it's your first time in one of my worlds or your fifteenth, I am so glad you're here.

ABOUT THE AUTHOR

Michaela Grey told stories to put herself to sleep since she was old enough to hold a conversation in her head. When she learned to write, she began putting those stories down on paper. She resides in the Texas Hill Country with her cats, and is perpetually on the hunt for peaceful writing time.

When she's not writing, she's watching hockey or blogging about writing and men on knife shoes chasing a frozen Oreo around the ice while trying to keep her cat off the keyboard.

Tumblr: greymichaela.tumblr.com
Twitter: @GreyMichaela
Facebook: www.facebook.com/GreyMichaela
E-mail: greymichaela@gmail.com

Want to find out when her next book comes out? Sign up for her newsletter here or follow her on Amazon here

Keep reading for a sneak peek at Roughing!

ROUGHING

Chapter 1

SAINT REACHED the practice arena's side door and slipped inside quickly, avoiding eye contact with passersby. In the dimly lit hall, he stopped and took a deep breath. He could hear skate blades and cheerful shouting, smell the ice, the rubber mats, sweat, metal, and leather—it all mingled in his head and made the tension drain from his shoulders. This was home.

His phone buzzed and Saint pulled it out.

It was from his coach. *Upstairs, first conference room.*

Frowning, Saint took the stairs two at a time to the second floor and the conference room with the huge windows that overlooked the arena. He found the coaches standing at the window, talking in low voices as they watched the players in the rink.

Flanahan saw him first. A big man unafraid to

use his size to intimidate opponents into agreeing with him, he'd been the first to welcome Saint to Portland and the most vocal in his support when Saint took the captain's letter. Saint didn't like him very much—Flanahan was far too willing to throw his weight around to get his own way—but he trusted him, at least as far as the team went.

"Saint, glad you made it! How was your summer? How was Montreal?"

Rogelio Reyes and Velvet Brennan turned to greet him as well. Reyes was a tall, thin, watery man, pale eyes that blinked too much and hands that constantly twitched as though he was resisting the urge to wring them.

On the other hand, Velvet was vivid colors in bright contrast to each other. Her dark red hair was cut in a messy pixie cut that highlighted her pointed chin and sharp brown eyes, and her pantsuit was a neat, staid tan but the shirt under the jacket glowed a vivid jewel green. She gave Saint a real smile as Reyes nodded.

"It was great," Saint said. "Nice to catch up with friends, you know?" He hesitated. "I should be on the ice. Is something wrong?"

Flanahan glanced at his assistant coaches, who didn't look inclined to say anything. "Nothing's *wrong*," Flanahan finally said. "We've just made some changes to the roster over the summer that you as captain should be aware of."

Saint tensed. "You made changes without consulting me?"

Flanahan's eyes narrowed. "This isn't your team, son. You may be the captain but that doesn't mean you get to tell us how to fill the lines."

"No, of course." Saint ducked his head. "I'm sorry, sir. I didn't mean to sound ungrateful. I just wasn't expecting it."

Flanahan seemed to accept that. "Well." He rubbed his hands together, a beaming smile breaking out over his ruddy face. "Come see your new team."

His new *team*? Unease shivered through Saint as he joined the coaches at the window to look down into the rink. Some thirty skaters were on the ice, warming up individually, some batting pucks back and forth and others taking shots at the empty net.

Saint squinted. There was Roderick Murphy, off in the corner doing his stretches. And there—Jason Carlyle on the near side of the arena, skating through a complicated footwork drill. And Felix Papillon—Butterfly—the rush of relief when Saint saw him in net at the far end was almost dizzying. Most of his third and fourth lines seemed intact. But his first and second lines were almost unrecognizable.

"Coach—"

Flanahan cut him off. "Management's been busy while you were gone. Lot of deals, lot of paperwork back and forth, but I think we've got a real chance this year."

"Coach," Saint tried again, his throat dry. "Where's my team? *My* team?"

"Right there," Flanahan said, pointing.

"No." Saint shook his head. "The team I played with last year. The team I've spent the last *three* years developing. Where's March? Where's Branson? *Where's Flynn*?" He cut himself off as

Velvet made an aborted motion toward him, taking a deep breath and touching his thumbs to his fingers in a vain effort to calm himself. "Where's my team, Coach? And who are these people?"

"Be honest with yourself," Flanahan said, gripping Saint's shoulder. His grip was heavy, almost painful, thumb pressing hard against Saint's collarbone. "Were those players going to get us to the playoffs this year?"

"We had a shot!" Saint said, fighting to not pull away. "They were gelling, we were close to finding what clicked!"

Flanahan made a rumbling noise in the back of his throat but he let go of Saint's shoulder. "The owner and GM felt differently. So this year, *this* is your team."

Saint's head was spinning, dread and misery a cold, heavy lump in his stomach. "How did you even pull this off without me knowing?"

Flanahan laughed, a delighted bray. "You turned your phone off for the entire summer and you're surprised you didn't find out?" He sobered. "We told those we traded not to tell you, and we kept as much out of the news as we could. Not because of you, but because we want to control the narrative when we're ready to tell the hockey world. Besides, all you would've done is fret yourself to death up there in Montreal. The GM wanted you to enjoy your summer."

It made a Machiavellian sort of sense. Saint knew the general manager, Kevin Dumont, well enough to know this was the kind of thing he would pull.

Still. "You should have told me."

Saint couldn't help the stab of betrayal at the thought of Flynn—*Flynn*—not at least warning him. Flanahan he understood, but he'd thought he and Flynn were closer than that.

"There's one more thing," Flanahan said, all but rubbing his hands with glee. "You have a new D-man on your line."

Saint narrowed his eyes.

"Carmine Quinn," Flanahan announced, without even the decency to look abashed.

"You've got to be fucking *kidding me.*"

Flanahan's eyebrows shot up at the expletive. Saint ignored him.

"Carmine Quinn, who went out of his way to board me or slash me or trip me every time we were on the ice together the last time we played the Otters, forgetting the fact that he *fought* me during that game? *That* Carmine Quinn? The Carmine Quinn who fractured three ribs and put me out of commission for six *weeks*?"

"You still won," Flanahan pointed out. "The fight, if not the game. What's the big deal?"

"The big deal?" Saint threw his hands up. "I only won because I *fell* on him. The guy's a thug, Coach! All he's good for is throwing his fists. Can he even skate? Does he know what a puck is?"

"It's the black rubber thing, right?" The voice came from the door and Saint spun.

Carmine was standing there, hands in his pockets. He looked unbothered by Saint's diatribe, but closer inspection revealed lines around his mouth, tightness in his shoulders.

His eyes were dark, almost unreadable in the

fluorescent lighting, and the dimples Saint knew existed were nowhere to be found. There were shadows under his eyes, and he rocked back on his heels, raising one sardonic eyebrow.

"I could be wrong," he continued. "After all, I barely know one end of a stick from the other."

Saint opened his mouth and closed it again. Something in Carmine's bearing said an apology would be sneered at.

"Glad you made it!" Flanahan said, falsely hearty. "You know Saint, of course."

Carmine inclined his head, mouth tight.

"And my assistant coaches, Rogelio Reyes and Velvet Brennan," Flanahan continued. "We're all excited to see what you bring to the team!"

"Are you?" Carmine murmured. "Well, first time for everything."

Flanahan gestured for Carmine to join them. "Take a look," he said, pointing out the window. "Your new team. Some of them are from the Embers—the next few weeks will determine who stays. What do you think?"

Carmine stepped up to the glass, keeping Velvet and Rogelio between him and Saint. He gazed contemplatively at the players and Saint averted his eyes from Carmine's profile, perfect except for the broken nose that had healed crooked.

"I think 47 is weak," Carmine said. "He's slow and his reactions are shit. He's not going to be able to keep the puck, let alone score."

Flanahan peered dubiously down at the ice. "He's done well on the Embers."

"You know best, I'm sure," Carmine said.

"Can I get on the ice or did you need me for something else?"

"Just wanted to welcome you to the team," Flanahan said, waving him away.

Carmine nodded and left the room without looking at Saint.

Flanahan's eyes gleamed. "It's going to be a good season," he said. "I can feel it in my bones."

"Are we done?" Saint asked.

Flanahan made an impatient gesture, and Saint escaped.

He took the back way to the dressing room, the one with the lowest chance of running into anyone who'd demand conversation. Halfway there, he stopped and pulled out his phone.

What the fuck, he texted Flynn.

Flynn's response was swift. *They threatened to put me on waivers, man. :(*

Saint blew out a breath. Of course Flynn had chosen to save his career. But it still stung. *Where did they trade you?*

Wildfire, was Flynn's answer. *Too hot. I'm dying.*

Saint closed his eyes. Arizona was so far from Oregon, and now he'd never get the chance to find out if Flynn's lips were as soft as they looked, or if the heat in his eyes had meant something or if he flirted that way with everyone.

He shoved down and strangled the misery that welled in his throat. *They're lucky to have you*, he sent, and put the phone away before Flynn could reply.

The dressing room was silent and empty, and Saint thanked his lucky stars as he quickly changed and laced up his skates. The big C on his jersey seemed to be mocking him. *What exactly can you captain? Jack shit, that's what.*

No one noticed him as he stepped into the rink and made straight for Butterfly. Felix's eyes lit behind his goalie mask at the sight of him and he pulled Saint into a rough hug.

"Did you know?" Saint managed in rusty French, his voice wobbly.

Felix shook his head. "*Non, cher.* Not until I got here. I'm so sorry."

Saint rolled his shoulders. "It is what it is, right? We'll make the best of it. At least you and Roddy and Jase are still here."

Felix's green eyes were unhappy. "I would have told you. Had I known—I would have told you."

"I know," Saint said. He clapped Felix on the shoulder. "You wouldn't do that to me."

Roderick broke away from the group he'd been talking to and made for them. Tall and craggy, he'd long ago adopted the role of put-upon father to the team of rookies led by Saint. He held out his arms and Saint went into them gladly.

"Missed you, kid," Roderick murmured.

Saint let himself have a brief moment of comfort, closing his eyes as Roderick kept the world at bay, and then he gathered himself and moved back, forcing a smile. Around them, some of the new players were pretending not to watch them while others stared, unabashed.

"You're still on my line, right?" Saint asked.

"Like they could take me off," Roderick said.

There were dark circles under his eyes, but then, there were always dark circles under his eyes. He'd looked permanently exhausted for as long as Saint had known him, and yet his energy was seemingly boundless.

"Who else is with us?"

"Arkady something." Roderick gestured with his chin toward a lanky man a few years younger than Saint. Sandy blond hair curled against the nape of his neck and he caught sight of Saint staring and smiled radiantly at him, his eyes bright green and cheerful.

"Incoming," Felix said under his breath as Arkady skated toward them.

He skidded to a stop with an elegant spray of ice, careful not to snow any of them, pulled off a glove, and shoved a hand at Saint.

"Arkady Volkov," he said. "They call me Volly but you say Kasha, yes? Is an honor, Sinclair."

"Just Saint is fine," Saint said, shaking his hand. He let go as quickly as he could but Kasha didn't seem bothered, beaming at him. Up close, he was younger than Saint had realized, nineteen or twenty at most. Saint found himself liking Kasha's open expression, the way he shifted on his skates as if hoping Saint would approve of him. "Where did you come from, Kasha?"

"The Direwolves," Kasha said. "But I'm from Russia. Excited to be here!"

Saint eyed him but didn't challenge that. "How long have you been on the ice today?"

"Hour? Maybe two."

Saint nodded. "Tell me what you've seen."

Kasha perked up. "That one—" He pointed at

a big man out of earshot down the ice, the one Carmine had indicated. "Likes to fight, I'm think."

Saint glanced at Roderick.

"David Stahl," Roderick said in a low tone. "And Volly's right—he's itching to throw his weight around."

"What else?" Saint asked Kasha.

Kasha pointed at a slender player on the other side of the rink. Saint couldn't make out details from so far away, but he had dark curly hair peeking out from under his helmet.

"He is good," Kasha said. "Slapshot is *really* good. But footwork nice too."

"Embry Rather," Roderick said. "Second line center, I think."

Embry smacked a puck down the ice, right between the other goalie's knees.

Roderick whistled softly. "You're right, Volly, he's good."

Kasha beamed. He indicated a tall brunet, talking to the equipment manager by the edge of the rink. "Tye. Don't know last name. Good footwork, maybe needs puck time? Seems nice. D-man." He scrunched up his face then and pointed at Carmine, warming up alone in the corner. "Carmine Quinn. He—"

"I know who he is," Saint said, too harshly. He took a deep breath and tried to gentle his voice. "What do you think of him?"

"Good skater," Kasha said, shrugging.

"That's it?"

Kasha looked unhappy. "He is—I'm not know how to say. Bad stories about?"

"Bad reputation?" Felix offered.

"Yes," Kasha confirmed. "He fights. Too much. Is always taking penalties, for stupid shit. He not—*think*."

"Sounds about right," Saint muttered. He rolled his shoulders again. "What else?"

Kasha kept going, naming more players. He had an eye for detail and a dryly funny delivery that had Felix and Roderick laughing as he reenacted a scuffle between two defensemen earlier. Saint forced a laugh, unable to take his eyes off Carmine for long.

Carmine didn't seem bothered by the players milling around him, but he didn't speak to them, either. He stretched and did his warm ups and then began circling the rink in slow, easy laps. Kasha was right—he *was* a good skater, light on the blades and perfectly balanced, avoiding the slower and more clumsy players with ease. Saint couldn't help but wonder what he'd be like with a stick. Were his hands as deft as his skating? He shook himself. Carmine wasn't there for puck handling. He was there to start—and win—fights.

Saint looked away. "Kasha, shooting drills on Butterfly?"

Kasha's eyes lit as Felix groaned theatrically but picked up his blocker and got in his crease.

Saint took the first shot, moving slowly to give his muscles time to warm up. He was aware of the eyes on him, most of the players stopping to watch. Saint didn't bother with anything fancy—Felix would stop it anyway. Instead he skated toward the net at half-speed, watching as Felix dropped his left shoulder invitingly. Saint didn't take the bait.

Almost on top of him, Saint faked left, then scooped the puck up and over Felix's right leg, under his elbow. He couldn't help the grin as he skated back to Kasha while Felix shouted profanities at him.

"Slow is best on him?" Kasha asked, eyes intent.

"Only if you know which way he's going to block," Saint said, leaning on his stick. The other players were gathering, drawn by the action. "He'll try and draw you in, make you shoot a particular way. He's really good at blocking top shelf, go low on him."

Kasha nodded, grabbed a puck, and was off. More players joined Saint, and he nodded at them. A few smiled back, others avoided his eyes. Saint made mental note of those—he'd have to put in extra work with them. Down the ice, Kasha made a shot that Felix easily blocked.

Someone hooted. "Why don't you just bend over and let him have it?"

Saint stiffened.

Kasha skated back up to them, looking rueful. "You right," he said. "I'm try top shelf next time."

But Felix blocked the next shot too. The same player who'd chirped Kasha before laughed even louder.

"Maybe if you blow him, he'll let one in, eh?" he shouted. "Pretty boy like you, you'd probably like it!"

Saint whirled on him. It was David, the player Kasha had pointed out earlier, and he blinked at the fury Saint knew was clear on his face.

"That's enough," Saint hissed.

David shifted his weight. "It's just chirping, Cap. Doesn't mean anything."

"While you're on my team—" Saint straightened and lifted his voice so everyone gathered could hear him. "On this team, there will be *no* homophobic slurs, you get me? None. You go there, you get benched. No discussion, no debate —I won't put up with it."

Someone—Tye, Saint thought—raised a tentative hand. "Can I still call someone a cocksucker? Because like, I don't *care* if someone sucks cock, but that's kinda my go-to insult, you know?"

"Because you're about as creative as a bag of flour," someone else said—Saint couldn't see who the speaker was.

Tye scowled but didn't argue.

"Look," Saint said, gripping his stick harder. Carmine had drifted over to listen, but he said nothing, eyes intent. "I'm not going to be able to stop you from using *all* derogatory terms on the ice. I know that. But you start calling people 'pretty boys' and inferring they like dick just because of how they look or act, and we're going to have a problem. Get me?" He stared at David, who looked at the ice. Saint lifted his voice. "*Are we clear*?"

"Clear," the team chorused back.

"Then go back to what you were doing," Saint said. The players dispersed, all except for Kasha and Carmine, who was studying Saint intently. "What?" Saint snapped, more sharply than he intended.

Carmine lifted a shoulder. "Just interesting to

see the rumors are true." He skated away and Saint looked at Kasha, baffled.

"Rumors?"

Kasha shrugged. "I'm not know. Only thing I hear is Saint great captain, gonna save team, make playoffs, maybe even win Cup."

Saint laughed in spite of himself. "Fuck off."

Kasha grinned back at him. "Is true," he insisted. "Saint is best captain. Even if no playoffs, you best."

Saint ducked his head, cheeks firing. "Thanks," he mumbled. He glanced up. "So tell me more about yourself. I need to know you if I'm going to run effective plays with you."

By the time practice was over, Saint knew almost everything about Kasha, and a lot about the other new members of the team. Kasha missed Russia, but loved American hockey. He had a girlfriend he doted on and was thinking of buying a house in the area if they extended his contract. "Only one year right now," he'd said, making an exaggerated sad face. He loved punk metal, which made Saint tease him about never having the right to choose the music in the dressing room, and Bob Ross, causing Saint to double over with laughter.

"Is good painter!" Kasha insisted over Saint's giggles. "And so nice, yes? Is… calm. Peaceful. Makes me…." He made a frustrated face as if he couldn't find the word.

"Centered?" Saint suggested.

"Yes," Kasha said, nodding. "More should watch him. Like David, yes?" He grinned, sly, tip of his tongue peeking from the corner of his mouth.

Saint snorted another laugh. "You might be onto something there."

In the dressing room, it was raucous, packed with players trying to find their spots and arguing over the best ones. Saint ignored them as he got undressed and hung up his skates. He came out of the shower, toweling his hair dry, to find Velvet waiting for him.

Several of the new players were making exaggerated offended noises about a woman in the dressing room. Saint rolled his eyes and lifted his voice.

"First of all, she's seen way better than your shriveled excuses for dicks. Second, I'm pretty sure her wife isn't threatened, so stop acting like children and get back to what you were doing. Which hopefully involves showering, because you fuckers *reek*."

Velvet stepped closer as the dressing room chatter resumed, somewhat muted. "I *can* handle it on my own," she pointed out. "But thanks."

Saint tossed the towel aside. "It's fucked up, but sometimes they listen better when it comes from a guy. What can I do for you?"

"Coach wants to see you."

Saint groaned. "Again? Can it wait?"

"Unfortunately not." Velvet looked uncomfortable, which made Saint tense.

"What's going on?"

"He made me promise not to say," Velvet said,

glancing around the room. "But it involves Carmine."

"*Fuck.*"

⁂

HE TOOK the stairs two at a time, eager to get it over with, but Carmine was already in the conference room, drumming his fingers on the table.

Flanahan was sitting opposite him, in the middle of saying something, but he cut off when Saint knocked. "Good to see you, Saint, good to see you!" he said, as if he hadn't talked to him two hours before.

Saint nodded, glancing at Carmine, who wasn't looking at him. "Velvet said you needed to talk to me."

Flanahan looked pleased with himself, which was never a good sign. "Well. The thing is, management feels we've got a real opportunity here. A way to get people through the doors."

Unease crawled over Saint's skin but he said nothing, waiting for Flanahan to get to the point.

"The last time you two were on the ice together, you had a bit of a donnybrook, didn't you?" Flanahan said. He laced his fingers and rested his hands on the table. "And now here you are on the same team."

"No," Saint said flatly.

"You haven't even let me finish!"

"You're setting us up to be rivals," Saint snapped. "You've probably got at least one commercial with the footage from our fight ready to go, don't you?"

Flanahan didn't have the grace to look ashamed. He just shrugged.

"He's my *teammate* now," Saint continued. "Whatever my personal feelings, that all goes away when we step on the ice together. I will not participate in this dog and pony show you're putting on. I won't."

"Good!" Flanahan said, bouncing to his feet, and Saint blinked. "Because Carmine doesn't have a place to live right now, and you're all alone in that huge house with all those guest rooms and it's a perfect solution. You guys can carpool!"

Saint opened and closed his mouth. He'd somehow walked right into the trap Flanahan had set for him. He glanced at Carmine, who hadn't said a word, and back at the coach, who looked far too pleased with himself.

"You're not serious," Saint finally said.

Flanahan's smile showed too many teeth. "You may be the face of the franchise, but you still have to do what I say. And I'm saying Carmine is now your roommate."

"You can't tell me what to do outside this barn!" Saint protested.

"Maybe I can't *force* you," Flanahan said thoughtfully. "But it sure would be unfortunate if a news outlet got hold of the information that Carmine's living in a hostel because you refused to let him bunk with you."

"For how long?" Saint demanded.

"We're thinking three months," Flanahan said, and Saint flinched. "That'll give us time to really build the narrative the way we want."

Saint swung toward Carmine, panic swelling under his ribs. "*You* can't be okay with this."

"Why not?" Carmine said. "Rent-free, nice place—I'm assuming—not too far from the rink? If it's a big house, we don't even have to see each other."

The panic was crawling up Saint's throat. If he opened his mouth, he'd scream. His stomach cramped and twisted. *People*, in his space. Not just people but a person he intensely disliked. *Living with him.*

"Excuse me a minute," he managed. He spun for the door and made it to the bathroom down the hall before his stomach rebelled and he vomited in the toilet, clinging to the porcelain.

Felix found him there. Saint was slumped against the bathroom wall, pale and sweaty. Felix said nothing, just dampened a paper towel and knelt to wipe his face.

"Coach sent me," he said when he was done. There was deep sympathy in his eyes.

"I can't do it," Saint whispered.

Felix sat down beside him, stretching out his legs with a sigh. "Hard practice today. The new guys all want to prove they're good enough. For you."

Saint closed his eyes. "It's too much."

Felix put a hand on Saint's thigh. "For someone on their own, maybe yes. You're not alone, though, are you? You have me. You have Roddy. You even have Velvet—you know you're her favorite. And I think… I think you have Kasha."

Saint rolled his head sideways until he could

rest it on Felix's shoulder. "I just want to play hockey."

"And you will," Felix said. "With us."

Saint looked up. "If they traded you, I'd walk away. I would. I don't even care what they'd do to me."

Felix's eyes creased with affection. "Probably good I just signed a five year contract, eh?"

"You did?" Saint sat up straight and Felix grinned at him. "Five years, Butterfly, that's great!"

Felix shrugged, but he was still smiling. "I don't wanna play unless it's with you either."

Saint leaned back against the wall. "How's your girlfriend?"

"Broke up over the summer, which you'd know if you turned your phone on." Felix nudged Saint's side. "Met a cute guy a few weeks ago, though. Gonna maybe see where it goes."

"Do you ever wish you could be out?"

"Sometimes." Felix sighed. "I don't wanna do it alone though, you know? Too much… attention." His smile turned sly. "Come out with me, eh? Twice the news, half the attention."

Saint laughed. "You're full of shit." He pushed himself upright. "I should go back." He rinsed his face and mouth with water from the sink before acknowledging that he was delaying. "Butterfly."

Felix, on his feet and smoothing the wrinkles from his pants, glanced up. "Hm?"

"Thanks," Saint said. "I'm—thanks."

Felix smiled at him. "You can do this. Text me whenever you need a break."

www.ingramcontent.com/pod-product-compliance
Ingram Content Group UK Ltd.
Pitfield, Milton Keynes, MK11 3LW, UK
UKHW021036270726
13967UKWH00013B/2694

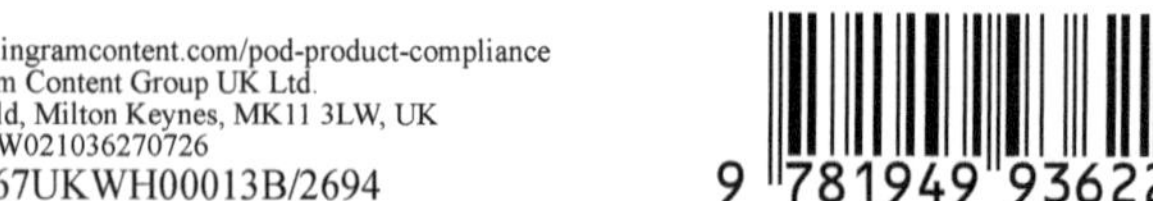

9 781949 936223